Praise for

"An explosive ending . . . What a righteously nasty imagination Huston has. If you don't know this perfervid writer of thrillers (*Caught Stealing*) and comic books (*Moon Knight*), this stand-alone novel is a great place to start. . . . Huston terrifically re-creates the time period."
—*Entertainment Weekly*

"Hard-boiled fans can't go wrong with Charlie Huston's *The Shotgun Rule,* an affecting look at what it was like to be a teenage boy in the 1980s, wrapped up in the guise of an adrenalin-packed suspense novel."
—*Los Angeles Times*

"Huston adds depth and pathos to already likable characters. As a result, the brutality and intensity of the remainder of the book hit hard. This is Huston's first stand-alone . . . and it's a winner."
—*The Kansas City Star*

"Huston has developed a reputation for his own brand of noir fiction, by turns side-splittingly funny and gruesomely violent and repugnant. Any male over the age of twenty will recognize elements of adolescence they had unconsiously buried—and will cringe or howl at the accuracy of this rendering of his childhood."
—*Rocky Mountain News*

"Memorable characters, hard-edged dialogue and graphic violence make this searing portrait of evil an exciting addition to new crime fiction."
—*Tucson Citizen*

"Moving like a fireball this is an engrossing read that feels kind of like a shot of cheap tequila, in the fun way."
—*Crimespree Magazine*

ALSO BY CHARLIE HUSTON

The Mystic Arts of Erasing All Signs of Death

IN THE JOE PITT CASEBOOKS

Already Dead
No Dominion
Half the Blood of Brooklyn
Every Last Drop

IN THE HENRY THOMPSON TRILOGY

Caught Stealing
Six Bad Things
A Dangerous Man

The Shotgun Rule

The Shotgun Rule

A NOVEL

Charlie Huston

BALLANTINE BOOKS

NEW YORK

The Shotgun Rule is a work of fiction. Names, characters, places, and incidents are the products of the author's imagination or are used fictitiously. Any resemblance to actual events, locales, or persons, living or dead, is entirely coincidental.

2008 Ballantine Books Trade Paperback Edition

Copyright © 2007 by Charlie Huston

Excerpt from *The Mystic Arts of Erasing All Signs of Death* copyright © 2009 by Charlie Huston

All rights reserved.

Published in the United States by Ballantine Books, an imprint of The Random HousePublishing Group, a division of Random House, Inc., New York.

BALLANTINE and colophon are registered trademarks of Random House, Inc.

"Memories of Tomorrow," written by Mike Muir
Copyright © AMERICAN LESION MUSIC (BMI)/Administered by BUG.
All rights reserved. Used by permission.

Originally published in hardcover in the United States by Ballantine Books, an imprint of The Random House Publishing Group, a division of Random House, Inc., in 2007.

ISBN 978-0-345-48136-8

Printed in the United States of America

www.ballantinebooks.com

2 4 6 8 9 7 5 3 1

Book design by Stephanie Huntwork

To Jeff Kaskey.
Role model.
Though he'll be horrified to hear it.

and

To the kids who don't know any better.
The ones with the attitude problems.
What the hell are they thinking?
Man, believe me, they aren't.
That's the point.
We never do.

The Shotgun Rule

The Sketchy House

I t's a bad house. Sketchy. They should know better than to go in. But if they were the kind of kids who knew better they wouldn't be here in the first place.

George races down the street, hits his front brake, and leans over his handlebars, popping the rear end of his bike into the air and holding the wheelstand for a beat before dropping back to the blacktop. He turns circles in front of the house, checking it out.

It's dark. The peeling Dodge Dart in the driveway sits over long dry oil stains, untrimmed juniper bushes edge the lawn and screen the bottoms of the front windows. The gate to the backyard hangs askew, a piece of yellow nylon rope keeping it from swinging open. The sidewalk streetlamp is broken, unrepaired from when he shot it out with the pellet rifle last night.

Yeah, the house is sketchy. But that doesn't change anything. They're going in. He whips the bike out of its circles, knobby tires buzzing on the asphalt.

The others wait for him. Hector kneeling next to his bike, fiddling with the chain, putting on a show as if it has become derailed. Paul straddling his own bike, lifting one leg to lean far over the crotchbar, rescuing a half smoked Marlboro Red from the gutter. Straightening, he flicks some grit from the filter and puts it in his mouth while feeling at his pockets for a light.

Andy sees the gesture and crams his hand in his own pocket, yanking out a cardboard fold of matches too quickly, flipping the pocket inside out and sending matches, loose change, and a small piece of plastic to the ground.

Paul shakes his head.

—Nice going, *Andrew*.

Hector smiles, but doesn't say anything.

Andy drops his kickstand and climbs off his bike, snagging his pants cuff on the seat and sending it crashing down.

Paul drops his head.

—Man. No wonder that bike is such a piece of shit.

Andy tilts the bike upright and balances it on the wobbly kickstand.

—Yeah, it's pretty crappy, man.

Paul leans and scoops the matches from the ground. His free hand stays half tucked in the rear pocket of his faded jeans as he folds one match backward over the matchbook and snaps it alight with his thumb before bringing the flame to the crooked halfsmoke in his lips.

—Heads up.

Still picking up his change, Andy looks up and sees the matchbook arcing easily toward him. He panics, any tossed object an opportunity for embarrassment, and rather than catching it bats it straight up, bobbles it several times, and finally slaps it at the gutter and watches it drop through the steel grate covering the storm drain.

Mid drag, Paul laughs so hard the butt shoots from between his lips and hits Hector in the back of his head. Already giggling, Hector falls apart now, laughing while running fingers over the shellacked crest of his bleached mohawk, making sure it hasn't been bent out of shape.

Andy laughs, too. Worse things than being clumsy. At least they didn't catch him picking up the little plastic twenty sided die that fell on the ground along with his change. He squeezes it in his hand, running his thumb over the little triangular facets, picturing an equation that would describe a twenty sided object.

Paul dismounts to reenact Andy's fumble. He juggles his hands and skips in place, then freezes to watch an invisible matchbook cut a slow arc across the sky before dropping down the storm drain.

Hector raises his hand in the air and Paul slaps five as they both laugh.

Andy drops the die in his pocket, trying not to laugh at himself, and, failing, honks and snorts through his nose.

Paul picks the still smoldering butt from the ground, takes a drag and passes it to Andy to finish off.

—Here, spaz, put this in your mouth and stop that fucking noise.

Andy pinches his fingers over a slight tear in the paper and takes the last hit, sucking the smoke into his lungs, feeling it burn, but not coughing.

Paul grabs a fistful of Andy's hair, jerking his head back and forth before letting him go with a little shove and a slap on the shoulder.

George rides up, kicking out the rear wheel of his bike and skidding to a stop.

—You fags done fagging around?

Paul gets back on his bike.

—Fuck you, queerbait.

Hector stops messing with his chain.

—We were talking 'bout fucking your mom.

Andy pats his pocket once and flips up his kickstand.

—Is it sketchy?

George is standing up on his pedals, fingers wrapped loose around black rubber handgrips, balancing perfectly on his chrome and gloss black Mongoose.

—Yeah, it's sketchy. Let's go rob it.

Part One

Piece of Shit Bike

It started with Andy's piece of shit bike.

—What the fuck were you doing not locking it up?

—I just went in for a second.

—*I just went in for a second.* How long do you think it takes to steal a bike, dickweed?

—It was right next to the window.

—Yeah, that'll do it; no one ever steals shit that's next to a window. Numbnuts.

George is kneeling next to a bucket of water, submerging the half inflated innertube from his bike's front wheel. He looks once at Paul, then back in the bucket.

—Don't be such a dick, man, he lost his bike.

Paul picks up a rock from the huge pile that occupies half the driveway. He shakes the rock around in his hand.

—He didn't *lose* his bike.

He tosses the rock, bouncing it off Andy's back.

—He let someone *steal* it.

Andy feels pressure behind his eyes and fights it. Already cried once coming out of the store and finding the bike gone. Can't cry again.

He picks up a rock of his own.

—I didn't *let* anyone steal it.

He throws the rock at Paul.

—It was *stolen.*

Paul stays right where he is, the rock skipping across the pavement and into the street without coming near him.

—Yeah, big diff.

George is still shuffling the innertube between his hands, looking for the string of bubbles that will point to the slow leak that's been plaguing him for days.

—Don't throw the fucking rocks around, dad'll have a fit.

Andy kicks at a couple rocks, nudging them back toward the pile. His and George's dad had them shovel the rocks from the back of his 4×4 two weeks ago. This weekend he'll rent a rototiller and plow up the back lawn and they'll have to move the rocks a wheelbarrow load at a time to spread over the yard. It's gonna suck and he's not even going to pay them. He says they should be thanking him for plowing under the lawn that they hate mowing and weeding.

A line of bubbles shoots to the surface of the water. George covers their source with a fingertip and lifts the tube from the water.

—Hand me that rag.

Andy bends to pick up a scrap of chamois that's lying next to the toolbox. Paul takes a quick step and places his foot over it.

—George, don't let this guy help with your bike. He's bad luck. He touches your bike and it's gone.

Andy yanks on the rag.

—Get off, dickmo.

—Make me.

—Get. Off.

Andy pulls harder and Paul lifts his foot and Andy falls back on his ass.

—You're such a feeb.

—Dick!

George holds out his hand.

—Give me the rag.

Andy throws the rag at him.

Some big brother. Think he could take his side against Paul just once. Just today. Fucking bike. Still can't believe he was so stupid not to lock it up.

George lifts his finger from the puncture in the tube and starts drying the rubber around it.

—Did you see who took it?

Andy gets off his ass, takes the puncture kit from the toolbox and pops the shiny tin lid from the cardboard cylinder.

—No. If I had I would have kicked their ass.

Paul reaches up, grabbing a lower branch of the maple tree alongside the driveway and chinning himself on it.

—Yeah, George, what are you thinking? If he'd seen them he would have kicked their ass. He's such a *badass ass kicker*. Asses all over town are afraid of him.

Andy flips him off and hands George the top of the puncture kit.

George drops the rag, takes the lid, and uses its ridged upper surface to score the rubber around the puncture.

Paul hauls himself up onto the branch, hooks his knees around it and dangles upside down, long curls falling over his face.

—Come kick my ass, Andy, I'll just hang here and you try to kick my ass.

Andy stays where he is, watching George fix the leak, taking the lid back and handing him the metal tube of cement.

He's imagining picking up the hammer from the toolbox and swinging it at Paul's face. He's picturing finding whoever stole his bike and stabbing them in the throat with a screwdriver.

Paul puts one arm behind his back.

—C'mon, man, one handed and upside down! You gotta be able to kick my ass.

George rubs the cement over the puncture.

Paul puts his other arm behind him.

—No hands. *No hands.* It's never gonna get easier than this, man. C'mon and take a shot. You know you want to. Remember that time I pantsed you on the quad? Here's your chance to get back at me.

Andy remembers. First day of his freshman year, bad enough that he'd been skipped a year to start high school early, but there was Paul, greeting him by running up and yanking his hand me down bell bottoms to his ankles while the entire student body was crisscrossing the quad on their way to homeroom.

He pictures standing in the middle of that quad with a machine gun in his hands, pulling the trigger and turning in slow circles until he is all alone and it is quiet.

He shakes his head sharply, trying to jar the image loose. He fails.

He takes the cement back from George, caps it and drops it in the kit, chews the inside of his cheek.

Paul swings himself back and forth a few times.

—What's the matter, spaz? Looks like you're getting twitchy over there. You gonna freak out and start throwing things again?

George picks up one of the rocks, cups it like a marble and flicks it at Paul, bouncing it off his forehead.

Paul laughs.

—You're off the hook, Andy, your bro's fighting your battles again.

George sets the innertube aside, carefully draping it on the frame of his upside down bike. Andy hands him a large piece of patch and a small pair of scissors.

George clips a small square from the patch.

—I ain't sticking up for the puss, dickhead. I'm just sick of hearing your shit. Our dad's gonna unload on him tonight and I'm gonna have to listen it.

George squares his shoulders and lowers his voice.

—*Opportunity, boys, that's what a thief looks for. Turn your back for a second, your property will be gone. Always lock up your bike. It's not just a toy, it's a responsibility.*

Paul rubs the spot where the rock tagged him.

—Whatever.

George peels away the bright blue backing from the patch, careful not to touch the sticky underside, and picks up the innertube. Pressing the patch over the hole, using his thumbs to smooth away any air bubbles trapped under it, he looks at Andy.

—What're you gonna tell him?

Andy stares at the patch, the violence in his head finally fading as he draws blood from his cheek. Why does he have to think about that kind of shit? It's not like he's like Paul. Paul likes to fight. But fighting sucks. Getting punched sucks. And hurting someone else, that almost sucks worse.

George kicks him in the shin.

—Dude, what are you gonna tell dad?

Andy shrugs.

—Dunno.

Paul unclamps his legs and tumbles to the ground, bracing with his arms as he lands.

Andy flips him off.

—Nice move, grace.

Paul doesn't move, just lays there with his eyes closed, his face suddenly pale and sweaty, skin drawn tight over his forehead.

George is focused on the tire and doesn't notice.

Andy does.

—You OK?

Paul doesn't move, just breathes deeply.

Andy steps closer.

—Migraine?

Paul opens his eyes, wipes the sweat from his face. He sits up slowly.

—I'm fucking fine. You're the one with problems. Better tell your dad you locked it up.

Andy bends to pick up the patch backing that George discarded.

—He won't believe someone could steal it from in front of the store if it was locked up.

George nods.

—Tell him you had the wheel locked to the frame, but not locked up to anything. Someone could have tossed it in the back of a truck. He'll buy that.

—Whatever. I'm still gonna have to walk everywhere.

A car swings around the corner, a '78 Firebird T-top, "Another Brick in the Wall Part II" blaring from the stereo.

Paul watches it all the way to the end of the street.

—Wouldn't have to walk if we had a fucking car.

Andy nods.

—Yeah, that would be sweet.

Paul reaches out and slaps the back of his head.

Andy does nothing, atoning for the imaginary hammer he smashed into Paul's face.

Hector barrels up the driveway.

—Hey!

He skids to a stop, leaving a streak of black rubber on the pavement, his front wheel scrunching into the rock pile.

—Hey, Andy, what's up with your bike? I just saw one of the Arroyos riding it around.

They all look at him.

Paul hawks and spits.

—Which one?

—Timo.

He sticks a finger in Hector's face.

—You fucking sure?

Hector knocks the finger away.

—Yeah, asshole, I'm fucking sure. We may all look alike to you, but I can tell my Mexicans apart.

Paul picks up a rock.

—Fucking Timo.

He heaves the rock, sending it far down the street in the same direction as the Firebird.

—Sweet.

———————

It couldn't be better. Sweet enough it was one of the Arroyos that stole Andy's bike, better yet that it was Timo.

That shit that happened when they played city league soccer, the year they were under twelves, Paul still thinks about that shit. Just about every day.

It's a City finals match and Paul's playing fullback, Timo is a forward on the other team. In a scrum down by Paul's goal, everyone going up for a header, Timo flails his elbow into Paul's face, sending him to the sideline with a split lip and a bloody nose. In the second half, cotton stuffed in his nostrils, Paul catches a deflection on his instep, traps the ball beneath his foot, waits for Timo to charge him, and drills the ball right into his gut. Timo goes down on top of the ball and before the whistle can sound Paul is kicking Timo in the crotch, not even trying to look like he's going for the ball. Redcarded, he argues that Timo was wearing a cup so no big deal, then walks from the field, screaming an endless string of fuck you's at the refs.

On his way home a gold flaked lowrider Impala rolls up next to him,

Timo and his big brothers Fernando and Ramon get out. Ramon has a switchblade. Shit, they all have switchblades, but Ramon, he holds the point of his to Paul's throat and tells him to take his cup off. Paul doesn't think they'll stab him, but that doesn't keep him from getting scared. His face goes red and tears run down his cheeks. The Arroyo boys say something about what a *puta* he is, the only Spanish Paul knows. Once his cup is out, two of them hold him upright while Timo sets up for a penalty kick from five yards away and pounds an Official Primera League futbol into his nuts. Paul goes down and coughs up the orange slices he ate at halftime.

Wasn't till that evening that George and Hector found him at the firebreak at the edge of their housing tract. Drunk on the three sixteen ouncers he'd grabbed from the fridge, head spinning from the smokes he'd bummed off a high school kid, telling George and Hector that Timo is dead. He's gonna kill that little fucking faggot. He tells them all the way home.

He doesn't tell them that he cried. And he doesn't tell them why he cried.

He doesn't tell them that reaching to pull his cup out of his athletic supporter, being told to put his hand down his shorts like that, made him think of his father.

———

—I'm gonna kill that fucking faggot.

George is sitting on the ground, turning his bike's front wheel in his lap, tucking the innertube back up inside the tire.

—Where'd you see him?

Hector is picking up tools.

—Over by their house.

—Was he fucking around or headed home?

—He was headed toward Fernando's pad.

George is using a screwdriver to flip the edge of the tire back inside the wheel rim. He stops.

—Fernando's?

—Yeah.

George goes back to work.

—Shit.

Paul is on his bike. He's already ridden it to the corner and back twice, Andy trailing him on foot both ways, saying nothing.

—So fucking what, he's going to his brother's; I'm still gonna kill him.

Hector shakes his head.

—Fine, man, go pedal over there and kill him. Not like Fernando won't be home. Not like Ramon didn't get out of Santa Rita last month. You see him since he got out?

—Fuck him.

—Looks like all he did in there was eat and pump iron.

Paul limps his wrist.

—And take it in the ass.

Hector turns away.

—I'm just saying, you know, you don't want to mess with Fernando and Ramon.

George has slipped the wheel back onto his bike's front forks. With a crescent wrench he gradually tightens the nuts on either side of the wheel, giving it a spin after each turn of the wrench to be certain that it stays true.

—When'd Timo move out of his folks'?

Hector has pulled out a nearly full pack of Marlboro Reds. He takes one for himself and hands the pack around.

—Don't know. My sister says he got in a fight with his mom and hit her in the stomach and his dad threw him out. Like, dragged him out the front door and threw him and a bunch of his shit on the lawn. So now he's at Fernando's.

The others are quiet as they each take a smoke from the pack.

George takes out a Bic sheathed in the stainless steel and turquoise case he bought at the Devil's Workshop head shop last summer. They all bum a light.

Hector takes the pack back and looks at Paul.

—And that's all. He's over there with his brothers. You ride over there and fuck him up, they're gonna kill you.

Paul bites the filter of his cigarette and gets back on his bike.

—Fuck 'em. I'll fucking kill those faggots if they let me take 'em one on one. Only way they can take me is if they gang up.

—Well, shit, man, that's what they fucking do.

George gives the wheel a final spin and packs the last of his tools away.

—Doesn't matter what they do. We got to go over there. They got Andy's bike.

And that's when they look around and realize that Andy's gone.

Such a Dildo

Andy was cool till Hector mentioned Alexandra and they all stopped talking.

Andy stopped talking because the thought of Alexandra always shuts him up. Shuts him up and makes his face hot so that he has to turn away. What sucks is that George and Paul stopped talking, too. Like they didn't want to accidentally say something in front of Hector about the sudden curves that have broken out over Alexandra's body. It'd be bad enough if Hector knew Andy was thinking about her that way. If he knew George and Paul had started checking her out, he'd have flipped. Pulled out the length of bicycle chain he keeps stuffed in his pocket, wrapped it around his fist and started swinging at his best friends.

Not that they really have to worry. Hector hasn't noticed the looks that follow Alexandra down the street. Hector still sees the same little girl he's always seen. But Andy's always seen her different, always seen how pretty she is. Not that she knows anything about it. Or anything about him.

But she knows about Timo.

Why couldn't it just be the damn bike?

Thinking about Timo on *his* bike, that sucks. That made him start thinking about ways of hurting Timo. Started a riot in his head. Dreams of finding Timo on his bike and pushing him off it and into the path of an oncoming eighteen-wheeler.

Another imaginary murder skidding across his brain. Leaving him wondering what the fuck is wrong with him. Why does he think about shit like that?

Which is stupid, because it's really his own fault the bike got stolen in the first place. If he'd not been so stupid, if he'd just locked up the bike, that piece of shit bike, Timo wouldn't be on it right now. Not Timo's fucking fault that he found an unlocked bike lying around. You don't blame a guy for picking up the five dollar bill you let fall out of your pocket. So what if Timo's never missed an opportunity to casually run him into a wall in the corridors at school? So what if Timo shouts *choke* every time he swings the bat in PE softball games? Lots of kids do that. Man, kids have been doing that shit to Andy since his first day of kindergarten. Since the first time he started getting noticed and people started talking about how smart he is. If he can't put up with that shit by now, what's the point? He pictures using one of the nicked and scarred aluminum PE bats to cave in Timo's forehead.

And repeats his mantra: *ImsuchadildoImsuchadildoImsuchadildo.*

The secret formula that halts the violence in his head. Most of the time.

But Alexandra.

Andy understands why she knows that Timo had been kicked out. She knows for the same reason that Andy knows many of the details of *her* life: because she likes Timo. God! Bad enough he catches Paul and George looking at her. Just now, after he's been looking at her for years. That's bad enough. And it's fucking gross. Bad enough that Timo might like *her.* But that she likes *him* back?

Isn't anything his? Isn't there one fucking thing that is worthless enough that he can have it to himself? His own pair of jeans that aren't George's hand me downs? His own smokes that aren't bummed from someone else? A crap pair of Cheetahs sneakers because his folks won't get him Pumas because he's just gonna grow out of them anyway? His water spotted books that come from some library sale of shit that's not good enough for the shelves anymore? The girl that no one else notices because she's quiet and scrawny and he's the only one who sees how pretty she is? His own piece of shit bike that his dad cobbled together from old Schwinn and Huffy parts that he salvaged from garage sales? Can't he at least have that? A bike that everyone makes fun of? Can't he have that without having to worry about someone fucking jerking it away from him and not giving it back till it's broken and used up and all

the fun has been taken out of it because it's just one more fucking re-
minder of what a dildo he is?

Fucking Timo!

The pictures come again, and he does nothing to try and stop them.

Fucking Andy!

George rides hard, trying to find his brother.

Sometimes? Sometimes, man, he just wishes he didn't have a brother
at all. How much easier would that make life?

Fifteen years since the little shit was born, and he's been underfoot
every single day of every single year. Always such a baby. Such a crybaby.
From the moment Mom came home from the hospital with him he was
crying. God! The years of sharing a room with him after he was too old
to sleep in mom and dad's room but before dad put in the attic room,
was there anything worse than that? Six years old and the kid was always waking up with nightmares, crying.

Dad off on the graveyard shift at the quarry back then, mom so tired
at the end of the day you could throw rocks at the wall and she wouldn't
wake up. Having to climb out of the top bunk, the one Andy wouldn't
take because he was afraid he'd roll out in the middle of the night, and
sit on the edge of his mattress and rub his back until he stopped being
scared and went to sleep. And then being awake for an hour after that
before *he* could get back to sleep. Getting in trouble the next morning
for not getting out of bed right away when mom came to wake them.
Years of that shit. Walking downtown together to go to a matinee during
the summer, having to walk slow because Andy couldn't keep up. Andy,
the little super genius, always so special. Always such a pain. Teachers
and people looking at George, wondering what went wrong with him,
why he didn't get to take the gifted classes. But finally getting to high
school, having it to himself, two years before having to worry about
Andy, before having to worry about wiping his nose and making sure he
didn't get initiated too bad. And then the little punk goes and gets
skipped a grade and it turned into only one year without him. Fine, they
were still in different buildings. Then he got skipped again. Straight
from freshman to junior. All last year, his little brother on the same

schedule, walking between classes at the same time, taking the honors versions of the same courses he's taking. And it's gonna be worse when school starts again. Senior year, class of '84. Should be nothing but good times, nothing but ditch days and double lunches and make work and senior trip and barely having to be around the fucking hellhole because the senior classes are such a joke. Best year of his life and he's gonna have Andy with him for every day of it. Every single day. Why couldn't he get skipped *again*? Why couldn't the little freak be going straight off to college like everybody knows he's going to do? Sometimes he'd swear the kid could have skipped if he wanted to, could have worked a little harder, but didn't. Worked just hard enough so he could catch up to George and drag around behind him like a fucking boat anchor.

He pumps down the street, cutting across the heavy traffic on Murrieta, the shaft of the ball peen hammer stuffed in his back pocket banging against his lower back. He coasts for a moment so he can reach behind and shove the head of the hammer deeper into his pocket, making certain it doesn't fall out. He doesn't want to lose the hammer. If the Arroyos hurt his little brother he's gonna use it to smash their teeth out.

Andy watches from the little league fields behind the elementary school as George rides past on the street. Paul already came by, taking his bike straight across the school's blacktop playground. Hector will be riding the longest way around, all the way down Murrieta to Olivina before cutting toward the Arroyos' neighborhood. They'll have split up the routes to catch him before he can get himself into any trouble. And if it were a race, they would catch him, any one of them could run him down easy. But he's not racing, he's hiding, and no one can catch him when he's hiding.

Out after curfew, when a cop car rolls up and they all break in different directions, Andy is the one who's never caught. He's not sure how he does it. The hiding places aren't even that good sometimes, but he knows when the spot is the right one.

When George goes on a rampage in their house because he's realized that Andy borrowed one of his favorite albums without asking and then put it back in the wrong jacket, he has a checklist of hiding places to look in. Cupboards, under the stairs, cracks behind large pieces of furniture, the roots of shrubs, high branches of trees even though he knows his brother fears all heights, in the hatchback of their mom's yellow Fiesta. Once, he opened the sofa bed, certain Andy had figured a way to close it and replace the cushions with himself folded inside. But in the end George always has to do the same thing. He stands in the middle of the house and yells. *Come out right now and I'll only punch you once, make me wait and I'll fucking kill you.* And when Andy comes out he hits him. Twice.

Now George passes and Andy stands up from where he's been sitting in the shadow of one of the bleachers, trots across the blacktop, over the white painted basketball and foursquare courts, his pockets loaded with rocks he sifted from the dirt while he hid. The new twenty sided die he bought today, the one that drew him into the game shop and caused him to leave his bike unlocked outside, squeezed tight in his hand.

Hector takes the long way around. All the way down Murrieta and then across on Olivina and then up on North P. Like Andy is gonna go that way on foot.

But George is right, they have to cover it. It would be like Andy to take the long way around just because they would be thinking he'd never take it. But it's also too obvious a dodge, so there's still no way he'd take it. But maybe it's *so obvious* a dodge, he might take it. Freaky little kid. They have to cover it. And Hector has to ride it.

Partly it's because he can ride the longest without getting winded. George can beat him in any sprint and can out trick them all when they start pulling stunts. Paul will take his Redline over any jump, pedal full out down any gravel strewn hill and bang off any other BMXer on the homemade dirt track all the kids ride on in the fields beyond the firebreak. But for distance it's Hector. He can ride all day, all night, he can ride full out for a mile and hop off and start swinging.

The other thing is, George and Paul think they're better fighters. Well, they talk more about it, and Paul gets in more fights than anyone, but that's because he's always mouthing off and starting them. He just doesn't know how to keep his mouth shut. Doesn't know how to keep shit inside. Doesn't know that if you want to kick someone's ass you just do it, you don't talk shit about it. Hector knows that's how it's done. Just stand there and stare at the sidewalk while some redneck calls you spic and wetback and makes fun of your mohawk and the safety pins in your earlobe, and when he turns to his friends to laugh at you, you pull your fist, wrapped in eighteen inches of bicycle chain, out of your pocket and start punching him in the side of the head.

George and Paul think if there's trouble at the Arroyos' it's best they be the first two showing up. They think they'll be able to do something. They're wrong. They could all three show at the same time, leap off their bikes and dive straight into a hook, but if Fernando and Ramon are there they won't stand a chance.

Regarding Your Mother's Pussy

The Arroyos were legend long before George, Paul, and Hector got to high school.

Bantamweights, they brawled their way through the school system until they emerged at high school, having moved up several weight classes.

Fernando was the first. He spent five years at the high school, leaving behind him a shattered and exhausted administration and a faculty that was to a soul nothing but grateful that they had survived. He had taxed the personal behavior codes to the limit, twisted them, and found loopholes so obscure the entire rule book had to be revised upon his departure. And yet, despite the physical damage he had done to the campus and assorted classmates, despite the psychological scars he had left on his teachers, despite all this, the football coach and athletic boosters had campaigned relentlessly to have a special grading curve installed to keep his GPA hovering in the vicinity of a C+, just that fraction across the border from C that would have allowed him to play varsity football. Their efforts had been inspired by the havoc he had wreaked as both an offensive lineman and linebacker in j.v. ball.

Any opposing player unlucky enough to have to line up opposite him, any bullrushed quarterback, any running back or wide receiver required to pass through his domain on the field, was inclined to trip and fall while he was still yards away rather than endure the rib cracking nose breaking concussion inducing hits he routinely laid down. If the ball was fumbled, every player, his own teammates included, ran from it, terrified of the prospect of ending up in his clutches at the bottom of a pile. His heavily taped fist pounding your groin, fingers gouging at your eyes, a barrage of

Spanish curses regarding your mother's pussy screamed in your ear. But, gamer though he may have been, his all but flawless record of nonattendance in class kept him from advancing to the varsity squad.

State, Coach sometimes mumbled drunkenly at the Rodeo Club, *we had had that Arroyo muchacho, we woulda gone State.*

In his third junior year he turned eighteen and passed finally into adulthood and the clutches of the criminal justice system. His record as a minor was admirable enough that his first adult arrest earned him a conviction (sentence suspended), and a final expulsion.

With Fernando gone, the school board heaved a brief sigh of relief, then began preparing for the arrival of Ramon.

The preparations were insufficient. Ramon commenced upon his own Sherman's March the first day of his freshman year. Announcing his presence by egging the entire faculty parking lot at midday in full view of the sixty eight year old campus security guard, who had been phoned at home the night before and told that if he ever called the police on an Arroyo he would have a Colombian necktie the next morning. He didn't know exactly what a Colombian necktie was, but, recognizing Fernando's voice over the line, he knew he didn't want one.

Ramon lasted barely one year, doing as much damage in that time as Fernando had done in five. But shortly after summer vacation began he was arrested for armed robbery and assault with a deadly weapon. The deadly weapon being a hacksaw he wielded like a machete when a clerk at the 7-Eleven refused to open the register for him. He was convicted and sent to juvy and was never seen on campus again. As a student anyway. As a former student he was often seen in Fernando's Impala, spinning donuts on the grass. The school left the lawns torn and unseeded until Ramon earned his first conviction as an adult and was sent to county for three to five.

Both were long gone when George, Paul, and Hector began their freshman year, but Timo was in their class.

It seemed Timo had watched Fernando's and Ramon's progression and decided it wasn't for him. He played j.v. and varsity soccer and starred on both squads. He maintained a dead on C+ average that never faltered, the product of a series of *tutors* who were paid to write his papers and prep cheat sheets for his tests.

One of the school's five letterman Mexicans, and altogether different from his brothers, Timo cruised through high school, far and away the number one Mexican citizen. Also, far and away the school's biggest pot dealer. Stoners were compelled to buy his shit brown ditch weed even when there was an abundance of green buds to be found. The penalty for not purchasing his goods being a visit from one of his older brothers.

He sported his brothers' lowrider style: khaki chinos, black leather shoes with white socks, long sleeved plaid shirt buttoned at the collar and wrists but open all the way down the front and left untucked to reveal the white wifebeater underneath, a net over his blow dried jet black hair, and a thin mustache he'd been cultivating since sixth grade. He wore the look, but minus the switchblade in his back pocket or the bag of reefer tucked in his sock or the Newports in his shirtfront. His lackeys carried these for him. He was always clean, ready for a patdown. A fine athlete, he was always welcome at the top jocks' table. Sleepy eyed and handsome, watched not just by the Mexican girls but by the white chicks as well. Cowgirls, cheerleaders, brains, and jockettes had an eye for him.

All of this concealing from the faculty what an enormous dick he was.

Infamous Hacksaw

Rounding the corner onto Fernando's block, Andy envisions hurling fistfuls of rocks and broken glass into Timo's face. Throwing things, always his opening bid in a fight.

Whenever his brother and the guys throw down on a pack of cowboys or some jocks who have been talking too loud about their ragged jeans and torn Zeppelin Ts, he gets pumped to the gills with adrenalin, spazzes out, and runs ahead of the guys, hurling whatever comes to hand before lowering his head and throwing himself into whatever's in front of him. And man, when his fist makes first contact, when a rock has actually bounced off some asshole's forehead, for that split second, it's the best feeling in the world. Then it all goes wrong. All the bloodlust, wanting to grab hair and yank it off along with bleeding bits of scalp, wanting to bite into the cheek of some dick twice as big as him, it goes sick inside him and his imagination takes over. What would happen if one of those rocks hit someone in the eye? What if he actually did bite through someone's cheek, snapped the line of their lip? What if a lucky punch or kick shattered a bone and sent it splintering through skin?

What if he really *hurt* someone?

Once that gets in his head he's done.

The sad part being, he's never gonna land a good punch. He hits like a girl.

Such a dildo.

And then he gets knocked around and put on the ground and the guys are left to finish things up. And they do. They could give a shit if they hurt the pricks they're fighting. Jesus Christ, it's a fight, man, that's the point.

The guys don't really fuck with him about it. After all, he's up for the fight. And it's kind of cool when he goes berserker and leads the way screaming gibberish. *Fuckfuckkillshitbreakyouyoufuckingfuckingdildobreath!*

Far as they're concerned, he never lasts because he can't fight worth shit. How much can you expect from him? He's a kid.

So when he rounds the corner, it's pretty much the same old story. He sees himself throwing shards in Timo's face, and then sees himself trying helplessly to stop a torrent of blood pumping from a severed artery in the asshole's neck.

He sees an entire funeral and grieving family.

He sees the revenge Timo's older brothers have taken, not on him but on George.

His brother lacerated by Ramon's infamous hacksaw.

And when he sees Timo just up the street, on *his* bike, bunny-hopping it on and off the curb with an ease he could never equal, he opens his hands and lets the rocks spill out and walks to the middle of the street.

—That's my bike.

Timo hears him, looks up, and glides over. He stands up on the pedals and swoops around Andy, circling him once, twice. Andy doesn't move, doesn't turn his face, just stands.

—That's my bike. You stole it.

Timo gives the pedals a couple pumps, just enough to keep the bike cruising in slow circles.

—This bike? This is your bike? This shitty bike?

He circles.

—Shit, man, you want this shitty bike from me?

Circles.

—All you got to do is take it.

He puckers his lips, makes a kissy noise.

Andy doesn't move.

Timo tightens his circle. Makes the noise again.

Andy stares up the street.

Timo circles closer, reaches out, slaps the back of Andy's head.

Andy does nothing.

Timo stops, puts his feet down, straddles the bike right in front of Andy. Waits.

Andy doesn't move.

Timo gets back on the bike, circles him one last time, and rides back up the street.

—Mujera.

He laughs and Paul skids around the corner, cutting off the path to his brother's house.

Timo turns back and finds George braking to a stop next to Andy. Further down the street, Hector's blond mohawk.

Timo rides up onto the sidewalk. George pushes off, chasing him. Paul cuts toward the gutter, popping his front wheel in the air, taking his bike hard over the curb. Timo swerves onto someone's front lawn and scoots past him.

Paul skids across the same lawn.

—Get off the fucking bike!

George stays in the street, paralleling Timo.

—Don't be a dick, Timo, get off my brother's bike.

Timo lifts a hand from the grips and flips him off.

He's starting to leave Paul behind, but George paces him, searching for a spot where he can put on a little burst, get around one of the cars parked at the curb, and cut his bike in front of Timo's.

A car door opens in front of him.

He hits front and back brakes, skids, releases the front brake, kicks his rear wheel out and edges around the door further into the street as an El Camino comes around the corner, horn blasting.

Hector has reached Andy and they both watch as George wrenches the bike back into the side of the parked car, bounces off it, and falls into the street as the El Camino drives on.

Andy starts running, Hector riding ahead of him.

George lifts his head from the pavement. He can feel the scrapes on the side of his neck. He wants to turn his head to check on his bike, but he can't take his eyes off of Fernando Arroyo as he climbs out the open door of the parked Impala.

Paul jumps off his bike and lets it run into the ice plant bordering the driveway at the house next to Fernando's, leaving Timo to ride up onto his brother's porch and straight into the house. Running to his best friend, he's forced to pull up as Ramon emerges from the driver's side of the Impala.

Fernando looks down at George, takes a hit off the joint he and his brother have been smoking in the car.

—You fucking with my little brother, Whelan?

George is still seeing the primer spotted hood of the El Camino scraping past him. One of Fernando's shiny black shoes smacks him in the thigh.

—I say, you fucking with my little brother, puta?

Standing on the opposite side of the car, Paul sees that Hector was right about Ramon; he's fucking huge. His sweat stained wifebeater is stretched tight over mounds of jailhouse muscle covered in jailhouse tattoos. He's come out of the car armed, the hacksaw, his weapon of choice, dangling from loose fingertips.

Eyes hidden behind wraparound black shades, Ramon waves the rusty bladed saw conversationally.

Timo comes strolling back out of the house.

—Fuck 'em up, bro.

Ramon shakes a finger at him.

—Settle down, ese. Don't be getting all bloodthirsty right after running away and shit. Don't look good.

He smiles at Paul.

—So, big Paul Cheney. What's up, man? You wanna fight?

Paul blinks, looks from Ramon's face to the saw.

—Drop the saw, I'll fight.

Ramon looks at the saw, points at it with his free hand.

—This, ese? I drop it I might bend it or some shit.

—Fucking drop it, pussy.

—Pussy?

He looks over the roof of the car at his brother.

—Yo, vato. Called me a pussy over here. Thinks he can get away with that shit.

Fernando kicks George again.

—This one don't say shit.

—What you gonna do to him?

Fernando hits the joint, flicks the roach away, and gestures at Timo.

—Stick me up, joven.

Timo joins his brother, reaches into the car, and brings out a green and gold minibat from an A's game and gives it to his brother.

—Here, bro. Bust him up.

—Gonna bust him. Gonna break his head.

He raises the bat.

Ramon nods, looks back at Paul.

—I'm gonna cut this one, cut his dick off.

He takes a firmer grip on the saw, slashes it through the air a couple times.

—Cut that shit off so Timo can bounce his futbol off it whenever he wants.

Timo giggles.

—Cool.

Paul goes for Ramon's face.

Two handfuls of rocks pepper the back end of the Impala, pocking and scratching the flawless gold flecked deep burgundy paint job.

Tableau.

George on his back in the street. Fernando over him, bat raised to smash into his face. Timo behind him, leaning in to get a better view. Paul ready to seize Ramon's throat. Ramon ready to scythe Paul's fingers off.

All of them, their heads turned, looking at Andy, fifteen feet behind the car, hyperventilating, Hector next to him.

Fernando tilts his head back and screams at the sky.

—My car!

Tableau broken.

Hector flings the eighteen inches of bike chain he's held bundled in his hand. It smashes into the rear window of the Impala, wedging itself in its own hole.

—Fuck your shitty car!

It is as if Fernando never left the game of football, it is as if a ball has just been fumbled into the midst of the scene and everyone else on the field is scattering from it as he charges to scoop it up.

He barrels at Hector, whirling the minibat above his head, Timo dodging out of the way.

Hector spins himself about and begins to pedal away. George scrambles to his feet. Paul yanks his bike free of the ice plant, Ramon ignoring him and starting to climb back inside the Impala. He makes it halfway inside before Fernando returns and raps him across the back of the neck with the minibat and shoves him across the seat, climbing in behind the wheel, Timo diving into the back.

George and Paul are both on their bikes, riding in the opposite direction from Hector.

Fernando hits the hydraulics, boosting the Impala high on its shocks, screeching away from the curb in a tight circle that takes him after the rapidly disappearing Hector, and reveals Andy, where he has been hunched at the rear of the Chevy, now utterly exposed, but with no one left to see him.

He stands there.

Across the street, three small girls are frozen in the midst of a hopscotch they've chalked on the sidewalk. Andy waves at them and they run shrieking into their house.

Rocks and broken glass outline the space the rear half of the Impala occupied at the curb. His eye catches on some flecks of blood; his brother's. In the middle of the street is the hammer that slipped from George's pocket when he went down. Andy bends, picks it up, looks both ways along the street, walks over the sidewalk across the dead lawn and onto the Arroyos' front porch.

George and Paul ride around the corner.

George's handlebars were twisted to the side in the crash and he has to ride with them at an angle. They both pedal onto the lawn.

Paul picks some ice plant from his front spokes.

—What are you doing, dipshit?

Andy points the hammer at the open door.

—Gonna get my bike.

George and Paul look at each other. The left side of George's neck is badly scraped, a trickle of blood runs to the hollow of his throat and stains the collar of his *Double Live Gonzo!* T.

He nods.

—Fuck yeah, let's get it.

They hop off their bikes and wheel them onto the porch.

Andy offers the hammer to George.

—Hector OK?

George takes the hammer.

—They'll never catch him.

—They're in a car.

Paul shakes his head.

—Don't matter. He'll hit the fields by the railroad tracks before they can catch up.

Hector rides up the driveway.

—Hey.

He stops, kicks one of the empty beer cans littering the front walk.

—What's up?

George points at Andy.

—Getting his bike.

Hector joins them on the porch.

—Cool.

Andy squints.

—What happened?

—They chased me to the fields by the tracks and had to park and come after me on foot and I lost them in the weeds.

—Cool.

—Yeah.

They all stand there on the Arroyos' porch.

George touches the blood on his neck.

—Let's get the fuckin' bike before they come back.

They go in, Paul, George, and Hector wheeling their bikes with them.

From Fighting With Chain

Their eyes adjust to the darkness inside the house.

Paul leans his bike against the wall.

—Fucking A.

The livingroom is littered with the mutilated carcasses of several dozen bikes.

Hector picks up the gear assembly from a ten speed.

—It's a fucking chop shop.

Paul kicks a milk crate full of pedals.

—Bike thieves suck.

Andy bends and lifts his own bike from where Timo dumped it on the floor.

—That's a movie.

They all look at him.

Paul starts picking through the pedals.

—What the fuck are you talking about?

—*The Bicycle Thief*. It's a movie we watched in Humanities.

He's inspecting his bike, searching for outward signs that Timo has ridden it. Marks he'll have to avoid looking at for fear that they'll remind him of what a dildo he was, not locking up his bike.

George lifts the edge of a blue plastic tarp to look at whatever is tented beneath.

—They show movies in Humanities? Fuck, why didn't we take that class?

Paul chucks a rusty pedal at Andy's foot.

—Because we're not super mutant brains like your mutant brother.

Andy ignores the pedal, clutching both the brake levers on his han-

dlebars, making sure the action has stayed springy in the two hours the
bike was gone.

—It's not that brainy of a class. Just reading and talking and stuff.
Writing a few papers.

George shakes his head.

—And watching movies. Only movie we ever got to see was the car
crash movies in Driver's Ed.

Hector is squatting next to a snaked pile of chains. He finds a broken one and unclasps the master link, leaving himself with two lengths,
neither the perfect eighteen inches he prefers.

He chooses the shorter of the two and drops the other.

—It is a good movie?

George stares at him.

—It's a bunch of people who got creamed on the highway.

—No, the movie Andy's talking about, the bicycle thing.

Andy remembers the movie, the way it made him feel.

—Yeah, it's, you know, it's sad, depressing. But it's a good story. Black
and white. It's in Italian. You have to read the subtitles.

Paul has picked out two matching chrome pedals. He drops them
back in the crate.

—Black and white movies give me a migraine.

Hector whips his piece of chain back and forth a couple times. It's a
little rusty. He wraps it around his hand, over the scratches and thin
white scars on the backs of his fingers that come from fighting with
chain. He flexes his encased fist.

He walks over to Paul.

—Everything gives you headaches.

—Fuck you, they're not headaches, they're migraines.

Hector punches the wall, cracking the plaster and leaving a series of
deep parallel tracks.

—Whatever, your head's always hurtin' and you're always whinin'
about it.

—You ever had one you'd know the fuckin' diff.

He turns and jabs Hector's forehead with the tip of his index finger.

—And I don't whine, fag.

Hector slaps the finger away and takes a boxing stance.

—Whiner.

Paul slaps at his head.

—Fuck you, puss.

They spar for a minute, Hector jabbing, Paul letting him hit his shoulders and chest and reaching out to deliver open hand slaps to the side of Hector's head.

Hector goes up on his tiptoes.

—*Oh meee, I got a miiigrane. It hurts sooo bad.*

—Fuck you, mama's boy.

—Hey.

They look as George whips the tarp away and reveals the final product of the Arroyos' chop shop.

Resting on top of several flattened cardboard boxes are two custom BMXers built around Mongoose frames. The bikes are flipped upside down, balanced on their handlebars and seats, the brake cables unattached but the other hardware in place.

Hector squats next to the electric blue one and runs a finger over the graffiti lettering that runs down the crotchbar.

—Oh, man, this is trick.

Andy looks over his shoulder.

—What's it say?

—Chupacabre. It's like a Mexican demon.

Paul picks up a box cutter from the floor and slips the blade in and out.

—Fuckin' bike thieves still suck no matter how good they put shit back together.

George takes a look at the yellow bike with the chopped forks.

He points.

—The blue flames are rad.

Paul clicks the box cutter all the way open.

—We should trash that shit.

Andy looks at his own piece of shit bike and then at the two works of art.

—What?

—We should trash 'em. Teach the Arroyos' a fuckin' lesson for stealin' bikes.

He takes a step toward the BMX chopper, box cutter in his hand.

Andy gets in front of him.

—No, man, leave 'em alone.

Paul points the cutter at Andy's bike.

—Fuck do you care? They would have done that shit to your bike, chopped it up and used it for someone else. 'Cept your bike is so lame they probably only could of used like the sprocket or a couple spokes. They stole your bike, man. Let's do something about it. Don't puss out.

—I'm not pussing, I just. You know, we should just get out anyway, they're gonna be back.

—Fuck that. They stole your bike, we're not going anywhere until we do something about it.

Paul's voice is rising, his face turning red.

Andy sees him wince.

—You OK?

Paul closes his eyes.

He breathes. He turns his back to his friends, lets his mouth drop open, relaxes the muscles in his neck.

He dreams.

He's dreaming about Chargers and GTOs and Mustangs. He's dreaming about driving. He's dreaming about the four of them piled into a black '72 fastback with red detailed louvers over the sloped rear window and a fat yellow racing stripe down the middle of the hood. Dreaming about laying rubber out the exit of the bowling alley. Dreaming about speeding after a European sports car full of fucking jocks and cutting it off and piling out the doors and fucking them up because they can't just drive away after they scream shit at them on the sidewalk. About nailing chicks in the backseat.

He's dreaming about walking out the front door of his house and getting in a badass set of wheels and driving it away and deciding never to go home and no one ever being able to catch him.

Andy touches Paul's back.

—You OK?

Paul turns and slaps his hand away.

—Don't touch me, puss, I'm fucking fine.

He drops the cutter.

—So leave the bikes alone, whatever, but I'm robbing these mother-fuckers blind.

And he sets off down the hall toward the bedrooms.

Andy looks at George and Hector, points at the door.

—C'mon, guys, we got to get out of here.

George and Hector look at one another.

And they follow Paul.

—Fine. Whatever. I'm getting out of here.

Andy goes to the window and looks out. The girls are back across the street, playing on the sidewalk. He touches his bike, imagines the havoc if the Arroyos come home with them still in the house. Imagines the feeling if something were to go down without him being there, and then he goes down the hall.

He watches the doorways as they toss Fernando's and Ramon's rooms and sees Hector find the fistfuls of stolen gold and silver chains hidden in the body of a donkey piñata. Sees Paul sweeping Fernando's dresser top clear of combs and hairnets and bandanas and a small shrine of the Madonna, sees him finding the rolls of singles and fives and tens stuffed to the back of the underwear drawer. He goes back into the hall and opens a door and finds the closet Timo's been dumping his stuff in and picks through it, taking a single photograph and walking away and pulling open another door and looking into the garage.

—Hey, guys!

They all come out into the hall.

George moves toward the bikes.

—They back?

Andy is still looking in the garage.

—What is this shit?

George comes over.

—Oh, fuck.

Andy looks at him.

—What is it?

George looks over his shoulder at Hector and Paul.

—What'd you think?

Paul takes a look.

—Fuck me.

Hector moves Andy aside so he can see.

—What? Oh fuck.

They stare at trash bags spilling hundreds of empty cold and allergy medicine boxes, bottles, and foil packets; at gallon jugs of iodine tincture lined against the wall; heaps of matchboxes with the strike surface cut off; various cans and bottles of acetone, Red Devil Lye, methanol, muriatic acid, and Coleman's camp fuel. A pingpong table in the middle of the garage is covered with an assortment of PVC fittings, flasks, Pyrex bowls, and pie tins. Baking sheets line a catering table against the wall, and two blow dryers are plugged into sockets next to a toaster oven with a shattered glass front. The row of tiny windows in the garage door are taped over with the same lowrider and skin magazine posters that cover the walls.

Paul takes a step forward.

—Fuck. Me.

George hooks the back of his shirt.

—C'mon, man, this shit can blow up.

Andy squeezes past Hector.

—What is it?

Paul jerks free of George and looks at the baking sheets, all of them covered in a coarse powder.

—Looks like the Great Brain doesn't know it all. It's a crank lab, man.

—What?

George grabs his brother's shoulder.

—Stay out of there.

Andy shrugs him off.

—Fuck you.

He goes to Paul, points at the powder on the sheet.

—That it?

Paul shakes his head.

—No, man, that's like a stage you go through. Jeff told me about it.

Hector steps into the garage, toes the plastic jugs next to the wall.

—How's he know?

—Working for Security Eye. He was guarding that house out in

Springtown for an insurance company, the one that burned down. That
was a crank lab that blew up. He talked to a detective or something.
Guy told him.

George steps into the garage.

—See, the shit blows up, that's what happened to Richard Pryor.

—That was freebase, fuckwad.

—Same thing.

—No it's not. Freebase is smoking coke. Crank is crystal meth.

—Fuck you.

—Fuck you. I know.

—I don't give a fuck what it is, let's get out.

Hector whips his new chain at one of the lowrider pinups, ripping it
through the middle and leaving a gash on the dirty drywall behind it.

—Arroyos are dealin' crank. Bikes must be a fucking hobby.

Paul rummages in a cardboard box. Dirty kitchen utensils, tangles of
rubber bands, newsprint coupons for Mountain Mike's Pizza, more bits
and pieces of bicycles and PVC.

—Maybe. Might just be making it. Selling to a dealer.

George is looking at the homemade chemistry set cobbled together
on the table.

—Jesus, they're making a lot.

Andy opens a paint smeared Kelvinator refrigerator in the corner.

—Yeah, they are.

Paul is fingering a rusty Buck knife with a broken tip, he looks up.

—What?

Andy points at the contents of the fridge.

—They're making a lot.

The top shelf of the fridge is loaded with six large Ziploc storage
bags, each stuffed full with yellow crystals.

Hector, about to slash a *Oui* centerfold, pauses to look.

—Shit. Holy shit.

Paul drops the Buck knife and comes over. He picks up one of the bags.

—Man. Oh, man. Fucking A.

Andy picks up a bag.

—How much is this?

George grabs the bag and puts it back in the fridge.

—It's a fucking lot. C'mon, let's go.

Paul opens his bag.

—I don't know, man. A quarter gram is like this much.

He holds his thumb and index finger about an inch apart.

—That costs twenty.

He hefts the bag.

—This is like, man, gotta be a pound. How many grams in a pound?

Andy blinks once while his brain arranges the numbers and they appear on the inside of his eyelids. He reads them off.

—Four hundred fifty three and a half. Well, a little more than a half. Like point five nine and change.

—Four hundred fifty three, point five nine and change times four?

—Eighteen hundred fourteen, point three six.

Paul licks his lips.

—And that times twenty?

—Thirty six thousand two hundred eighty seven, point two.

Paul squeezes the bag, it rustles, and the crystals crunch.

—That's a car, man. That's the most bitchin' car ever. Fuck, man, that's four decent cars.

George takes the big bag from Paul and hands it to Andy.

—Put everything back like it was, man. This is not a car. It's fucking crank and you have to sell it to get the money to buy the car and you don't know how to sell it and you get busted and end up in Santa Rita playing bitch to some fuckstick like Ramon.

—Fuck you, man. What's easier than selling drugs? Your aunt deals pills. She does OK.

Andy finishes arranging the bags and steps back.

—That's it.

George looks.

—You sure? It looks different.

—Maybe move that one on the end to the right a little.

George pushes the bags around. Hector's found a can of WD40 and is using it to loosen up his chain.

Andy looks at his brother's back, nudges Paul with his elbow.

Paul gives him a shove.

—Knock it off, fag.

Andy rolls his eyes, nudges him again.

Paul raises a hand to give him a slap.

—What did I just fucking?

He sees the bag of crank Andy is holding behind his back.

George closes the fridge and turns.

—That shit's more trouble than it's worth. I told you that story about that guy.

He has told them the story. They've all heard the story from last summer when he was making pill runs for aunt Amy.

———

He was dropping a vial of ludes with a guy who needed them to come down. A crankhead who'd been binging for like a week. George went in the guy's apartment and the guy wouldn't let him go.

George was still freaked hours later when he told them the story.

The guy just kept fucking talking shit and spazzing out and making me play Monopoly. Wouldn't let me be the dog like I always am, didn't want to be the dog himself, he was the fucking racecar, kept going Zoomzoom-zoom, but I couldn't be the dog. Just played and played and kept talking about nothing, just spewing shit and just when it seemed like he was winding down I'd make a move toward the door and the guy would do another couple lines and start jumping around and get pissed if I tried to leave the kitchen. Guy finally went bankrupt and started crying and saying that he lost everything and he was gonna kill himself and went to the closet to get a gun he said he had and I shoved the guy in the closet and slammed the door and ran the fuck out of the place. Told aunt Amy that's it, man, no more fucking crankheads. Rather drop a bag of bennies at a biker party than do another lude run for a crankhead.

And he's been down on crank ever since.

———

Paul holds up a hand.

—OK, man, whatever.

Through the garage door they hear a car pull into the driveway, the sound of Fernando screaming at his younger brothers, then the two of them screaming back at him as "Beat It" blares from the Impala's stereo.

Paul makes a face.

—Fucking Michael Jackson.

By the time the Arroyos are coming in the front door the guys have run out the back with their bikes, thrown them over the rear neighbor's fence, and gone over after them. Their pockets crammed with the money, jewelry, a bag of loose joints from Timo's stash, a pearl handled switchblade, a box of Trojans, and a few copies of *Oui*. Paul with the bag of crank he's taken from Andy shoved down the back of his pants.

By the time the Arroyos have stopped screaming at each other and Fernando has broken Timo's nose for being a smartass and squared off with Ramon in a no holds barred fistfight that has Timo hiding behind the legless couch, by the time the fight is over and Timo has gone for a doobie to kill the pain of his throbbing nose and found everything trashed and told his brothers and they've run to the garage and found that a half kilo of crank is missing and Ramon has gone for his little chrome .22 automatic, by that time the guys have cleared the neighbor's yard, ridden to the Senior Taco in the P&X shopping center, and ordered sixteen tacos with fries and milkshakes.

———

They know being a rat sucks, but the Arroyos are gonna know who robbed them and if they don't do something those crazy fuckers will. Paul's ready to do it. It was his idea they rob the place, if someone has to rat the Arroyos, it's him.

But as they're talking and waiting for their food, Andy gets up and makes the call. Not that he still wants revenge for the stolen bike he's leaned against the phone booth, but he does want to make the call himself. He just can't help it. Finding the school picture of Alexandra when he was digging through Timo's shit was too much; the little photo clipped from a large sheet of them; *Te quiero, Timo* written in the corner in red ballpoint, in her own hand.

So he dials 0 and asks for the cops and anonymously reports a disturbance at 1367 North P Street. Some kind of fight or something.

The cops know that address. Small town heat that they are, they like nothing more than to bust the chops of the local spic hooligans. So they send a couple cars right over there.

Paul has just grabbed the last taco from the pile in the middle of the table and peeled off the grease stained orange paper and crunched into the taco, biting it in half, when a few blocks away the cops arrive at the Arroyos' just in time to see Ramon stepping out the front door, tucking the bright silver .22 into his waistband.

They don't bother telling him to drop it.

The Sketchy House

They roll their bikes up the driveway as if they live there, Paul flipping his new Buck knife open with the edge of his thumb the way Jeff showed him, the razor edged blade slicing clean through the hank of yellow rope, the crooked gate creaking open on rusted hinges before creaking closed behind them.

George loops one of the loose rope ends around the gatepost to keep it from swinging open. He peeks through a wide crack between the gate's warped planks and watches the street. No one comes out on their front porch to gaze across the street. No bright lights shine out from the cracks between curtains as someone looks from their kitchen window. The street is TV time quiet. Everyone parked in front of the tube watching *Magnum P.I.*

He turns around. Andy is lining up the bikes, turning them so they face the gate, enough room between them so that they can all jump on and start riding without being on top of each other.

Paul is at the side door. He turns the knob. Shakes his head. George joins him. The window peeking into the garage is covered on the inside. Tinfoil and black duct tape.

Hector has gone around the rear corner of the house, trying the back windows for one that's unlocked.

He stays low so the tall crest of his mohawk can't be seen from any of the other backyards. The guys wanted him to wear a cap or something over it. Fuck that. Thing takes almost as long to do as his sister's hair. Besides, these old houses off Junction Avenue have huge yards and tons of big trees that are like a hundred years old or something. No one is gonna see shit. What the guys really wanted was for him to cut it off.

They're uptight that if someone gets a look at them going in or out the mohawk is gonna get them all busted. Sure, there's only a couple other guys in town that got 'em. And he's the only Mexican. But that's the point. Looking different is the point. Having your appearance spit in people's faces and piss them off is the point. Cut off the hawk and it's like caving in. Fuck that.

And where the fuck's an unlocked window for fucksake?

He's checked the whole back of the house, tried the kitchen and bedroom and livingroom windows and they're all locked. Normally, you could slip a jimmy into the crack between the sliding glass door and the jamb, but the owners have a piece of 1×2 laid flat in the door's guide slot or whatever the hell it's called. Pop the lock and try to open the door and it'll just get jammed against the stick.

And, man, it's a mess in there. Boxes and shit piled all over. Stuff that just looks like garbage. A shitty old couch and a lamp. Not even a TV. What kind of stuff they supposed to find in a place like this?

Fuck it. Not his problem.

He peeks around the corner into the narrow space that runs between the far side of the house and the fence. One of those little louvered bathroom windows is cranked open. He goes back around the other side of the house and gets the guys.

He tells them what the deal is, and they all look at Andy.

Andy keeps his hands in his pockets, his right hand fingering the twenty sided die.

The Worst Thing That Happens

Bob Whelan stands at the foot of the stairs, sipping coffee and looking up at the door to his older son's room. He thinks about going up and kicking the foot of George's bed and getting his lazy ass up and dressed and out to the job site with him. Been weeks since the kid's come out for a day's work. It'd do him good to get out there and make a couple bucks instead of screwing around with his pals all day.

Cindy shuffles into the kitchen, rubbing her eyes and yawning. Barely looking at what she's doing, she gets a mug from the cabinet, fills it with coffee, rips open two packets of Sweet'N Low, dumps them in the mug, pours in a drop of milk and stirs it with her index finger before taking a big swallow.

She looks at Bob at the bottom of the stairs.

—You should go get him.

He shrugs.

—Not gonna force him to make money he doesn't want to make.

She reaches under the XL T that reaches halfway down her thighs and scratches her stomach.

—If you want his company all you have to do is ask.

Bob walks away from the stairs.

—Not about wanting his company. Doesn't matter. He'd rather mess around with Paul and Hector.

She picks up the coffee pot and tops off his cup for him.

—So take Andy. Andy would love to go.

He rolls his eyes.

—Honey, if you'd been there the time I took him. That kid on a construction site is like the opposite of a bull in a china shop. Thought he was gonna kill himself, wandering around daydreaming.

—So give him a broom and have him sweep some stuff up.

—It's not like that. Can't just stand off to the side. You have to be on the ball and pay attention to what's going on around you. He'll be out there sweeping and thinking about math problems and Dungeons & Dragons and whatever else and end up under a grader or something.

—Take them both. George can keep an eye on Andy and you can spend some time with both of them.

Bob's cup bangs on the counter when he sets it down.

—I'm not trying to arrange quality time with my sons, Cin. I was just thinking George should be working a little more this summer and fucking around a little less. OK?

Cindy shakes her head and starts for the bedroom.

—Fine, Bob, whatever you say. I've got to get dressed for work. You want to wait a few minutes I'll make you some breakfast.

—I'll get something from the cater truck.

—Suit yourself.

He watches her disappear down the hall, looking at her legs, the bruises on her thighs from where she's banged them against the checkout counter at Safeway where she spends her days at the cash register.

He thinks about what it would be like if his wife didn't have to work. His mom never had to work. Well, she worked plenty on the ranch, but she never had to go and take a job outside the house. Not till pop lost the ranch anyway.

Could have been different.

He stares into his coffee cup and thinks about what he could have done to make it different.

—Hell with that.

He walks to the front hall, sits on the little bench Cindy found at a yard sale and stripped and sanded and stained so it would look nice in the house. He sets his cup down, pulls on one of his scuffed steel toes and laces it up.

Things could have been different. Doesn't mean they would have been better. Not for him. Not for Cindy. Not for the boys.

He stands and stretches and tries to remember how much gas is in the truck and whether he has any cash in his wallet to fill it up.

—Hey.

He looks at Cindy, coming toward him in her bikini pants and bra, running a brush through her hair, Andy's cesarean scar across her stomach, a good looking woman.

She taps the brush against his arm.

—I'm just saying, you could tell George you want him to come with you. It doesn't have to be a contest to see who says something first.

—It's not a contest.

—Well you sure act like it is. Both of you.

—Cin, the boy is getting older. I'd like to see him making some decisions on his own that don't involve riding his bike to the bowling alley or copping a few extra bucks so he can get someone to buy him a six pack.

She reaches up and loops her arm around his neck.

—Just because the apple doesn't fall far from the tree, that doesn't mean it'll grow the same way.

He pulls out from under her arm.

—What? Where the hell did that one come from? That a Hallmark card?

—You know what I mean. Even if he's like you, you worked out just fine.

He looks at the wall, the series of pencil marks that rise up it, charting the growth of his sons.

—I got lucky.

He goes out the front door.

———

—Almost through with that?

Paul doesn't look up, just folds the newspaper and places it on the table in front of his father's chair.

Mr. Cheney pours himself a cup from the Mr. Coffee.

—Don't have to give me the whole thing. Finish reading what you were reading.

Paul gets up and takes his cereal bowl and spoon to the sink and washes them and puts them on the dish rack. He picks up his own coffee cup from the table and starts for the kitchen door.

His dad is at the table, fingering the corner of the front page.

—You got in late last night.

Paul stops.

—Ya huh.

—Out with the guys?

—Ya huh.

—How are they?

—I'uh nuh.

Mr. Cheney takes a sip from his cup.

—What are you doing today?

Paul stands in the doorway, back to his father, shrugs.

—Summer almost over. Got any big plans?

Another shrug.

—Never see the guys anymore. Used to play over here all the time.

Paul walks.

—My head hurts. Goin' to my room.

Mr. Cheney moves to the door.

—Need anything?

Paul keeps walking. His father watches him disappear down the hall, then sits at the table and waits.

He hears it when Paul slips past the kitchen and into the garage, hears the automatic door swing up, and knows his son has ridden off on the bike he bought him for his sixteenth birthday in lieu of the car he really wanted.

He gets up and goes to the cabinet next to the refrigerator and squats to reach behind the stack of newspapers Paul hasn't taken to the curb for recycling in weeks, and takes out the jug of Delacort brandy hidden there. He holds it up and checks the level against the mark he made on the label last night. No change. He takes the bottle to the sink, pours half his coffee down the drain and replaces it with brandy, makes a fresh mark on the label and puts the bottle back behind the papers.

He swirls the coffee and brandy and takes a drink. Need to pick up a new bottle today. The Liquor Barn in Pleasanton this time. Haven't been there in a few weeks. Not that he's got anything to hide. Just nobody's business how he lives his life.

Unfolding the paper, knuckling his glasses higher up on the bridge of his nose, he reads the story about Ramon Arroyo being shot in the leg by police and he and his brothers being busted on an assortment of charges: stolen goods, drugs, weapons, resisting arrest.

Good lord.

He thinks about Caesar Arroyo, the boys' father. The squat bundle of calluses and muscle that he used to see swatting his boys' ears at soccer games when they didn't play up to his standards.

He'd tried to have a word with the man once. Walked over to him on the sideline and smiled and suggested to him that his boys might play better, have a better time if they didn't feel quite so much pressure. Caesar had stared at him, then waved one of his boys over. Ramon? Fernando? How long ago was this? Could it have been the youngest one? The one Paul had that trouble with?

The boy had come over and, staring Kyle Cheney in the eye, Caesar had slapped the boy hard. And stood there waiting until Kyle walked away, back to the adjoining field where Paul and George's team was playing.

Bob Whelan had been there. He'd seen what Caesar was doing and looked away. He could have done something about it. Whelan is the kind of man who could have said something to Arroyo and made him think twice about knocking his kids around like that. At least made him stop doing it out on the soccer fields where the other kids saw it and got freaked out. But he didn't do anything. Just like most people. Most adults just don't have the kids' best interest at heart.

Any wonder the Arroyos have grown up like they have? A drug lab. Here. In his town. When do these things happen? How do they happen? Don't people know they have to monitor their children? Care for them? Love them? Otherwise, things like this happen.

Tragedies. Family tragedies.

He gets up, tops off his cup again. Marks the bottle. Then goes down the hall to his son's room.

He fingers the Master Lock Paul mounted there last year. He takes out the duplicate key he had made the afternoon he was doing laundry and found Paul's key, forgotten in the pocket of his dirty jeans. He opens the lock and goes into his son's room and sits on the bed.

He remembers the room as it was, before it became plastered with posters of Iron Maiden and Van Halen and Ozzy Osbourne and Ted Nugent and AC/DC and The Scorpions and Judas Priest and all the others dripping blood and wrapped in Spandex and surrounded by skulls. He remembers when the floor was littered with Legos and Lincoln Logs instead of microwave burrito wrappers and empty matchbooks and torn copies of *Rolling Stone* and crushed beer cans pushed under the bed and discarded cigarette pack cellophanes. He remembers this room before it smelled of spilled beer and smoke and the stale incense that's meant to cover it all up.

He gets up, takes a long drink, sets his coffee cup on top of the dresser and starts to search the room, just as he does every day.

An empty half pint of Fleischmann's vodka and the same old stash of *Playboy* back issues with Bob Whelan's address label on the cover.

Booze and dirty magazines. Kyle Cheney knows there's worse somewhere.

When Paul first started changing, when his mother took off and left them alone six years ago and he started talking back, that's when he'd had to start this. She'd driven a wedge between him and his son. That's what he couldn't forgive her for. Not the stupid way she left them, but the things she'd said to the boy, the things she'd said about *him*. Things she'd screamed that scared Paul. Things Paul was just too young to understand.

Things that confused him about their relationship.

What it was.

What it meant to him.

When he started finding the boy's door blocked, a dresser shoved in front of it, that's when he knew the extent of the damage she'd done. The damage she'd done to their trust.

Paul stopped talking to him. And he'd had no choice but to take things into his own hands, to find out what his son was up to.

And he found things. A few joints. Pills. A boom box and someone's class ring, both obviously stolen. Girls sneaking in the window in the middle of the night. Girls he'd seen, and heard. Stood in the hall outside the boy's room and heard them.

But it wasn't enough. None of it was enough to make him feel like he was still inside his son's life.

He just had to keep looking. Keep looking until he found the secret that would open his son back up to him.

———

Hector wakes up, reaches for his turntable and hits play.

The tone arm jerks and drops heavily onto the album that's cued up and waiting to start his day. The speakers hiss and crack and then explode into "Memories of Tomorrow."

The sound yanks him from bed and he pogos around the room, flailing his arms and bouncing off the walls.

Suicidal Tendencies got it right.

The Pistols were a great start. Dead Kennedys and Black Flag carried him for awhile. He thought it might be the Bad Brains that did it for him. But it was Suicidal Tendencies that took it all the way. He heard about them after taking the bus to Hayward and riding the BART train into San Francisco for a Kennedys gig at Mabuhay Garden. He had to wait another month for the album to come out. It was worth it. It's perfect and he's been listening to nothing else ever since.

He jumps on his bed, jumps from it to the twin his little brothers sleep on, bounces back and forth between them. The little fuckers must be up already. Up and outside, fighting with each other and talking back to their mom. Little pieces of shit.

Alexandra opens the door.

—Turn it down!

He bounces high off the bed and lands in front of her, smiling and jumping up and down.

—What?

—Turn it down, Hector, it's awful! Turn it down.

He pogos higher, arms plastered to his sides, leaping.

—Turn it up?

—Down! Down!

—Louder?

—Heeeectooor! Stooooop iiiiiiit! It's awwwwwfuuuuuul!

He grabs her hands and drags her into his room, pulls her up on the bed and bounces.

—Dance, mija, dance to the music!

She tries to jerk free.

—Noooo, it's not dancing! It's not music! It's awful!

He wraps his arms around her, bouncing, laughing.

—Dance with me, little sister.

—Moooooom! Muuuuuhhoooooom!

But she's jumping with him now, her perfectly blownout hair mussed, her sharply creased khakis wrinkled, heavy eye liner smeared by tears as she laughs at her crazy big brother.

He lets her go and they jump up and down on the bed.

Their mom comes in.

—Mijo!

He flies off the bed and crashes off the wall, the record skips once, plays on.

He dances.

His mom puts her hands on his shoulders and tries to push him down, to stop the bouncing.

—Mijo! So loud! So loud!

But she can't stop him. She's laughing.

—Mijo, no, it's too early. Come eat breakfast. Turn it off! Come eat.

He bounces to the turntable, lands, thrashes his head back and forth at the end of the song and takes the needle off the record, becoming still.

Alexandra climbs off the bed, running a fingertip under her eye.

—Hectooor, you ruin my makeup. Mooom, look at my face.

She runs out the door and into the bathroom, where she'll spend the next hour redoing her hair and makeup.

Their mom is still laughing.

—You look like a dancing fish, mijo. A fish.

He smiles.

—C'mon, Ma.

He puts the needle back down on the beginning of the song, bounces back to her and grabs her hands, pulling.

She jumps up and down a few times with him, then frees her hands and covers her ears.

—Enough, mijo, enough! Too loud. Come eat.

She reaches out and grabs a fold of his belly skin between her thumb and index finger and gives it a twist.

—Eat!

He bounces free and moshes around the tiny room.

She waves her hands in the air and walks away, still laughing, the song thundering and ripping new cracks in the taped up speakers.

Through the open door he watches her walk back to the kitchen, where she spends her life minding pots of rice and beans and stewed pork and chicken.

His dad is in the livingroom, asleep on the couch already, his ruined leg propped on a kitchen chair, a bottle of his painkillers sticking out of his bathrobe pocket, a half empty gallon jug of Gallo on the floor.

Hector pushes the door closed and dances, slashing his hand up and down over the strings of an invisible guitar. The guitar he'll have one day when high school is over and he takes BART into The City for the last time.

He'll crash in a squat full of punks and put together a band and play that guitar when they gig at Mabuhay and he'll take it on the road and he'll see shit that he's never gonna see if he takes a job at the quarry and marries one of the pachuco chicks from the neighborhood and has three kids by the time he's old enough to go in a bar. Fuck that. He's gonna buy a guitar and be a fucking punk.

He is a fucking punk.

And he sings.

Mass starvation
Contaminated water
Destroyed cities
Mutilated bodies

I'll kill myself
I'd rather die
If you could see the future
You'd know why.

It's hot in George's attic room. All summer long he wakes up sweating. Today he wakes up sweating and screaming, having dreamed the El Camino running him over.

He sits on the edge of the bed, sweat coating his scalp under his long hair and running from his pits and down his sides, soaking the seat of his Fruit of the Looms. He gets up and goes to the mirror over his desk and looks at the scrapes running from his jaw down the left side of his neck.

When he and Andy came home yesterday he told their folks he pulled an endo on a jump at the firebreak. His dad asked if his bike was in one piece while his mom cleaned the cuts with hydrogen peroxide. Andy had gone straight to his room.

You don't want Andy around when you're lying to mom and dad. Little spaz gets restless and starts talking too much and fucks it up.

But it wasn't a big deal. Mom was relieved it was nothing that required a trip to the emergency room. Dad was satisfied that the bike wasn't messed up. But he gave one of his speeches: *Got to value the things money buys, the hard work that goes into making that money. You'll need that. You're not gonna be getting a scholarship anywhere like your little brother, you're gonna be working for a living. Nothing wrong with that. Nothing wrong with you. That's the way it is. Life's not fair. Sooner you learn the truth that work sucks and working for someone else sucks even worse, the better. Got to put value on what you earn when you hate doing what you have to do to get it.*

Big Bob Whelan, saying it like it is. Again. Telling him that everything has a cost. There's no free rides and life's not fair and there's always assholes wherever you go. Work, work, work and get by and take a break on weekends and crack a beer and watch a game and show your kids how to mow a lawn and drywall a house and shovel rocks and play hard and there's no such thing as second place winner and be nice to your wife and she'll be nice to you and don't take anything for granted and clean your plate and as long as you live under my roof you live under my rules and there's no such thing as a free ride and if it ain't easy that just means you should work a little harder, doesn't it?

The lesson of life: You get what you work for, if that.

George turns from the mirror and goes to the bathroom at the foot of the stairs. He gets in the shower and blasts it cold to stop the sweat. He should have brought his jeans down with him, his jeans and the Aerosmith *Toys in the Attic* T he plans on wearing today. Getting dressed up there, he'll just start to sweat again. He thinks about the money from yesterday, wonders if there's enough to buy an air conditioner for his room, a window unit. No. His dad would want to know where he got that much cash. But a fan, he could probably get away with a fan.

He thinks about the money, but that makes him think about the Arroyos' house, and that makes him think about hitting the street and the El Camino just missing him and what it might have felt like to go under the wheels.

He could have died. But according to dad, that's not the worst thing that happens to you. The worst thing is that you work for someone else and have to put up with assholes telling you what to do, that's the worst thing.

But it doesn't have to be like that. Be smart enough, and maybe it doesn't have to be like that. If he can get to be good at something else, he won't have to work. Not really.

————

Andy makes a map.

He starts with a blank piece of graph paper. Sitting at his little desk, wearing the glasses he hates, tracing heavy black lines over the light blue lines on the paper, creating a world.

Not a whole world, just a part of it. A tiny secret corner filled with puzzles and traps and treasures and monsters. A dungeon for heroes to explore and plunder.

With one hand he draws. With the other he fingers a set of geodesic dice, tossing them one at a time or in combination, glancing at the numbers and applying them to secret formulas only he knows. The results dictating which way a tunnel will twist, where a crevasse will open suddenly, a goblin leap from a recess, a potion of healing be found.

He could design it all. Lay it out in his head and put it on the paper, but randomness is cool. It injects chaos into the game. Chaos is cool. He wouldn't have thought of that on his own, but reading about it lately, it's cool. The way order is just an illusion, something we create in our heads and lay over the world to try and force it to fit all these ideas we have about the way things should be. But the world's not really the way people think it is. Or maybe it is. Hard to really say for sure. But chaos seems to make more sense than anything else.

It explains a lot.

Like how you can be so smart about some things and so dumb about others.

Like stealing the methamphetamine and giving it to Paul.

Now that was stupid.

He stops drawing for a second and bangs his forehead against the desktop. Really, really stupid. Man, why is he so damn stupid?

Imsuchadildo.

He lays his head on the desk, still fiddling with the dice, letting part of his brain play with the numbers. Letting the smart part of his brain play.

Stealing the crank is either the coolest thing he's ever done or the lamest, he's not sure which. Order or chaos.

Paul's into it. But there was never any question that he'd be into it. Paul likes all the ups. He likes getting baked and drunk and dropping a lude, but he really likes the beauties and the whites and the greens. Any kind of speed. Like Paul needs to be *more* high strung. Like they need Paul to be more high strung and starting any more trouble than he already does. Half the hooks they end up in are because Paul is so uptight and can't keep it together.

Some jocks walk past laughing, probably talking about the time one of them farted in remedial English, and Paul thinks they're laughing about him and starts calling them fags and telling them to say whatever they have to say to his face. They take one look at the four of them; big Paul with the curly hair and acne scars on his cheeks, Hector with his mohawk and safety pins, skinny George with his pretty face that all the girls dig, and Andy, short and scrawny with the long unwashed hair; and it's on.

Fag this and *fag* that and *kick your fucking ass* and *do it if you're gonna do it stop talking about it and fucking do it, fag,* until one of them explodes from the pressure.

Chaos.

Fists and kicking and going down on the pavement with someone's arm around your neck and your hair getting pulled as your brother tears that guy off you and seeing someone's legs in front of you and grabbing their ankles and pulling them and hoping the fucker doesn't split his head open when he hits the ground and Paul always going after the biggest one and getting him down and sitting on his chest and punching his face over and over until someone drags him off.

A dozen fistfights play out in Andy's head. He throws a grenade into the middle of them all and watches the body parts fly and winces and bangs his head again and rolls the dice and only stops rolling when the sum of their faces divided by the number of dice he's rolled totals a prime.

Order.

Yeah, Paul thinks the crank is cool. And if he does like he was talking about and sells it and gets enough money for a car they can all cruise around in, then stealing the bag will be cool. If he ends up whiffing it all himself and getting higher strung than he already is, then it's just the lamest idea ever.

And he can't even tell George what he did.

George'll be pissed.

Just have to wait and see what Paul does. He'll either tell the guys he has it and make like he was the one who took it and tell them it's too late to do anything about it now and start figuring a way to sell it. Or he'll keep his mouth shut. And if he keeps his mouth shut, it's because he's snorting it.

He lifts his head, rolls the dice, puts a trap in an empty room. Then changes his mind and replaces it with treasure.

The Smartest Boy in Class

Paul rides his bike into George and Andy's garage. The cars are gone. Their mom and dad already at work. He leans the bike against the toolbench and lights one of the Marlboros from the pack he bought yesterday with the Arroyos' money.

It's so cool George and Andy don't have to worry about their folks being around during the day. Not like his dad. He's always around. Teaches computer classes at the community college down the 580. Staggered schedule. Night classes, day classes, morning classes. Summer, winter, fall, spring. Sooner or later, every fucking day, he pops up. Asking questions, nosing in his business like it's not enough already. Like he hasn't gotten enough and wants more, more than he's already had.

He grinds his smoke out, tossing the butt in the coffee can full of sand that Mr. Whelan keeps out here, lighting another.

He smokes. And finds something else to think about, taking out of his back pocket the tightly folded copy of the *Valley Times* that he snatched off someone's lawn on the way here, and unfolding it on the workbench.

So much for the Arroyos.

Those fucks are gone. Only part of it that sucks is that he never got a chance to beat the shit out of Timo. Or Ramon. Would have liked a crack at Ramon without that saw in his hand. Fucker's big, doesn't mean he can fight. Doesn't mean he can take it. Paul can take shit those vatos never heard of.

He remembers all he's taken.

Lightning crackles between his eyes, the first flash of a migraine.

He drags hard on his smoke, the cherry flares. He lifts the bottom of his T and touches the tip of the cigarette to his stomach, adding another mark to his collection. The migraine recedes, blown over the horizon.

And the pictures of what he's endured go away.

He drops his shirt, the cotton stinging his stomach when it touches the fresh burn. He drags on his cigarette, tasting his own skin.

He can take it.

He can fucking take it.

He touches the wad of the Arroyos' money in his pocket.

His money now. He boosts himself up on the bench and pulls the cash out. After the food and the smokes and the bottle of tequila they got a college guy to buy them at the QuickStop by the freeway, there's a little over two hundred left. Fifty and change each.

Fifty bucks for weed and booze and pills and video games at the bowling alley. Fifty bucks to finish off the summer. Before senior year. Before he has to get serious about classes.

Serious enough to pass a few. Just enough to graduate. Just enough to get a diploma. Just enough to get that piece of paper so that there won't be any question about the Army accepting him when he turns eighteen next June thirteenth and goes to enlist that same day. Next stop basic training. Next stop after that, the other side of the fucking world. Never to return, man. Never to return.

So fifty bucks worth of partying before that grind starts.

And the crank.

Sitting on the can this morning, door locked, bag of crank on his lap. Fingered a couple crystals out of the bag and set them on the edge of the sink and thought about crushing them with the bottom of his water glass and spooning up the powder on the end of his nail clipper and doing a couple whiffs. Enough in that bag to keep up for weeks. Keep up and clear. Keep him focused. Keep the shit that comes into his mind on the outside.

But if you could sell it.

And not like dealing it, George is right about that. Get into trying to deal it, say around the bowling alley with the loose joint dealers pedaling their bikes around and whispering, *Loose joints, man, loose joints, one for two or three for five, loose joints,* get into that scene and a bust is on its way. Cops always cruising the bowling alley. There's the parking lot at the Doughnut Wheel. But those acid dealers from the other high school, they got that lot staked out. Besides, who knows how long it will take to sell it all?

Better to sell the whole bag at once. Won't be worth as much, but still a lot. Enough for a car. But who the fuck has that kind of money? George and Andy's aunt might be able to hook him up with someone. Or she might freak out. She doesn't like crank. Stays away from dealing it herself.

Jeff.

Jeff doesn't have the money himself, but he knows people. He talks all the time about stuff that *fell off the back of a truck*. Half the parts he gets for his Harley are hot. And he's done some stuff himself. Talked about some of the places he's guarded for Security Eye, goin' in when he's alone, boosting shit. He knows people who buy shit. And he knows dealers. Jeff knows everyone. And he won't give a crap it's crank.

Just got to handle it right. Got to be cool about it. Don't just knock on his door with a bag of crystal and drop it on the table and ask what he can get for it. Start with the other stuff. Take him those chains and see how that goes. Maybe mention to him there's some other things to talk about when the rest of the guys aren't around. Yeah, be cool about it.

And then, the look on the guys' faces when he rolls up in a couple weeks in a car? Sweet. They'll have to work out some kind of deal. Park it at Jeff's or Amy's. Take turns with it. Hector can take it into the city to those punk gigs instead of having to go on the bus and BART. George can take his chicks for a ride instead of having to rely on them to borrow their dads' cars. Andy, well, Andy can learn to drive in a badass set of wheels.

Sat on the can in his old grass stained soccer shorts and the George Blanda jersey he sleeps in, staring at that bag. And he did the right thing, dribbled those crystals right back inside. Then got a roll of athletic tape from beneath the sink, taped the bag closed, lifted the lid from the back of the toilet, and taped the bag to its underside before replacing it.

Dad'll find anything you leave in the room. Checking it every day. Using that key he left in his jeans that time. Sure, let the old man dig around in there, that way he doesn't dig around anywhere else. Don't have to be as smart as Andy to figure out that kind of shit.

Course, the cherry on top of the morning was the newspaper. Saw the story about the Arroyos on the front page of the paper. Almost choked trying to keep from laughing and blowing milk and Cheerios out his nostrils.

———

Kyle Cheney jiggles the handle on the toilet, but the plug still doesn't drop. The chain is snagged again. He lifts the lid off the back of the tank and sets it on the seat. Sure enough, snagged chain. He reaches in and untwists the tangled links and flips the plug down over the drain and the tank starts to fill with water. He fiddles with the handle, pressing it down and releasing it, trying to see why the chain only snags when *he* flushes.

Paul says it's because he's doing it wrong.

Flushing the toilet the wrong way.

He wipes his fingers on a hand towel and picks up his cup from the sink. Almost all brandy now. He drains it.

When did that happen? When did he become the kind of man who flushes toilets the wrong way?

It wasn't always that way.

He'd been far and away the smartest boy in class. Not a prodigy maybe, not like Andy Whelan, but valedictorian nonetheless. He'd gone to college when that really meant something in this town. Not just college, but Berkeley. And a scholarship. Partial, yes, but a scholarship. And perhaps at Berkeley he was no longer the smartest, but he worked plenty hard. So, not top of his class, but good enough to be accepted for postgrad work in computer science.

And computers! That had been thinking ahead. He'd been dead right about that. It was one thing to say computers were the future, it was quite another to have the strength of your convictions and commit yourself to that path.

If he'd just finished.

If he'd just not let himself get distracted by Paul's mother and her campus politics and idealistic crusades. And then, pregnant. Of all clichés.

With the PhD he'd still be there, teaching at UC Berkeley in one of the most prestigious departments in the country. Tenured. Perhaps a chair by now.

Well, he has a chair. At the satellite campus of a community college. An institution that specializes in GED prep courses and AA degrees.

Department chair.

Lord, he's the entire computer department himself. Teaching data entry and machine language to borderline high school graduates.

Should have been more focused when he got the IBM job. Be a project manager by now. But Paul was born by then. And he'd fallen so in love with the boy.

His son.

Taken sick days just to spend more time with him. Margaret had loved that at first. Didn't give a damn about his career. So many of the other men at IBM, complaining about their wives and how all they could do was shop and rag on them about getting ahead. But not Margaret. As long as there was food on the table and a roof over Paul's head she didn't care about money at all. He could hang about the house playing with his son all he liked. She was moved by what an attentive father he'd turned out to be.

But then she stopped loving it. Started saying things about it. As if it was wrong that a boy's closest friend should be his father. That a father's strongest friendship should be with his son. As if it were wrong.

Jealous is all she was.

And unreasonable.

She just could not listen to reason when he tried to explain it to her. Imagine, threatening to take his boy from him.

Nonsense.

Well, in the end it was her own fault. What happened was her own fault. No one told her to get so drunk and say those things and scare Paul so much he went running from the house. No one told her to go speeding off like a crazy woman looking for him. If she'd exercised just a little self control she never would have lost control of her car.

That had been hard. Explaining to Paul that his mother wouldn't be coming home.

The look from the boy.

Like it was his fault.

The toilet tank is full now.

He lifts the lid from the seat and his fingers graze something and he flips it over and sees the plastic baggie held to the underside by a large X of white athletic tape.

And for the first time in years he knows just what to do.

Summer Job

—What about when they get out?

Paul snorts, blows smoke and passes the joint around.

—Get out? A crank lab in this town? They're never fucking getting out. Something like that here, that's like cheating at cards in the Old West. Hanging offense, man. They're done.

Andy looks again at the paper spread across his dad's workbench.

—Think Ramon's OK?

Paul turns his back and walks to the other side of the garage.

—Somebody else please slap at the back of numbnuts' head this time.

George slaps at the back of his brother's head.

—Who gives a fuck if he's OK, numbnuts?

Andy ducks, the slap glancing off the top of his head and sending his unwashed hair into his eyes. He tosses it back.

—I didn't say I cared, I just asked if you thought he's OK. That's all.

Hector finishes counting the money they took from the Arroyos' and sets it on the newspaper.

—Ramon is a psycho, man, kind of guy they shoot twenty times and keeps coming. Bullet in the leg means shit.

Paul points at the money.

—How much?

—Two fifty eight altogether.

Andy nods.

—Sixty four dollars and fifty cents each. Two of us get sixty five and give the other two fifty cents to make it even.

Paul takes a hit from the joint.

—Gee, I'm so fucking glad we have a rocket scientist here to do our math for us. Don't know how us retards would have figured that out with the fifty cents and all.

Well baked, Andy giggles helplessly.

Paul hands the joint to George.

—Better keep this away from Mr. Lightweight. Looks like he's over the edge again.

George hits the joint, watching his brother spaz helplessly, caught in a giggle fit that is clearly going the distance.

He passes the joint to Hector.

—I don't know, man, I've been thinking about this. Maybe the secret, maybe the secret is to get him higher.

Andy is panting, shaking his head, tears starting to pop from his eyes.

Hector takes a hit, sucks the smoke in deep, holds the joint out to Andy.

—Take another hit, man, don't listen to them, you're handling this shit just fine. No, seriously, man, you got it all under control. Cops, teachers, parents, whoever, they'd never know you're stoned out of your mind. Take another hit, go on, man, you're fine.

Andy waves his hand at the joint, sides heaving, gasping through the giggles, in danger of pissing his pants.

Hector holds the joint up, strikes a pose. *Eureka!*

—He wants help hitting it!

Paul nods.

—Supercharger.

George nods.

—Definitely a supercharger situation.

Andy whips his head from side to side, tries to hold his hands up in front of him to keep them away, but clutches his aching sides instead.

—Nuhhhooo! Nuhooo!

Hector turns the joint around and puts the cherry inside his mouth, puffing his cheeks, while Paul and George take hold of Andy. He puts his face close to Andy's and blows. A thick stream of smoke jets from the tip of the joint.

Andy wheezes most of it in through his flaring nostrils and gaping mouth, instantly choking.

They release him and he doubles over, coughing and laughing and sneezing, ropes of drool and wads of snot hitting the concrete floor of the garage.

George pounds him on his back.

—Don't puke, man, that would be a breach of good taste.

Still bent over, Andy reaches back and slaps his brother away, the giggles fading as he gags a few more times.

Hector has taken the joint from his mouth. He blows some ash off the cherry.

—Looks like the supercharger did the trick.

Paul is laughing now, near silent hisses that slip in and out of his open mouth.

George looks at him.

—It's catching. Lightweightness is catching.

Andy is straightening, wiping his mouth with the back of his hand.

—You guys are dicks, I thought I was gonna choke to death.

Paul slaps the toolbench, mouth still hanging open, tiny seal barks coming from the back of his throat.

George points at him.

—Supercharger, man?

Paul bends, puts his forehead against the top of the bench, banging his fist on the scarred wood, tears streaming.

Hector waves the joint in the air.

—He's gone over the edge, man.

George bites his lip.

—Definitely on the dark side now.

Andy is at the sink that their dad uses for washing paintbrushes and their mom uses for bleaching things. He splashes water on his face, rinsing away the mucus around his mouth and nose.

—Man, he's losing it, he may never come back. No wonder you guys laugh at me when I'm like that, he's a mess.

Still bent at the waist, Paul lurches across the garage, shouldering Andy to the side and sticking his head under the tap.

George goes and stands right behind him.

—That's a good strategy, wash that shit out of your system. Nothing like a quick shower to help reestablish some fucking self control. You want me to wash your hair for you?

Paul comes up, flinging his head back and shaking it from side to side, water flying and spraying the others.

—Oh fuck, man! Whew! Oh my God. I lost it, man.

He shoves Andy.

—You busted my shit up.

Andy grabs a dirty bath towel from the basket sitting on top of the washing machine and dries his face.

—Yeah, nice to know when I'm choking to death it's good for a fucking laugh.

Paul snags the towel from him and rubs his hair.

—Fucking A right about that.

Hector holds out the joint.

—So who's ready for another hit?

They all fall out, staggering into the open air and sunlight of the driveway.

Across the street, Mr. Marinovic comes out of his house and stands on the porch shaking his head at them. He walks down the cement path to the driveway and swings his garage door open and walks around the side of his '78 Bonneville. Pulling into the street, he stops for a moment and watches them standing around their driveway, laughing and screaming and pointing at each other.

He rolls down his window and leans his head out.

—You should be working. It's summer. Why don't you have summer jobs?

The laughter stops. They all stare at him. The laughter starts again.

Mr. Marinovic rolls up his window, adjusts his rearview mirror, and puts the car in drive.

The boys watch Marinovic's car turn the corner as they snort a few last laughs out their noses, shaking their heads, exhausted.

George walks to the curb and looks up and down the empty street. Paul joins him. A Cessna buzzes by overhead on its way to the municipal airport. It's quiet again.

Paul blows out his cheeks to make himself look fat.

—Why don't you have a summer job? Blah. Blahblahblahblaaaaaah. George nods.

—Fuck him. We *have* a summer job.

—Fucking A. Let's get to work.

And they run across the street into the open garage and through the unlocked door that leads inside Mr. Marinovic's house.

The house smells like bug spray and TV dinners. Plastic runners laid across the wall to wall carpet lead through the livingroom and down the hall.

They ignore the kitchen. Nobody hides shit in the kitchen. They ignore the color TV and the console stereo and anything else that's just too big. They go to the master bedroom and Paul hits the medicine cabinet while George goes through the dresser drawers. If there's cash or jewelry stashed, it'll be in the dresser or the nightstand or the closet.

He runs his hands between neatly folded shirts. Squeezes rolled pairs of socks to see if anything offers resistance. He finds a box of condoms and a business card from the massage parlor across town, a phone number written on the back in green ballpoint. Which is all pretty gross. But at least the guy's wife is dead. So it's not as gross as it would be otherwise.

Paul comes out of the john rattling a brown prescription bottle. George looks at the label. Phenobarbital. He remembers something Aunt Amy told him.

—Shit's for epilepsy.

Paul opens the bottle and looks at the pills.

—Does it get you sideways?

—Fuck yeah.

—Think Marinovic is epileptic?

—He's got the pills.

Paul pours his palm full of pills and caps the bottle.

—I'll only take half.

He puts the bottle back where he found it and goes to check out the spare room.

George is going through the pockets of the clothes hanging in the closet. He spots something on the top shelf, reaches up and pulls down a jewelry box and opens it. Mrs. Marinovic's old jewelry.

Five bucks a week allowance for doing chores around the house doesn't even cover smokes. And the few extra bucks to be made some weekends when his dad takes him to a job site where they need a couple kids to clean shit up? Four bucks an hour to shovel plaster fragments and splintered plywood and bent nails and haul the shit out to a dumpster. Sweeping up and packing tools away in the sun and a half hour for lunch and all the guys on the site calling him kid and giving him shit about his long hair and the silver and turquoise necklace and ring he wears.

Only way he's ever really made money was running pills last summer for Aunt Amy while his mom and dad thought he was doing custodial at the water treatment plant by the airport.

She robbed the pills from the hospital dispensary on her RN shifts and dropped two bucks on him for each delivery. He spent last summer ducking in and out of her house on Rincon Avenue to see if she had anything for him to run. She told him not to tell the other guys, especially not Andy, but he couldn't keep it to himself. Running dope, man, it was too cool not to tell them about it. Plus, they knew he wasn't mopping any fucking floors and he wasn't gonna lie to his brother and his best friends about how he got the cash for his Mongoose.

He kept doing it after school started, just a couple deliveries a week when he had time, cigarette money and shit. Hell, he'd still be doing it except they got in a fight about a delivery that came up short. A few ludes and a couple whites and she pitched a fit. Like it hadn't happened before. But all of a sudden it was a big deal this time. Fuck it. By then he had the bike. He walked out of her place while she was yelling at him.

Acting like she was a boss or something.

Only time he'd seen her since was when she came over for last Christmas. Gave Andy a Star Wars model, an X-Wing. Gave him a sweater with a reindeer on the front. Whatever. They'll make it up sooner or later. She's too cool not to be friends with.

Totally different from his dad. Which is why his dad can't stand her.

Delivering the pills had been cool. Hanging on Aunt Amy's couch and smoking her Marlboro 100's and helping her sort the pills she stole from the dispensary into baggies and cranking twist ties around their tops and tucking the bags into his pockets after a few calls had come in. Hustling over to Shovelhead's, pounding on the door to be heard over Steppenwolf playing "Pusherman." Folding the cash into a tight bundle and slipping it into his sock. Taking a hit off Shovelhead's huge neutronbong and bouncing two blocks to Tiny Red's. Swapping a quarter gram of pharmaceutical coke for sheets of Mickey Wizard blotter acid, tiny pictures of Mickey Mouse in his *Fantasia* costume printed on each tab. Hanging with some of the younger guys, the cooler ones. Like Jeff. That'd been alright.

But it was still a job. It was still someone telling you where to go and what to do and how to do it.

This is different. Going in someone's house when they're not there? Better yet, when they are? That's like the total opposite of doing what you're told. That's blazing a trail and doing it your own way. Whatever you find, cash, drugs, some silver or gold that you can take out to Hayward on the bus and hock, it's all yours. You take the risks and you get the rewards. Get caught, well that's just your own fault. It's all on you. No bosses. No coming home like his mom and dad, burned out and sleepwalking through the evening and dropping into bed and struggling through the next morning to do it again. None of that shit.

———

He takes Mrs. Marinovic's engagement ring and her wedding ring and a set of tiny diamond earrings and a pearl choker and puts the box back on the top shelf, and he and Paul head out.

In the street, Hector and Andy toss a football back and forth. Hector lobbing the easiest passes he can, Andy dropping them anyway, then chucking the ball way too low so that Hector has no chance to catch it and it ends up under a car half the time.

George whistles from inside the garage and Hector and Andy look up and down the street and give a thumbs up and George and Paul run out and they all trot back into their own garage.

Paul doles out the phenobarbital, two each and three for him, and they add the rings and earrings and pearls to the chains from the Arroyos and look at the pile.

Paul tosses a pheno in his mouth and dry swallows.

—Fuck the bus ride to Hayward. Let's bike over to Jeff's and see if he can help us move it here in town.

His Son Reeling

Paul leads them in a pack across the field to Portola. They cut across the QuickStop blacktop, go under the arching sign for the Rancho Vista Trailer Park, and down the gravel drive that runs between the trailers. They round a bend, pass a double with a mini white picket fence running around an Astroturf lawn patrolled by a toy poodle, and there's Jeff on the porch of his own single.

Rust streaks down the yellow and white siding, weeds standing knee high all around, a corrugated tin awning shading the porch, cracked plastic tiki lamps dangling from its lip. Two beat to hell '63 VW Beetles, one being cannibalized for parts, the other consuming them; a '70 Datsun 240Z on blocks; and a sometimes functional '69 Chevy pickup, stand in front leaking oil, antifreeze, and radiator water into the weeds.

In the shade of the awning, Jeff sits on an upside down milk crate, the stripped carburetor from his '76 Harley XLH 1000 Sportster spread on a flattened cardboard box at his feet. The guys crunch up, and he waves oily fingers at them, pulling a filterless Camel from between his lips.

—Hey, fuckos.

Paul leans his bike on the 240Z and Jeff waves his cigarette.

—Hey, whoa, no, not on the wheels.

Paul moves the bike, leans it against the porch.

—Sorry, Jeff.

Jeff puts the smoke back in his face.

—'S no problem. What up with you guys?

Paul stands at the foot of the steps leading to the porch, the guys are still straddling their bikes, looking at rocks, trees, weeds. He pulls out a Marlboro.

—Kinda wanted to talk.

—Yeah?

—Yeah.

Jeff goes back to work on the carburetor, dipping a rag into an old baby food jar full of gasoline and using it to clean a residue of black carbon from inside the carburetor.

—What about?

—Some shit.

Jeff cleans. The guys stand around.

Paul takes a step up.

—Jeff?

—I'm still here.

—Yeah. Could we maybe talk about it inside?

Jeff rubs his wrist against his chin, takes the smoke from his mouth and tosses it in the dry weeds.

—Look, guys, I got to be at work in a couple hours and I want to get this thing back together so I can ride. Sick of the damn bus. Something's up, get to it.

Still straddling his bike, Andy waddles forward and steps on the smoldering butt before it can ignite the oil soaked weeds around the cars.

He looks at Jeff.

—We stole some stuff and we want to know if you can hock it for us.

Jeff gets up, wipes his hands on the ass of his jeans, opens the front door and points inside.

—Everybody out of the fucking water.

————

By sitting on the kitchen counter and leaning his face against the far end of the window over the sink, Mr. Cheney can see all the way down the street to the front of the Whelan house.

He's watching when Hector rides up, that disturbing wedge of hair jutting up from his head. He'd been such a sweet quiet boy when his family moved into the neighborhood. The first Mexican family on the block. Well, the only one actually.

He reaches for the brandy and tips more into his coffee cup, no longer bothering to mark the label or put the bottle back in the cupboard after each drink. It's nearly empty now, so why bother? A quick run to the Liquor Barn and he'll have a full one. Or maybe not, a drive into Pleasanton seems rather far. The Safeway is closer. Except that Cindy Whelan will be working there. Well, a few groceries to surround the bottle then, just to keep her minding her own business.

Oh nonsense!

Dave's Liquors is right next door to the Safeway, if he's going to drive to the shopping center he can just go to Dave's. To hell if anyone sees him going in there twice in one week. Three times? Hell with it anyway. And he can get a pint at Dave's, something for the glove box as well as the bottle for the house.

He empties the last of the brandy and leans his forehead against the window as the boys tumble out of the garage, laughing.

They're high. Christ, they're stoned out of their minds. He saw enough of it. From Paul's mom. Woman could barely get up in the morning without smoking a joint.

His son is reeling around the driveway, mouth open, too far away for his father to hear the sound of his laughter.

Mr. Cheney remembers when he could make his son laugh like that. The boy was so ticklish. Under his arms. Tickle him under his arms and he would kick and scream, tears running. Not any more. Now he has to get stoned to have a laugh.

Damn that woman.

If only she had left sooner. If she had taken her drugs and her rock and roll and her *Disarm Now* posters and gotten the hell out of here sooner. Maybe it's not kind to say, but if only she had died sooner, maybe then his son wouldn't be the mess he is today.

But that will be changing soon. Paul may ignore him, ignore his attempts to communicate and to return their relationship to what it once was, but he will have to listen when confronted with the contents of that bag.

He's not a stupid man, after all. Top of his class. He knows amphetamine when he sees it. And he knows enough about his son's history with the Arroyos to see that the bag is somehow connected to their arrests. Paul will have to listen to him in the face of that knowledge.

Not that he wants to threaten the boy. Not that he'll handle it that way. A conversation is all it will take. A conversation explaining that he doesn't want to see his son getting into trouble that he can't get out of.

And what's he asking for anyway? Nothing. Just to be included. Just for them to spend time together. Just for his son to be available to him.

He brings the cup to his lips, but it's empty again.

He looks at his watch. His first class begins in two hours. A quick trip to Dave's and then out to the campus will take half an hour. That gives him another ninety minutes to watch his son. Mr. Marinovic stops his car in front of the boys and says something. He watches as the old man drives off and Paul and George run across the street and out of his view. And he's still there, face pressed to the glass, five minutes later when they run back into the Whelans' garage followed by Hector and Andy.

By the time they're on their bikes and riding down the street hurling insults at one another, he's called the school and told them he's too sick to come in today and is crouched low in the driver's seat of his car.

He drives around the block, going the opposite direction from the boys, and rounds the corner in time to see them taking their bikes across the field where the old elementary school used to be. He ignores the stop sign at the end of the block and turns onto Murrieta in front of a speeding station wagon with fake wood paneling on the side, forcing the other car to hit its brakes, the driver leaning on his horn.

As he takes a left on Portola, the boys have broken from the field and are skidding from the sidewalk into the QuickStop lot and on under the sign for the trailer park. He parks in the Orchard Hardware lot across the street and waits.

Baking in the sun that pounds through the windshield, looking at the liquor display in the QuickStop window.

The Little Brothers You Never Had

Jeff takes another sip of lukewarm beer, looking at the pile of jewelry on his counter, teasing one of the chains loose from the tangle.

—See, what you have here is mostly shit. The silver, the fourteen carat gold stuff, it's crap. The twenty four carat chains and these ones here, these two are platinum, these are worth something. The diamonds and the pearls, I don't know. Could be something, could be crap. Problem is, pawnshops are full of this shit. They buy it because it has intrinsic value and it takes up no space. Way better than a TV or some stereo or some shit like that, but still they got tons of it and it's a buyers' market so you get, maybe, I don't know, ten percent of value. If you're lucky. So, you know that, you've hocked shit before. But, also, most places, you walk in with a handful of gold and silver chains and they don't want to fuck with them. A couple at a time, even from kids like you, that's whatever, no big deal, but a handful of hot jewelry, that's a no no. Whatever you guys have heard, seen on *Baretta* or *Hill Street Blues,* whatever, pawnshops aren't all fences. Not professionals anyway. And the ones that are, go in with something like this, all in a pile like this, next time the owner gets in trouble with the cops you're gonna be one of the guys he snitches.

Sitting on the filthy carpet, his back against the wood paneling, just underneath an *Easy Rider* calendar, Andy blinks when he hears the word snitch.

Paul is perched on the fold down kitchen table, having cleared space in the mess of magazines, used paper plates and assorted scraps of the cars out front.

He sips his own warm beer.

—OK, but it's worth something, right? It's got to be worth *something*. Jeff looks at the kids.

How'd he end up with this crew hanging around? Wouldn't have happened if George hadn't been delivering pills for his aunt last summer. First time Bob Whelan's kid showed up on his porch with a baggie of ludes, he just about shit his pants.

Truth is, if he hadn't been tripping three days straight and desperate to crash, he never would have let the kid in the front door. Not that there's anything especially wrong with scoring off a high school kid, just, you know, Bob Whelan's son? That's begging for trouble. But, man, he'd needed those ludes something desperate. Turned out the kid's mellow as hell. Totally solid. No chance that kid's gonna lose his cool and say the wrong thing around his dad, let him know what he's up to. Bob probably wouldn't mind the kids over here, but he'd flip if he knew about the pills. Found out Jeff scored off his son, it would not be pretty at all.

Yeah, George is definitely a chip off the old fucking block. But he doesn't have a clue what his dad was like back then.

'64 to '68, they had themselves a time. Might still be having a time if Bob had handled things a little different. Well, that was then. Dude turned grim after he had the second kid and took the job at the quarry. For awhile he was still looking to party on a Friday night, blow a joint, go down to the Rodeo Club have a couple drinks and some beers. Then he stopped coming in at all.

Now? Say hi when they cross paths at the gas station or something, but haven't hung out for years. Too much baggage. Too much water under the bridge. Something like that.

But blood is blood. Whatever went down, whatever trip Bob got into with grinding the 9 to 5, his kids haven't bought in. Close your eyes around George, sometimes you'd swear you were hearing Bob talk. Got that thing, that easy mellow, makes people listen to what he has to say, makes people trust him. Fucking gift, that is.

And once he got his foot in the door, the others just seemed to squeeze in after him.

His brother is just a total spaz. Where that weedy little braniac came from is a mystery. Couldn't be more different from Bob. Cindy, she was a smart girl, a real bookworm, but hard to see a chick that hot having a kid that geeky. He is a trip. Picked up that copy of *The Tao of Physics* and whipped right through it. Took Jeff the better part of a year to read that.

Hector's cool, too. Knows more about rock and roll than any other Mexican. Tried to bring some of that punk shit in here and play it, turn him on. Fuck that. Loud and hard is loud and hard, but you got to know how to play your fucking instruments, sing a little, man.

They're all OK kids. Why shouldn't they hang here, play his albums, have a place to bring a chick every now and then? Long as they sometimes bring their own bottle or a couple Js, it's no big deal.

Paul's the one spends the most time here.

Cuts classes so he can come around and work out with the DP weight bench on the porch. Hangs around and passes tools while Jeff tries to get the 240Z running. Hell, come home from the Club some nights, find the kid crashed on the shredded vinyl easy chair out front. Middle of last winter the first time it happened.

Came home drunk as hell, weaving the pickup all over the road, ran over that old bitch's toy fence across the way. The chick he was with screamed when she saw Paul on the porch. Sweatshirt and a patched Levi's jacket, arms wrapped around himself, hands stuffed in his armpits, curled up and passed out in the chair. Tried to slap him awake and send him home, but he was out. Chick felt sorry for the kid, made Jeff bring his ass inside. Next day he woke up around two, chick was gone along with twenty two bucks from his wallet; Paul was outside pulling weeds. Next time it happened he wasn't passed out, just asleep. Kicked him in the foot, asked him if he wanted to crash inside. Kid said he was cool on the porch if it was OK. Told him to get his ass inside. Found a sleeping bag and put him on the floor. Kid's wearing one of Jeff's Harley caps right fucking now. Weird. Kind of like having a little brother when you never had one your whole life. 'Cept he's not. Just some kid needs a place to hang and get out of his own house. And, shit, who the fuck doesn't know what that's like?

He finishes his beer and balances the empty can on top of the overflow erupting from the garbage bag under the sink.

He looks at George, over there leaning against the wall with his arms crossed.

—How's your dad?

George shrugs.

—He's cool.

—That right? Your old man's cool? He get to be cool all of a sudden?

George scratches his armpit.

—He's fine. You know, work. Whatever.

—Your mom?

—Same.

—Uh huh.

Andy's still picking fuzz from the carpet.

—That right about your folks, that's what they're up to, working?

Andy rolls his head back.

—Yeah, you know. Work. Dad's doing stuff in the yard. Tearing it up. Mom wants a rock garden.

—Rock garden.

Jeff thinks about their mom. Cindy Hunt. She'd been a piece of ass. One of those smart hot chicks. Did they make out that one time? Shit, can't remember if that was her or that other chick. Rock garden. What the fuck happens to people?

Hector is flipping through his albums.

—Your pop, what's he, still at the quarry?

Hector keeps looking for something recorded later than '75.

—Disability.

—How'd that happen?

Hector flips past Grand Funk Railroad and Jefferson Airplane and The Average White Band.

—Had a front loader drop a couple tons of gravel on his leg and got put on disability.

—What's he doin' now?

Hector pushes the stack of records back together with a thump.

—Sitting around taking painkillers and drinking wine.

—There's worse things.

—If you say so.

—I say so.

He pokes Paul in the shoulder.

—What about your dad, what's up with him?

Paul plucks at the pull tab on top of his can, playing the "In-A-Gadda-Da-Vida" guitar riff.

—I'uh nuh.

—He's still teaching, right?

Paul twists the pull tab back and forth, trying to tear it free.

—Hey, man, wake up. He teaching, yeah?

Paul wrenches the tab loose.

—Yeah, whatever, he's teachin', what the fuck, that's what he does.

Jeff picks up the wad of chains.

—So, safe to say none of your folks know about this shit.

Nothing.

—Safe to say they'd be pretty pissed, they ever found out.

Nothing, all of them just watching the floor, waiting.

He hefts the knot of chains a couple times on the palm of his hand. He thinks about his shitty minimum wage job with Security Eye and the cash he just dropped on a rebuild kit for the Harley's carburetor. He thinks about if Bob heard he helped his kids hock some hot jewelry.

—Yeah, they'd be pissed. And if I get involved in trying to move this shit, they'll be more pissed at me. And the cops, they'd be really pissed at me and hit me with receiving and possession of stolen shit and contributing to the delinquency of minors and all that crap.

Paul puts down his empty can and grabs at the chains.

—So fuck it, we'll get rid of it ourselves.

Jeff pulls his hand back, still full of gold and silver.

—*Get rid of it yourselves.* This much shit, get busted is what you'll get.

He puts the chains on the counter, out of Paul's reach.

—I know a guy. He moves stuff sometimes. Buys shit. I look at this, I think I can get him to come up with a hundred, maybe. I'll take twenty percent for setting it up, leaves you with twenty bucks each.

—Fuck, man. It's got to be worth more than that.

Jeff shrugs.

—Hey, it probably is to the right people. *You* know who that is? Cuz I sure as shit don't. Who I know is a guy who knows those people. And his price, what he'll pay is, I think, a C note. I mean, look, you're always gonna be disappointed with what you get. You know that. First eight track player or whatever you ever boosted, bet you walked into the hock in Hayward expecting fifty bucks. Lucky if you got five. Lucky if the guy didn't laugh at you and tell you to fuck off with that shit. If everybody got rich at being a thief, that's all there'd be in the world. It's never gonna be as much as you want it to be. Snatch the Hope Diamond, know what you're gonna get? Less than you believed was possible. So look, I don't want to fuck with you guys. I'm just telling you, I think I can walk out that door, be back in about half an hour with a hundred bucks. That's no shit, that's not a bad deal. Your aunt, ask her, she'll tell you it's not a bad deal. Right now, what you got is a worthless pile of shit that you don't know what to do with them all together and all they're gonna get you is busted. You can piece them out for the next couple months and take the bus back and forth to Hayward and end up making maybe a hundred and fifty. Sounds like a drag to me. Or we can Monty Hall this thing right now and take what's in the envelope. Which I'm pretty sure will be a hundred. Less my twenty.

George shoves himself away from the wall.

—We'll take it.

Jeff opens a drawer, digs out a crumpled brown paper lunch sack, shakes it out and drops the jewelry inside.

—You gonna hang here?

Paul shrugs.

—If it's cool.

—Yeah. Like I said, maybe half an hour.

George works his Marlboros out of his hip pocket.

—What about work?

—I'll be late. Fuck do you care? There's beer in the fridge. Make sure you leave me a few. And don't run the fan, the PG&E bills are killing me. If it's too fucking hot in here hang on the porch. Just keep the beers down so I don't catch shit from the hag across the way.

He goes on the porch and out from under the awning and gets pelted by the high Valley sun. August in this town. A month of limitless blue sky over brown hills with never a breeze or a cloud. He looks at the pieces of carburetor. That'll have to wait till tomorrow now. But he's gonna make it worth his while.

He climbs into the pickup.

—Hey, Jeff.

Paul is coming down the porch steps.

—Hang up a sec.

Jeff cranks down both windows, trying to get some air to move through the cab.

—What?

—This guy you're going to see?

—Yeah?

—He handle other stuff?

—Like what?

—Like whatever. I might have some other shit.

—You guys on a crime spree? Gonna hit a bank?

—No. Other stuff. Like shit, you know.

Jeff adjusts himself on the hot black fabric of the pickup's bench seat.

—Like? What? Like shit?

—Yeah. You know. Maybe. I might be able to. Maybe. Get some stuff.

—Pot?

—Other stuff.

Jeff tugs a heavy ring of keys out of his pocket.

—Could be. You want me to?

—No. Don't. I could have something. Or not. So, just to maybe know if there's someplace to take it. Maybe.

Jeff slides a key in the ignition.

—Sure. I'll see what I can find out.

—Cool. Thanks, man. Thanks for taking care of this for us.

—Sure. No problem. So go inside and crack another beer. I'll be right back.

He watches Paul go inside the trailer, leaving the front door open.

He has to tease the pickup to get it to start up, pump the gas pedal four or five times so it's on the edge of flooding, then hit the ignition and let the fucker *wahwahwahwah* till you'd swear it's never gonna catch, and then it does. He revs it, black smoke coughing out the exhaust, and yanks the gearshift into reverse. It bitches and grinds, but it goes. He pulls out, then jams it into first and starts down the gravel drive, first gear whining all the way. Second is shot and it'll stall if he tries to drive this slow in third. He could give a damn about the park speed limit, but the property manager's been up his ass about the late rent on the lot and he doesn't want to give him any excuses to come around being a dick.

The drive curves to the right. His own trailer is well out of view when he pulls up in front of a shiny new double just a couple slots from the rear exit to the park. A swing set and a litter of kid's toys on the small sod lawn. A line of pinwheels shaped like sunflowers borders a short flagstone path that leads to the bottom of a carpeted porch that's stocked with a gas grill and a set of iron lawn furniture.

He takes the bag of jewelry from the seat and climbs out, the cab door grinding shut as he slams it. He could have walked over here. But he doesn't want the kids to know how close the guy lives. Better they think he has to take a little trip to get this done. Expend a little elbow grease. Especially as he's pretty damn sure he can pull down a hundred and fifty for this stuff.

Not that he's ripping the kids off. He'll pocket fifty on his own, plus another twenty. That's less than fifty percent. That's what a fence gets. And he's the one acting as the fence here. Try explaining that to the kids, they wouldn't buy it. End up trying to unload it themselves and they'd wind up getting taken. Worse, they'd end up getting busted. See what Bob would think of that. This way is better. Take care of it himself, take care of the kids so they don't get screwed over.

He goes up the steps. This should be easy as hell. Geezer's always in the market for shit like this, and whatever pills or acid Paul's maybe got his hands on.

Just that there's no reason at all to mention Geezer's name to the kids. For that matter, there's no reason to say anything to Geezer about George and Andy being Bob Whelan's boys.

The Sketchy House

Andy doesn't like to go in. The Arroyos' was one thing. His bike was in there. But mostly, when they do this kind of thing, he stays outside and watches the street, keeps an eye on the bikes. He gets panicky inside the house. Short of breath. Once, he passed out and Paul had to throw him over his shoulder and carry him out.

He just doesn't like going in.

But that bathroom window Hector found. That tiny fucking bathroom window. He's the only one who can fit through it.

So he watches as Paul wiggles the last of the glass louvers out of its slot and passes it to George, who stacks it neatly with the others on the ground.

George looks at Andy, bends and laces his fingers together and holds them down low.

—Let's go, little brother.

Andy stares at the window.

Paul gives him a shove.

—Get in there, man.

George straightens and puts his hand on Paul's chest.

—Dude, just chill. He's scared.

—Fag *should* be scared. He passes out in there before he lets us in, who's gonna carry him out?

Andy jumps up and grabs the bottom of the windowsill and tries to pull himself up. Hector grabs the bottoms of his feet and lifts him.

—Got it?

Andy heaves his upper body through the window.

—Got it.

His favorite T, the one with the dragon silk screened on the back, snags on one of the empty louver brackets and starts to tear.

—Hang on.

Hector stops lifting.

—What?

—My shirt. Unsnag my fucking shirt.

Paul grabs his calves and starts to shove.

—Fuck the shirt, get in there.

The shirt rips a little more. Andy grabs the window frame to keep himself from being pushed inside any farther.

—Fuck you. It's my favorite shirt.

Paul pushes harder.

—You can get a new shirt. Get in there.

The fingers of Andy's right hand slip off the window ledge and he flails his arm, grabbing the shower curtain. Two of the curtain rings pop loose. His upper body hangs in the air.

—Fucking stop it, I'm gonna fall and rip the shirt. Unsnag it.

Paul starts to push again.

—Fuck the shirt.

George grabs his brother's ankles and tries to pull him back.

—Stop being a dick, unsnag his shirt.

—I'm not being a dick, he's being a pussy.

Hector jumps up, grabs the corner of the window frame with one hand, wall walks two steps, reaches in and unsnags Andy's shirt with his middle finger before dropping back down.

—Fags.

Paul and George let go of Andy's legs and he falls headfirst, the curtain rings popping off the metal rod, a stack of titty magazines on the back of the toilet slapping to the floor. He puts his arm out and jerks the last few rings free, the bar coming down with them, crashing down into the chipped tub and ringing off the cracked wall tiles.

They all freeze. A car drives past out front.

George hauls himself up and sticks his face in the window.

Andy is on the floor, half of the curtain draped over his legs.

—You OK?

Andy looks at him, a little blood on his lower lip from where his teeth sliced it when his face hit the floor.

—Yeah, thanks, fag.

—It wasn't me, it was Paul.

Paul punches George in the back of his leg.

—Fuck off.

George kicks at him.

—Stop being a dick all the time for a change.

Hector heads for the glass door.

—If he's OK, tell him to let us the fuck in.

George adjusts his grip, pulls himself up a little higher.

—You cool to let us in?

Andy is getting off the floor, looking at the hole in his shirt.

—I'll be there in a sec.

Still inspecting the hole, he opens the bathroom door and Fernando is standing there and he punches Andy in the face and starts kicking him when he hits the floor while George screams and tries to claw his way through the window that's far too small.

Things That Look Different but Are the Same

Geezer untwists the neck of the paper bag and looks inside. There's a word for this. The moment he sees the jewelry he knows there's a word for what has happened and what will happen as a result.

—*Un* something.

Jeff blinks.

—What?

—An *un* word. *Un* something. When there's just no fucking excuse whatsoever for it. The kind of thing you cut people's eyes out for.

Jeff runs a hand down the length of his ponytail.

—Unconscionable?

Geezer looks up from the bag.

—That's it. *Unconscionable.* That for which you cut some fucker's eyes out.

He rubs his nose.

—Kids?

—Yeah. Teenagers anyway.

—The ones you got crawling around your trailer all the time?

—Yeah.

—One of them knows somebody or something. What's the deal on that?

—One of them, he.

—*One of them he,* what?

Jeff looks at the bullfighter in black velvet hung over Geezer's head.

—He was running Amy Whelan's shit for a while.

Geezer upends the bag in his lap. He picks out an engagement ring he doesn't remember being with the rest of the jewelry when he told the spics they could keep it.

Amy Whelan.

Could have swore she was clear on the concept. Went over there and made a point of showing her that Oakland holds this town, that as far as that's concerned, he's Oakland's hand here. Showed her how the Oakland boys handle shit. Thought she was clear. Should have known better. Doesn't matter how together a person seems, how well they got their priorities in line, they start seeing drug money roll across their table and they get greedy and stupid. The two being pretty fucking much . . . fuck.

—The word?

Jeff shifts from foot to foot.

—The word?

—When two things mean the same thing? Two words got the same meaning. Not when they're spelled the same but mean different things, the opposite of that.

—Synonymous.

Geezer rubs at the small stone in the engagement ring.

—That's it. *Synonymous*. When two things look different, but they're the same.

Greed and stupidity. Synonymous. Amy Whelan's done gone and got greedy. Got stupid. Got some kids involved in his shit. Fucking up shit for everyone. Upsetting his personal applecart, creating friction with Oakland, interfering with supply and demand. The supply of cash that Oakland demands for staying out of his ass.

Unconscionable bitch.

—Where they now?

—My place.

—This all they got?

—One of the guys, this kid Paul, the big one who's over there the most, he said he might have something else.

Geezer runs his palm over the slick nylon of his shiny gold sweat suit.

—More jewelry?

—No. I don't think so.

—Guns? He pick up a couple pieces somewhere?

—Maybe. Sounds more like he got his hands on someone's stash. A bag of coke or something.

Geezer wraps his fingers around the handle of his grabber, squeezing, making the plastic claw at the end of the aluminum pole into a fist.

—Yeah. Coke. Crank, maybe?

—Um, I don't. You know, that's *your* thing, man. I don't know where they'd get crank that didn't come from you.

—Said one of 'em works for Amy Whelan?

—Used to.

—So maybe she wants to get some new business going?

—I don't think so, man. I mean, everyone knows that's your deal. No one's gonna mess with you, Geez.

—Sure. Of course. Kid got his hands on a couple eight balls, wants to move one of them.

—Yeah, probably.

—OK, look into that.

Geezer scoops the jewelry out of his lap and back into the bag and sets it next to him on the black leather couch.

—How much they want?

Jeff looks at the bullfighter again, looks at the gilded plaster sconces that bracket it dripping plastic grapes.

He shrugs.

—Shit, Geez, they're kids, you know? They'll take whatever you give and be happy with it.

Geezer smiles, leans back, the couch creaks as his fat rearranges.

—And you, you gonna be happy with whatever you can get?

—I'm just doin' them a solid. Shit ain't mine, they just brought it to me.

Geezer looks him over.

Loser. Guy should have it stapled to his head. Stapled to his head. Could you do that? Probably not with a regular stapler. A contractor's stapler, a big industrial one that would go in the bone, the kind they use to staple into concrete and shit. Use one of those, you could staple a dead cat to a guy's head and it'd stick. Or a live cat. Or a weasel. Staple a live weasel by its tail and watch and see what it does. Or one of them . . . long and wormy . . . like a weasel, but?

—Like a weasel, but different?

—Um.

—Long and skinny and furry, a rodent, but it hunts other rodents.

—A ferret.

Geezer closes his eyes and laughs.

—Yeah. That's it. *Ferret.* A ferret by the tail. That'd be something.

He laughs until he coughs.

Jeff takes a step closer.

—You OK?

Geezer waves him off. Choking, he reaches over his stomach for the glass of juice on the coffee table, squeezing the grabber's handle, the claw closing around the glass.

He brings it close, removes the glass from the claw and takes a sip.

—Pluck your eye out with this thing. Best five bucks I ever spent.

He puts the grabber back in its place.

—So, you're just selling the shit for them, getting nothing out of it?

—Well, I get, you know, twenty percent. A couple bucks. Who can't use a few bucks?

Geezer nods, runs his fingertip around the Looney Tunes characters enameled on the side of the glass he got from Burger King. This loser. Had some moves back when. Now look at him. Security guard. Good for opening a lock and turning his back every now and then. Good for giving the Seville a tune up and detailing the mags. That's it. Should have cut him loose years ago. What you get for being sentimental, you get dead weight like Jeff Loller on your back.

Still, Amy Whelan's punks trust him.

He rolls his bulk forward, reaches between the black leather sofa cushions and pulls out a thick roll of bills.

—Two hundred.

Jeff wraps his arms around his torso, the cold air blasted into the trailer by the swamp cooler starting to raise gooseflesh.

—Two. Um.

—That's not what you were looking for? For the kids who'll take anything?

Jeff shakes his head.

Geezer snaps the rubber band off the cash.

—It's too much, right? I know it's too much. Don't go spastic because it's too much, Loller.

He pats the bag.

—This is good stuff. These kids, they might be good little thieves. I want to overpay a little, give them a little career encouragement. You take your twenty percent and forget ripping off whatever you were going to rip off. I want them to like me. Right?

—Hey, I wasn't gonna rip anybody.

—Really, who gives a fuck? Just don't do it. OK?

—Yeah, but I wasn't even thinking.

—Jeff, I'm not gonna apologize for saying the truth. Drop it.

—OK. OK.

—Two hundred?

—Yeah. Of course, man.

Geezer grunts and holds out the empty juice glass. Jeff takes it and puts it on the coffee table next to the lily pad shaped ashtray with the ceramic frogs waiting to hold a cigarette for you. Geezer licks his thumb and starts peeling twenties from the roll.

—Here we go. Come and get it.

Jeff takes the money and puts it in his pocket.

Geezer shoves his bankroll back in the couch.

—And see if maybe they want to do something for me.

—Like what?

—Steal some more shit. I know a place. Here, let me write this down.

—Sure, but I should split. Gotta get to work.

Geezer uses the grabber to pluck a notebook from the coffee table, brings it to his lap and scribbles, passes Jeff a scrap of paper clutched in the claw.

—Split. Have fun.

Jeff turns the knob, starts to open the door.

—And, Jeff?

Jeff stops.

—Yeah?

Geezer leans forward.

—You know where a guy would get a stapler? A big one?

———

Paul comes back into the trailer and finds Andy sprawled on the floor.

George is leaning Jeff's cabinet speakers together to form an A frame above Andy's face.

He looks at Paul.

—What'd you have to talk to him about?

Paul squats next to Hector, looking through Jeff's albums, looking for the perfect one.

—Seein' if the truck needed a push to get started.

Hector pulls Van Halen *Van Halen* from the stack.

Paul shakes his head and pulls out *Number of the Beast*.

Hector rolls his eyes.

—Shit may as well be pop.

—Fuck you, Maiden rocks.

—Rocks your grandma.

George leans between them.

—I don't know what you guys are fucking around for. There's only one way to do this.

He grabs an album and slides it from its sleeve.

Hector stands up.

—All this shit is tired anyway. It's like Day on the Green Greatest Hits or some shit.

George puts the album on the turntable.

—Fuck you, you like going to Day on the Green as much as anyone.

—I like going and getting fucked up and checking out the chicks, but the music is dinosaur rock. Beat and tired.

Paul puts an elbow in his ribs and heads for the fridge.

—Metallica is not beat.

Hector jumps on his back.

—One decent fucking band! A whole day of tired music and one decent headbanger in the whole lineup.

Paul crashes into the sink and falls to the floor with Hector clinging to him, the two of them wrestling on the linoleum.

—You're dead, fag.

He goes after Hector's hair, Hector slapping at his hands.

—Not the hawk, not the hawk, man! That's not cool!

Paul is rubbing his hand over Hector's head, demolishing the hawk.

—Gonna scalp you this time. You wanna look like a injun, you can die like one.

George turns away from the spectacle and kneels next to his brother and offers him a chromium blue sneak a toke made out of spun aluminum.

—Here.

Andy takes the bomb shaped pipe and sucks a hit out of it and hands it back to his brother.

—Thanks.

George turns to look in the kitchen as the garbage can is kicked over and empty beer cans spray across the floor.

He looks at the pipe in his hand and then at his genius brother.

—What the fuck are you doing here, Andy?

Andy is staring up into the angle where the speakers meet, thinking about Pythagoras. The sum of the three angles will be equal to two right angles. That's a fact. He focuses on trying to generate an accurate measurement of the angles by applying his estimations to the formula.

He has cottonmouth and sucks the back of his tongue to try and create some moisture.

—Hangin'. You want me to leave?

—No, man, I just. I mean, why aren't you doing something else?

George blows smoke at his two best friends rolling around in the mess of cans and cigarette butts and fast food bags.

—We got nothing better to do. You could be doing shit. You could be studying for the SAT. You could be working on science fair shit. You could be making one of your dungeons. Something, you know, creative or something.

Andy's looking for the trap. Is George being serious? If he answers him, will he grab his hair and call him a fag?

If the triangle made by the speakers and the floor had a right angle he could apply Pythagoras' Theorem and show that the square of the hypotenuse is equal to the sum of the squares of the other two sides. No one could argue that it is not.

—You guys are my friends.

George is looking at the floor now, his eyes hidden by the fall of his hair.

—You have other friends, man. You could be off playing Dungeons & Dragons with them. Not getting into trouble. Not burning up brain cells. You're going to college, man, you got better things to do.

Andy blinks.

College. What's so great about college? Everyone makes a big deal out of it. All college really means is going someplace and being all alone. Pythagoras was head of a secret society, he believed that at its deepest level, reality is mathematical. The inner circle of his followers were the *Mathematikoi*. They shared his beliefs.

—My other friends don't understand me.

George laughs.

Andy closes his eyes. Here comes his ration of shit.

George reaches for the stereo.

—Little brother, if you're hanging with us because you think we understand you, you are in the wrong place.

He flips the needle down and it hits the groove and "Children of the Grave" blasts Andy's face in perfect stereo.

He opens his eyes and watches his brother get up and kick Paul and Hector apart long enough to be able to get a beer out of the fridge.

He smiles and listens to the music, his favorite Sabbath song, the one his brother picked out for him.

Manners Worth Gold

Jeff angles the pickup into its spot between the 240Z and the Beetle that he hopes will be running someday. He kills the engine, keeping his fingers crossed, and the engine cuts without giving the particular shudder and groan that means it won't go anywhere else for the rest of the day. Thank God for that. Late enough for work now that the bus is no longer an option. The truck is gonna have to get him there.

He listens to the sound of top volume Black Sabbath coming from inside his place. It'll be par for the course if they've sucked down all his brews. He thinks about peeling a twenty from the money Geezer gave him. Just to cover the cost of the beers those punks drank. He gets as far as sticking his hand in his pocket, and then pulls it out.

Better not. Geezer ends up meeting the kids, someone might say something about how much money they got. He wants them to have two bills, it better be two bills. And he'll still come out of it with forty. So that's cool.

He walks around the 240Z, running his hand across a primered patch of Bondo. He remembers when he and Bob used buckets of the stuff to fill in the dents and creases on a '53 Ford Crestline they'd fixed up in high school. Man, they'd just about shoveled it onto that car. Sucker made some time, though. So did they. Lots of chicks took a ride in the back seat of that jalopy.

It was the right thing, not saying anything to Geezer about George and Andy being Bob's kids. Would have just queered the deal and they'd have been out the cash. Bad enough Amy's name came up.

He steps up on the porch, wondering if she really is dealing crank these days, pulls open the door of his trailer, and looks at the mess in the kitchen and the stoned kids scattered on the carpet.

—Fucking A.

Paul points at Hector.

—He did it.

Hector throws a beer can at him.

—Faggot.

Paul goes for him, but Jeff gets him by the scruff and trips him.

—Enough. Cool it. Don't care who did what, let's see some asses cleaning this shit up.

Andy gets up, moving around the trailer with the garbage bag, picking up the mess he had nothing to do with making.

Jeff points at the blaring stereo.

—And turn that down for a second. We got business.

George twists the volume down to nothing.

—What's the word?

Jeff has his head in the fridge.

—The word is I told you punks to leave me a couple beers.

Paul points at Hector.

—He did it.

Hector throws a beer can at him.

—Faggot.

Jeff stands with his hands on his hips.

—What the fuck are you guys on anyway?

Paul looks at George.

—What's it called?

—Phenobarbital.

Jeff's eyebrows go up.

—No shit? You get it from your aunt?

—Boosted it.

—Give me a couple.

George takes a pill from his pocket and tosses it to Jeff.

Jeff shakes his head.

—C'mon, one of these won't do shit for me.

—That all I got left.

Andy takes both of his from his pocket.

—Here.

Jeff nods.

—Cool. More like it.

He pops two of the pills in his mouth and washes them down with the dregs of the beer he takes from Paul.

—Hey, man, I was drinking that.

—No, man, you were finished with that.

Hector is taking the needle from the album on the turntable.

Jeff taps him on the shoulder.

—Any chance you could put on something mellow? Some old man music for a change?

Hector brushes back his demolished mohawk.

—You got some Carpenters in here?

—Fuck you. Put on some Marshall Tucker or something. Just give me a break for about five minutes, then I'll be out of your guys' hair and you can burn the place down.

He plops onto the bench seat torn from a '55 Bel Air.

—So anyone want to ask how it went? Now you're all wasted you no longer got the head for business? The big deal no longer bears the same interest for you?

George busts out a smoke and offers one to Jeff.

—There a problem?

Jeff lights up.

—A problem? Well, could be there was a problem. Could be I didn't get the price we were talking about.

Paul comes out of the kitchen.

—What the fuck? That's bullshit, man. That was a discount price. That was like a sweet deal for doing it bulk or wholesale or whatever. Don't tell me you took this guy's bullshit price, man.

Jeff wags his head.

—Hey, man, sometimes it's a matter of what the market will bear. Just got to take what you can get.

—Fuck! Fuck, man! Fuck!

Paul stomps out to the porch and kicks something.

Jeff leans forward on his seat and looks out the door.

—Don't be screwing with my tools and shit out there.

Paul kicks something else.

—I'm not screwing with your tools and shit.

He comes back in and takes one of George's cigarettes.

—I'm not screwing with any of your shit.

Hector has dropped *Searchin' for a Rainbow* on the turntable, shaking his head the whole time.

—How bad we get screwed?

Jeff reaches in his hip pocket and pulls out some bills and counts.

—Well, let's see. Got twenty, forty, sixty, eighty, aaand, ho, what's this? Hundred. Hundred twenty, hundred forty, sixty, eighty. Looks like two hundred to me. Who knows how to say thank you? Who can say *thank you, Jeff?*

Andy puts the garbage sack back under the sink.

—Thank you, Jeff.

George, Paul, and Hector all drop their heads.

Paul nudges George.

—What's it like having a fag brother?

—Man, I don't have a brother.

Jeff waves the money.

—Fuck them, Andy. Manners are worth their weight in gold. Come over here and get your cut first.

Andy brushes between his brother and Paul.

—Fuck you guys, manners are worth their weight in gold.

Jeff peels off a couple bills.

—Forty bucks for the kid with some manners.

George tosses his butt in the sink and runs the tap over it.

—Forty?

Paul points at the money.

—Should be forty five, man.

Jeff holds a couple bills up between his fingers.

—Two, minus forty for me, equals one sixty. Equals forty each for you guys.

—Forty for you?

—That's twenty percent.

Hector stands up.

—Said twenty bucks, man.

—Said twenty *percent*, holmes.

—Don't *holmes* me, man. You ain't no vato.

—Well you ain't, neither.

George comes out of the kitchen.

—Cool it, Hector, he didn't mean anything.

—Sure, sure, I know, but I don't need that shit. Get enough of that shit out there, don't need it from my friends.

Jeff puts out his hand.

—Hector, my man, it's cool. Didn't mean anything at all. You're right, it's all friends here. Be cool.

Hector takes his hand and they shake down, sliding their palms up, down, across, locking fingers and snapping them loose.

—I know, man. It's cool. We're cool.

—Alright then.

Jeff leans back.

—So, twenty percent. You guys tell me that's not what I said, it's not what I said.

Andy shakes his head.

—No, it's what you said. Twenty percent.

He looks at the others.

—It's really what he said.

Paul lifts his arms.

—Hey, man, who's gonna argue with the human computer. Fagmo says it was twenty percent, that's what it is. Let's just get to the cash and go hit the QuickStop for a bottle of Jack.

Jeff splits the money.

—And you guys gotta give the truck a push.

George takes his cash.

—How'd you get the price up?

—Started high, you know. Truth is, guy bit on my price so fast, I was probably asking too low. Looks like you guys got a better eye for this shit than I thought.

He gets up.

—Matter of fact, guy I was dealing with, he's looking for more of the same.

He heads for the bedroom.

—But he wants to get his hands on it fast. Has some deal of his own going.

Paul looks at the others and sticks his thumbs in the air, yelling down the hallway.

—How fast?

Jeff pops his head out of the bedroom.

—Fast. Couple days at the most. As much as you can get. Gold, silver, jewels, platinum. Coins. Whatever you can get your hands on, he'll take it.

George waves Paul down.

—Hey, man, that's cool and all, but we kind of lucked into this shit. Wouldn't know where to start actually finding the right houses for good stuff.

—Not a problem.

Jeff comes back down the hall, cracked black leather boots draped by the cuffs of indigo polyester slacks with a baby blue stripe down the side, tattooed arms hidden in the sleeves of a matching shirt with the Security Eye patch on the shoulder.

—He's got a house he says is prime.

The Sketchy House

Paul freezes, and watches George's legs as he's jerked into the bathroom, his jeans catching, pulled low, deep gouges being cut into his thighs.

He grabs his friend's ankles and digs his heels into the dirt.

—Let go! Let the fuck go! I'll fucking kill you if you don't let go!

George is howling, blood running down his legs.

—Paul! Paul! Letmegoletmego! Fucking Andy is! Letmego!

There's a sound like a piece of firewood hitting a gourd.

George's legs stop kicking.

Paul freezes.

His friend's legs are yanked from his hands, disappearing into the window and leaving behind a scrap of bloody denim and a single tennis shoe that falls to the ground.

Fernando's face appears in the window.

—You coming in, Cheney?

Paul runs.

He runs and boosts himself over the fence and lands in the front yard and runs some more and keeps running.

Nothing Like His Father

Mr. Cheney ducks low behind his steering wheel when the boys come out of the trailer park pushing a pickup. It jerks and a huge cloud of black smoke spits out of the tailpipe and the boys and the truck leap forward a few yards. Paul jumps in and slides behind the wheel as the driver gets out and heads into the store.

Good Lord, Jeff Loller.

How long has Paul been hanging around that overgrown delinquent?

Would barely know the man if Loller hadn't taken one of his intro computer classes last year. Didn't last. Once he realized they wouldn't be sitting around playing Tetris and Flight Simulator he dropped out. Before that he was just a vaguely familiar face. Memorable in high school mostly because he was one of Bob Whelan's cronies. By the time he'd come back from college and moved into the house down from Bob's, Loller had faded entirely from his memory. Until he'd slouched into class looking much the same as he had eighteen years before.

And now Loller is buying liquor for his son.

The appeal for Paul is pretty clear. Loller is much like any number of the boyfriends his mother's friends dragged through the house when he was small. Nothing like his father. Long hair. A motorcycle. Aimless. A bad cliché.

He watches his son in the other man's truck, revving the engine to keep it from dying. Does he know how to drive it? Of course he does. He smokes and drinks and takes drugs and steals things and has sex; of course he knows how to drive. Did Loller teach him? The thought.

Jeff comes out of the store with a brown paper bag. He lifts it to his mouth and takes a drink from the bottle inside, then hands it to George and gets back in his truck, Paul jumping out the other side.

After he's driven off and the boys have left with their bottle, Kyle waits several minutes, then runs across the street for his brandy. Just for a little relief.

————

—If you guys are gonna stay over tonight you can help with those rocks on Sunday.

Paul turns from the sink where he's washing his hands with a gritty bar of Lava.

—What if we're not staying over the whole weekend?

Mr. Whelan pops the tab on a can of Oly and pours it into one of the beer mugs he keeps in the freezer during the summer.

—Paul, if you manage to get through the weekend without spending a night here or eating at least one meal in my house, I will apologize on Monday for having made you shovel rocks. But until that jury is in, the cost of a hot and a cot is you lend a hand. Got it?

Hector takes his turn at the sink.

—I got it, Mr. Whelan.

Sitting at the kitchen table with his beer, George and Andy's dad looks at Paul.

—You got it?

Paul wipes his hands on a dish towel and hands it to Hector.

—Yeah, no problem. Sir.

—Can that *sir* crap.

—Yes. Sir.

Mr. Whelan is bent over, unlacing his boots.

—You still planning on joining the Army, Paul?

—Yep.

—That smartass crap will not float. I didn't serve myself, but I can tell you right now, that crap will sink like a turd made out of brick. And drag you with it.

Paul laughs.

—Yes, sir.

Mr. Whelan leans back and crosses his legs, flexing his toes in his filthy socks.

—See, if this was the Army and I was your sergeant, I'd be busy slapping you down and watching you do about five hundred pushups before I sent you down the hall to clean my toilet so my wife doesn't have to do it this week.

He leans forward and tugs the back of his wife's tanktop.

—How 'bout that, you like to have this punk clean the bathrooms for you this week?

She looks from the giant bowl of fruit salad she's making.

—It'd be a nice change of pace from the messing up he does in there.

Andy comes in from the bathroom.

His mom squints at him.

—You feeling alright?

He shrugs.

—Sure, fine.

His mom puts the back of her hand on his forehead.

—You feel a little hot.

—It's like a hundred degrees out. Everything's hot.

—Well, drink something cold. Drink some Kool-Aid.

He gets the jug from the fridge.

Hector grabs two glasses from the cupboard.

—Let me get some of that.

Bob Whelan drinks his beer and watches the boys jostle around the kitchen, enjoying the noise and the roughhousing.

George comes in, hair wet from the shower. He takes the Kool-Aid jug from his brother and starts drinking directly from the spout.

His mom throws her hands in the air.

—Hey. Hey!

He stops drinking and wipes his lips and looks at his mom.

—What?

—A glass? Is it so much trouble to open the cupboard and take out a glass and use it?

—I'm just having a quick drink, why get a glass dirty?

His dad knocks the bottom of his mug on the table.

—Don't talk back to your mom. You want a drink, you use a glass.

—Fine. Whatever. I'm not even really thirsty.

He opens the fridge door and puts the jug back and stands looking at the contents of the shelves.

His mom swings a towel at him.

—The door. You're using energy. What's in there isn't gonna change. And I'm making dinner right now.

—I'm just seeing if there's anything.

Mr. Whelan reaches with his foot and pushes the door closed.

—There's plenty. But your mom said she's making dinner and I'm paying the PG&E bills, so don't stand with the door open. Got it?

George moves closer to his mom and looks at what she's doing.

—Fruit salad?

—And sandwiches. It's too hot to cook.

Bob snaps his fingers; three sharp shots.

—Hey, I said, *got it?*

George faces his dad.

—Yeah, I got it. Don't stand with the door open. It wastes energy and energy costs money. I got it. You've said it a million times.

—So if you don't want to hear it, stop doing it. Got it?

—Got it. Got it.

—You keep going with that attitude, Paul and Hector are gonna be heading for home and me and you are gonna be outside shoveling rocks right now. You got *that?*

George looks his dad in the eye.

—Yes. I got it. I'm sorry.

His dad points at his mom.

George looks at her.

—Sorry, Mom, didn't mean to be a smartass.

She nudges him with an elbow and smiles.

—Mustard?

—Please.

She looks at her husband.

—Lettuce and tomato?

—The works, please. Thanks.

She cuts a cheese sandwich in half from corner to corner the way

Andy likes it, puts extra mayo on Paul's ham sandwich, and pickles on Hector's, and brings it all to the table.

The boys scrape chairs and grab sandwiches and fistfuls of chips and start eating, pausing between bites just long enough to breathe and to wipe their mouths with paper napkins.

Bob bites into his sub and nods at his wife.

—S'good, babe. Thanks.

Hector bobs his head while he chews.

—Yeah, thanks, Mrs. Whelan.

Andy picks grapes from his fruit salad and pops them in his mouth one by one.

—Good salad, Mom.

George and Paul grunt through their stuffed mouths.

Bob takes a long swallow of beer and listens to the boys argue about a band called Rainbow and whether its lead singer should be allowed anywhere near Black Sabbath.

This had never been the plan.

Being a family man, having a wife and kids, let alone playing troop leader to a couple strays like Paul and Hector, had never been in the cards at all. He'd had other things on his mind altogether. And a wife like Cindy? How the hell did he manage that? Her plan, her parents' plan anyway, had been Stanford. Hell, they'd never have crossed paths if she hadn't started tutoring Amy. That hadn't happened, Amy never would have brought her to that party, he never would have ended up making out with her, never would have gotten her pregnant with George, never would have gotten married. And all the rest that came after.

Cindy'd be living in a big house over in Blackhawk or something. Lawyer husband and a housekeeper and a BMW and the country club and all that shit. Well, *they* could have had that stuff. Don't have to be a lawyer to get money. Just need to have the want.

Bob thinks about the kinds of things a man can do to make money if he has the want. And he looks at his sons.

He watches George laugh and spray some chips out of his mouth and clean them from the tabletop and say *excuse me*. He watches the way Andy and Hector and Paul all watch him, take their cue from him. The leader of the pack. But not taking advantage of it, not lording it over his pals. Kid could be something special, just needs to put some elbow grease into it. So many things come easy to the boy, he thinks that's the way it's always gonna be. Bob knows that feeling. And it didn't matter how hard his pop tried to slap it into him, he had to learn different on his own.

Cindy scoops some more fruit salad into Andy's bowl. He picks through it, eating first the grapes and then the oranges and then the bananas and then the apples, leaving the little slivers of strawberry for last.

Bob shakes his head.

Where did he come from? And how in God's name did he survive in the first place? Six weeks early. Could rest on the palm of your hand. Doctors telling them not to get their hopes up. Telling them that if he made it he might not be normal. Shit, they were right about that one. Normal is the last thing his youngest turned out to be.

Nine days out of ten it's more fun to butt heads with George than it is to try and figure what the hell Andy is talking about. Pick him up from school on a rain day, he's chattering about some theory of how the universe is all made of empty space, how everything solid is mostly just air. Or not even air. Made of just nothing. Made of the chance that something might be in all the nothing. Or some shit like that. A little kid with stuff like that in his head. Still, it's better than when he starts in on Dungeons & Dragons. Might as well be speaking in tongues.

Man, if the apple's ever fallen farther from the tree, he'd like to know about it. Still, college. Two years early and all expenses paid. His son. If that doesn't make it all seem worthwhile, nothing else will.

He finishes the last bite of his sandwich, crumples his napkin and drops it on the plate and leans back in his chair. Cindy reaches over and kneads the back of his neck, and he runs his fingers over her bare forearm.

None of it in the cards. Thirty five. A woman like this. Sons like these.

They'd been taking bets on him fifteen years ago, most people who knew a thing about him would have had theirs on prison or a coffin. And it would have been safe money.

The Rocky Mountain High Incident

—Eurythmics, Culture Club, Duran Duran, Depeche Mode and the Talking Heads.

—I like "Psycho Killer."

—I know what you like, man, it's my fucking list and those are the five gayest bands in the world.

Hector rips open a bag of Doritos.

—There's not really anything gay about Talking Heads.

Paul grabs the chips from him.

—Just because you like one of their songs doesn't mean they're not gay.

George holds out a hand and Paul passes him the bag.

—I'm with Paul on this one, the Heads are pretty gay. I mean, what's up with the big suit?

—Fuck cares about the big suit, listen to the music.

Andy peels back the lid on a can of bean dip.

—I think Hector likes them.

—Fuck you. You don't even have a list. There's no music too gay for you.

Andy gets a chip from the bag and scoops a wad of dip.

So he likes a lot of music, big deal. Course, the problem isn't liking all kinds of music, it's liking mellow music. Not just a track like "Behind Blue Eyes," which rocks toward the end, after all, or even instrumentals like "Orchid," but really mellow shit. Jackson Browne. Journey. John Denver. Paul caught him listening to Denver once. Would have been better if he'd walked in on him jerking off.

For now he needs to keep his mouth shut. Otherwise the Rocky

Mountain High Incident will be mentioned and harped on for the rest of the night.

He dips another chip and rolls a four sided die on his notepad and writes down a number.

Hector holds up a hand and checks off fingers one by one.

—The gayest bands are. Culture Club.

George flips another page in the Monster Manual and looks at a picture of a fire elemental.

—Culture Club goes without saying. At this point we should really be doing the gayest bands other than Culture Club and Duran Duran.

Paul has moved and is sitting next to him on the bed, looking at the pictures over his shoulder.

—Fuck, that's cool. That's what I want to be. Andy, I want to be a fire elemental.

—You can't.

—Fuck can't I?

—There's no stats for them. I'd have to make it up again and it takes too much time. I'll give your character something with fire that's cool.

—Cool. Thanks.

Andy thinks about fire, he thinks about fire as a weapon and what it would be like to burn someone, and he sees what it would look like. He shakes the image away and rolls the twenty sided die.

At first he fought when the guys wanted to be monsters and shit, stuff that Dungeons & Dragons isn't designed for, but then he realized it was more fun that way. The more they ignored the way the game was supposed to be played, the more fun it became for him. Chaos.

He thinks about fire again, about fractals and how they can describe a natural phenomenon like fire. He thinks about whether there is a difference between what is random and what is chaotic.

Numbers arrange themselves for him and he writes them down.

Hector starts with his first finger again.

—Fine, no Culture and no Duran and Paul can't be a gay fire elemental. The five gayest bands are Devo, Depeche Mode, Flock of Seagulls.

Paul hits his own forehead.

—Hugely gay. The Flock. How'd I miss those cocksuckers?

—Wham.

—Massively gay. Again, how'd I miss that?

—And Phil Collins.

George slaps the Monster Manual shut.

—Not a band.

Hector stands up.

—You know, I don't even care. He's so fucking gay and his music sucks so fucking hard he has to be on the fucking list.

Paul takes the Monster Manual and flips it back open, looking for the fire elemental again.

—I'm still so stunned by Fuck a Seagull and Wham, I don't think he even needs Phil. You can D.Q. Phil and that is still the gayest list ever.

He nudges Andy with his toe.

—What say?

Andy writes a number for armor class and looks up.

—Mondo gay. Hector clearly knows his gay. His gayometer is in fine working shape. His recognition of gayness is noteworthy and admirable. All hail Hector, King of Gay.

By *gayometer* Paul and George have already fallen out laughing. They're helpless long before *King of Gay*.

Hector holds his hands above his head.

—So be it, King of Gay. Still better than being Mellow Lad, like John Denver over here.

Andy laughs and writes something on a paper and holds it out.

—Here's your character, *Hector, King of Gay*. He has a plus five to find gay.

One arm held out straight, Hector spins in place.

—Beep. Beep. Beep. Beep. Beep.

Slowing, stopping, swinging back in the other direction, bringing his arm down toward Andy.

—Beepbeepbeep. Beeeeeeeeep!

Pointing right at him now.

—Cool, it works. Guys, I just found some gay.

It's another half hour or so before they get started, spread around the room, *Diary of a Madman* in the tape player, the last of the bottle of Jack that Jeff bought for them making the rounds.

Andy doesn't remember how they ended up playing the game with him. Somehow, one of the days they'd started by fucking with him about it had ended with them playing. George had probably had something to do with it. Leading Paul and Hector from messing with him into letting him show them something new. And now they play just about every week. Getting stoned while Andy takes them through a new dungeon or a haunted forest or whatever. Playing until they get bored and just start saying *I hit it with my battle ax* every time they run across something that breathes.

—I hit it with my battle ax.

—I use my flame sword.

—I find its gay.

Andy starts dropping the geodesic dice back in the little leather bag he keeps them in.

—When do we meet Jeff?

His head stuck out the window so he can smoke, George holds up a couple fingers.

—Two. He'll drive us over to check out the house.

Paul crowds next to him at the window and takes the smoke from his hand.

—We should just hit it tonight.

—Let's take a look first. Could be a dog or it could have an alarm or some shit. You know how to do anything with an alarm? Cuz I sure as shit don't.

—But if it's cool, we should rob it tonight.

—The guy wants to pay us to do this shit, man. Let's be cool.

Hector squeezes next to them and takes the smoke.

—Yeah, let's do it when he says. Two bills for that shit we had. I want more of that.

George gets his cigarette back, takes the last drag and flicks the butt, the cherry trailing over the neighbor's fence.

—That's the point, man. If he can do this, tell us what houses have good shit, and he'll buy it from us? I don't want to fuck it up. Jeff says the guy says it'll be empty tomorrow night. We'll just take a look tonight. Make sure it's not too sketchy.

Behind them, Andy's eyes scan the dungeon he designed earlier in the day, mentally crossing off the rooms the guys have already traversed, the hazards survived, the riches plundered. More monsters and fewer traps next time. The guys like fighting more than they like figuring things out.

The Sketchy House

Hector hears the screams from the side of the house.

He wraps the chain around his hand and punches the plate glass door. It shatters, shards raking his forearm. He reaches down and flips the lock and pulls his arm out. He yanks on the handle and the door jams against the length of 1×2 he's forgotten about.

He throws rabbit punches at the glass, widening the hole.

The screams stop.

Someone is coming into the livingroom.

—Yo, Hector.

He stops punching the glass, stands there staring at Timo.

—Hector, I ever tell you what a piece of ass your little sister is?

Hector hits the glass again, spattering it with his own blood.

Timo is laughing.

—Keep coming, I want to talk to you about her. You pop her cherry yet? Or your old man beat you to it? Hope not, I'm looking forward to that shit. So far all she gives up is tit, but I'll be in her pussy in a week.

Hector kicks the glass, the hole is almost big enough to get through now.

Timo points at something.

—Hey, yo, what's that?

Hector sees the reflection in a hanging shard of glass just before Ramon limps up behind him and cracks him in the back of his head with his crutch.

The Rule of Shotgun

The pickup starts.

Jeff rolls out of the trailer park and pulls up at the QuickStop gas pumps. The gas is eight cents cheaper in the middle of town, away from the freeway entrance, but the guys here know him and won't give him shit when he leaves the engine running while the gas pumps. Let it die and it may never start again. He puts five bucks in the tank and heads out, a tallboy in a brown bag between his thighs.

A little breeze blows through the open windows and cools off the cab. Fucking Security Eye and their polyester uniforms. Couldn't they at least throw down for something made with a blend, something that might breathe a little? He uses his left hand to undo the buttons all the way down his front, exposing his sweat stained T.

He swigs the beer.

Should be at home. Sitting on the porch, finishing the rebuild on that carburetor. Should be getting the Harley back together so he can ride and not have to worry about the pickup starting, not have to worry about if he's gonna have to take the bus. Instead, gotta pick up the kids.

Damn it, Geezer. Fat slob doesn't have enough guys around he can get to rob his houses for him, has to get these kids involved?

Oh well, not like he can really do anything about it. Gonna tell Geezer how to do his business? Gonna tell the kids to knock this shit off and tuck in their shirts and go to class? Geezer's gonna do what he wants. The kids are gonna do what they want. Everybody's gonna do what they want, just like they always do. Everybody's gonna do this shit, no reason why he shouldn't help out here and there and make a few bucks himself.

But shit, gotta be tonight? Really want to get the Harley on its feet.

He pulls the pickup to the curb, finishes the last of the beer and drops the bag and the can out the window and lights a smoke.

Little fuckers best not be late.

—Hey, littering makes the Indian cry. Don't you watch TV? Ain't you seen the Indian cry when people litter?

The pickup lurches as Andy and Hector climb into the bed.

George strolls up, bends over and picks up the beer can.

—Crying Indians, man, that's no joke.

He holds out the can.

Jeff takes it from him.

—You guys high again?

—The word is *still*.

—Yeah, well you're *still* a punkass without a car. So get your ass in and let's go.

George sees Paul about to pull open the passenger door.

—Shotgun!

Paul flips him off.

—Fuck you, I called it on the way over here.

—You can't call shotgun until you see the car.

—Since when?

—Forever, man, that's always been a rule. No early shotguns.

—It's a gay rule.

George comes around the truck.

—Hector, what's the shotgun rule?

Hector sits on top of the wheel well.

—Got to see the vehicle in question, man.

George reaches in the back of the truck and pokes his brother.

—Andy?

Andy is on his back, looking at the sky.

—It's the rule. The only rule standing between us and the savages. It keeps the forces of chaos at bay. Scorn not the rule.

Paul starts to climb in the cab.

—Fuck chaos. I called this shit right after we climbed out the window. You can see the street from your window. You look, you can see your window through the trees. I called shotgun when we could see the truck.

George blocks him.

—You *can* see it. But *did* you see it?

—Man, are you splitting hairs with me on calling shotgun?

—Hey, you heard Andy, man. Chaos. You want to risk chaos?

Paul moves George's arm from his way and gets in the truck.

—Dude, I'll take my fucking chances.

Jeff looks at both of them.

—You ladies settled? Got that one all worked out? I just want to know so I can keep track of the gas I'm burning here so I know what to charge your asses for the taxi service.

Paul closes the door.

—Shotgun. It's a complicated issue.

George boosts himself into the bed of the truck and stands behind the cab and slaps the roof.

—We ride!

Jeff drops the empty beer can back in the street and pulls away.

—Fucking kids.

Andy raises his arm, pointing at the stars.

Calling out.

—Daring chaos by breaking the eternal rule of shotgun, they set out on their journey.

On the dark street off North L, Jeff drives the truck past the house, letting the kids get a good look. It's just another crappy house in another run down neighborhood. A couple lights are on. There's a streetlamp out front. Second time around the block Jeff dumps all the kids except George at the corner. George lies on his back in the bed of the pickup with the pellet gun Jeff dug out from behind the seats. He pumps it until it won't pump anymore. Jeff stops below the streetlamp, and George draws a bead the way his dad taught him years ago when they shot his grandpa's old .22 in the fields beyond the 580. The gun pops and the lamp goes black and Jeff pulls away as glass showers the street. They pick up the guys and go home.

———

Why doesn't he come home?

He stays out all the time. But tonight of all nights, why doesn't he come home?

Kyle Cheney sits in the livingroom, his back to the front door, TV tuned to NBC. *The Tonight Show* was on when he nodded off, but now it's only a cloud of static. All the lights are off. The scene is set. But his son won't come home.

He's at George and Andy's.

Where else would he be.

That's where they always end up. He watched them exit the trailer park, weaving their bikes back up the street, knowing where their next stop would be. After they disappeared he let himself go back to the QuickStop, ignoring the pints and half pints behind the cash register this time, going to the back where the proper bottles are. And then discovering he was 27 cents short. Having to dig through the change in the loan a cent on the counter. Sweaty, counting pennies out of the green plastic dish, the look from the Middle Easterner behind the counter.

Then heading for home and realizing he couldn't park the car in front of the house. If there was any chance of the boy coming home before midnight it would be ruined if he thought his father was there.

Parking the car two blocks away. Walking with the bottle in a brown paper bag, cradling it in the crook of his arm so it would be less visible.

People, nosy people, butting in.

Waiting. Sitting on the kitchen counter, peeking out the window, waiting. Waiting doesn't work. And it'd be worse if Paul found him like that, desperate like that. He got cleaned up, took a shower. Ate a Hungry Man. A few bites, anyway. Thought he should get the car, decided not to.

Maybe Paul will look out a window over there, late, see the car missing, wonder what's wrong, come looking for his father. Like any son would.

He needs not to be desperate when that happens. In control. Relaxed. In the livingroom, watching TV, back to the door, not concerned.

Don't let him know anything. Not until he goes to the bathroom and opens the toilet and sees the note. Then he'll be scared. Then he'll have to listen to what his father has to say.

When he comes out of the bathroom and sees his father with the bag of methamphetamine sitting right next to him? Paul will understand everything, without being told.

He reaches for the brandy bottle on the floor, misses, gets it on the second try, opens it and takes a drink. His eyes want to close again. It's the brandy. Too much today. Normally he has it under control. It's just that today was so stressful. Finding out your son is involved with drug dealers is stressful. Who wouldn't need a few drinks? The problem, the problem now, is to stay awake. Can't let the boy see how upset you are, but you also can't have him slipping in and out while you're asleep. Time for a little self discipline. He puts the cap back on the bottle and puts it down.

The TV hisses.

And his son doesn't come home. Doesn't see the missing car. Or sees and doesn't care.

Yes, the trick will be not letting Paul know how much he cares. He wipes the tears away, hiding the signs.

Date Night

—Mijo, where have you been? All night. All night.

Hector bends and kisses his mother's cheek.

—I was at George and Andy's. I told you yesterday, Ma, I spent the night like I told you.

—No, mijo, you didn't.

—I did.

She turns from him and stirs a pan of refried beans.

—No, Hector, you didn't tell me. I didn't sleep. All night I didn't sleep.

—Ma, I told you.

—No. You did not tell me. You did not. Do not lie to me.

—Ma.

—You tell me you told me, that is a lie. Lying to your mother.

—What did he do?

Hector's father stands in the open door of the kitchen, leaning on his cane, his bathrobe hanging open over his belly.

—What did he lie about?

She crosses the kitchen to him.

—Nothing, nothing, mi amor.

She puts a hand on his arm and tries to guide him to the table.

—Sit, I have your breakfast, sit.

He shrugs her off.

—I can walk. Leave me, I can walk to the table.

She smiles and nods and backs away toward the stove.

—Amor.

She starts filling a plate with beans and tortillas and a few links of Brown 'N Serve.

—Hector, take this to your father.

Hector takes the plate and a fork and a paper napkin and sets them on the table.

—You been lying to your mama?

—No, Pop.

—Bring me some water.

Hector fills a glass of water from the tap and takes it to the table. His mother keeps her back to them, tending the pots on the stove.

—Here, Pop.

His father takes the pills from his robe pocket and hands the bottle to his son.

—Two.

Hector opens the cap and takes out the pills and hands them over and watches as his dad washes them down with the water.

He puts the glass aside and cuts one of the sausages with his fork and pushes a piece of it around in his beans.

—What did you lie to your mama about?

—Nothing, Pop.

He puts the sausage and beans in his mouth.

—And now you're lying to *me*?

—No.

—Yes. Yes, you are.

He swallows the food.

—Go on. You came here to get some food, to change your clothes, to do that thing to your hair. Go on. Do the things you came here for. But don't come to my house and lie to my wife. You come home when you want to, I am not an animal, my son has a home, I don't kick my son out no matter what he does. But don't come home to break your mother's heart. Go on, go take care of your things. Just get out of the kitchen before you tell another lie.

—Pop.

—Go on, get out.

Hector puts a hand on his mother's shoulder.

—Ma, I didn't.

She shakes her head, brushes her hand in the air, doesn't look at him.

—Go on now, Hector, like your father says. Go on, it will be better right now.

—But.

His father bangs his cane on the floor.

—You heard your mama, go on. Go be with your friends and listen to your music. Go tell lies in their homes.

Hector squeezes his mom's shoulder.

—I'm sorry, Ma.

She smiles, but doesn't say anything.

His father points at a cabinet.

—Where's my wine?

Hector leaves the kitchen.

———

—Look at the bad penny.

—Hey, Amy.

—Don't let the cat out! Don't let the damn cat out!

Jeff sticks his leg in front of the cat, blocking its path, and snags it by the scruff.

—Got 'im.

He dangles the cat.

She puts her Marlboro 100 in her mouth and holds out her arms.

—Easy, easy, he's a old cat.

She takes the cat and rubs her ear against its neck.

—Aren't you? Just a little old man, aren't you?

She turns and walks back into the house.

—You comin' in?

—Yeah, sure.

Jeff follows her, watching her ass under the tight white jeans.

She climbs inside the bell of a wicker chair that dangles from the ceiling by a heavy chain, crossing her legs and putting the cat in her lap.

—What's up, what you looking for?

He settles on a Spirit of '76 souvenir beanbag from the bicentennial, the white patches turned gray by the years.

—They got me doin' splits again.

—Shit.

—Yeah. Graveyards, I can take a couple ludes the first few mornings, get used to sleeping during the day. This half and half shit, don't know when I'm up and when I'm down.

—Need help with the ups, huh?

—Supervisor drove by this parking lot, a parking lot I'm fucking protecting, I was crashed out. Finds me asleep again, says he's gonna suspend me. *At least*. Like I care if I lose the job.

—Uh huh. Want to get high?

—Yeah.

Amy points at an ashtray on the floor.

—There's a roach in there.

—Got a clip?

She bends forward, sticking her head out of the wicker cocoon, the chair tilting beneath her.

—Here.

She turns her head to the side and Jeff removes the feathered clip from her ponytail, opens the alligator jaws and places the roach between them.

He lights up, takes a hit and offers it to her.

—You in?

She waves the joint away.

—Go ahead, I already did a wake and bake. Got to be at the hospital in a hour. Doubling up my shift. Get too wasted and I'll be taking naps on the gurneys.

—I hear that.

She watches Jeff blow the roach.

Cute guy. He'd been a serious maybe at one time. Back in high school he'd been a definite yes. But she'd been Bob's little sister, fucker hadn't even noticed her. Not till her tits popped, then he noticed all right. By then she knew what she had, didn't need to be screwing her big brother's biker buds. But he'd stayed on the maybe list for a long time. If he'd tried a little harder he'd probably have got in. Made out that one time when they got drunk together on wine cooler. But some of the skanks he's walked out of the Rodeo Club with? Who wants to be on that list?

Still, he did give a good back rub. And he's a great kisser. And when she passed out he didn't even try to fingerbang her or anything.

So he's not on the *serious* maybe list, but he's not on the *no fucking way* list either.

She adjusts a bra strap, moves the cat so he hides the tummy she started getting in the last two years.

—Whites OK?

She pulls a baggie from under the chair's seat cushion.

Jeff sucks the roach dead.

—If that's what you got. What I could really go for is some crank.

—Don't got it.

—Not a little? Just a quarter for an old friend?

She leans back, deep inside the chair, her face disappearing in the shadows.

—I don't fuck with that shit. You know that.

—It's cool. I'm sorry. Just asking. No biggie.

—Why would you even ask that shit?

—No reason, just thought you might have changed the menu.

—Why? Where'd that idea come from? You ever hear me say anything about crank other than it's a shitty high? I don't deal in shitty highs. I'm a specialist, man. Pharmaceuticals. A little acid maybe. None of that cheap bathtub, do it yourself nose Drano.

—Got it, got it. I was out of line asking. Just.

—What?

—Nothing.

—Bullshit. *Nothing.* My ass. What?

Jeff opens and closes the roach clip, runs his fingers over the fluffy white and black feathers that hang from it on a suede cord.

—It's nothing. No big deal. Just something I heard.

She leans forward, the cat jumps from her lap and scoots under the couch.

—You heard what?

Jeff stands, gets a Camel from his pocket.

—Those whites handy?

Amy unfolds her legs, sticks them out of the chair, looks up at him through dirty blonde bangs, the same shade as her nephews'. She holds out a hand.

—Jeff, come here, baby.

He steps closer, offers her the roach clip.

She takes the clip from him, drops it on the floor and holds his hand.

—Baby, how long we know each other?

He fiddles with his unlit cigarette.

—Long time.

She runs her thumb across the back of his hand, massages an old white scar that covers an entire knuckle.

—Since we were kids. When did you and my brother first start hanging out? What were you, like, thirteen? I would have been nine. That's, what, over twenty years, man? That's crazy. You ever think you'd know anybody more than twenty years?

Jeff puts the cigarette away and takes her hand between both of his.

—Baby, I never thought I'd *be* twenty. Trips me out all the time.

She swings a foot back and forth, the basket chair rocks slightly.

—Being over thirty just blows my mind. And the way things change. Like the shit Bob was into when I was, like, the good little sister. And now look at him, and look at me. A trip. And like you and Bob were best friends and I was just his kid sister and now you guys don't ever see each other and me and you have been friends for a long time. Weird how that shit happens.

Jeff pulls lightly on her hand, adding to the chair's motion, rocking her.

—I like that part, baby. A lot of it, getting older, most of it is a drag, but I like being closer with you.

She holds his hands tightly, pulls, drawing herself closer to him.

—Well, I tell ya what, baby, you want us to be close, you want to ever have a chance of getting closer, you ever want to score another pill off me ever, you need to tell me where you got the fucking idea I might be holding crank.

She frees her hand from his and swings away, dropping her feet to the floor, halting the chair.

—Now, Jeff.

He looks at the floor, shakes his head, takes out the cigarette and lights it.

—Nice, Amy, nice way to be with a friend.

—Right now, you're barely a customer. You want to be my friend again, do something to show me that you are.

Jeff nudges the beanbag with his boot.

—Fucking.

—Jeff.

—Yeah, I heard you. Just, look, don't make a big deal out of this.

—Jeff.

He kicks the beanbag.

—Geezer. OK? Geezer said something about you and that he thought you were maybe dealing a little crank.

She points a chipped red fingernail at him.

—You fucker.

—Hey!

—You weren't gonna tell me. You knew that, and you weren't gonna warn me.

—That's not.

—You came in here. *Um, shucks, got any crank?* Wait a minute . . .

—Whoa, Amy.

—You. Are you here for him? Did he send you over here too?

—No. No way. No fucking way. You know me better than that.

—Do I?

She stands, the top of her head at his chin, a finger in his face.

—OK. OK. You tell, him, that fat fucking slob, you tell him no fucking way. I am not dealing crank. No. You tell him, tell him to stay away from me. Tell him, he comes around here, he comes, I see him on my lawn, tell him I'm calling every old man I ever had. Tell him I'm gonna have every biker in the Tri Valley on his ass. Tell him to stay away. Tell him to leave me alone, just leave me alone.

Jeff tries to touch her face, to wipe away some of the tears pouring over her cheeks.

She jerks away, stomps her foot, exhales and drops back into her chair. Head hanging, arms and legs limp.

—Geezer.

She pulls her legs up into the chair and wraps her arms around them.

—Oh fuck. Ohfuckohfuckohfuck.

————

—Let me borrow a shirt.

George looks down into the drawer of carefully folded concert Ts. He's standing in his underwear, his arms held away from his sides so he won't start sweating again.

—Why?

Paul pulls off his own shirt.

—Got bean dip all over mine.

George takes out a Stones shirt from their "Face Dances" gig at the Cow Palace.

—So go home and get one.

Paul lies back down on the sleeping bag spread on the floor.

—Fucking never mind.

George puts on the Stones T.

—Dude, don't be a girl, borrowing my clothes all the time. Go get a clean shirt.

—Don't be a rag, fucking lend me one.

George closes the drawer.

—No way, you get bean dip on your own shirts, not on mine.

—Yeah, now who's the girl?

He gets up and goes to the dresser and opens the drawer.

—Look at this, man, you wash these things in Woolite or what?

—Fuck you.

—They're just shirts, man. You wear them, that's what they're for.

—It's a collection, OK? It's a collection of shirts from concerts I've gone to and paid money for the shirts and taken good care of them because I want to keep them around and wear them. You five finger discount every concert shirt you ever had. No wonder you don't give a fuck if they get thrashed.

Paul takes a step back.

—Whoa. Sorry. Didn't realize I was talking to your dad here.

George pulls on his favorite cutoffs.

—Fuck you, man.

He grabs his smokes and lighter and shades and walks out.

—Do whatever you want, take whatever you want.

Paul stands alone in the room.

Fucking George. No joke, the guy can get like infected with his dad sometimes. Not that that should be a big deal. They all make jokes about how uptight Mr. Whelan is, but he's far and away the coolest dad any of them know. George doesn't know how good he has it, how easy.

He looks at the shirts, picks up the one from the Blue Oyster Cult show last December. He unfolds the shirt and looks at the front, the ankh and the reaper in a night sky, the tour dates listed down the back.

George loves his shirts, doesn't mean he has to be a dick about it. Knows how much it sucks to go home after staying out all night.

You OK? Everything all right? I wish you would call if you're going to stay out all night. Something is going to happen one night and I won't even know to be worried or to look for you. All you have to do is pick up the phone and call. Even if you need a ride. Especially if you need a ride. Don't ever get in a car with a drunk driver. If you've been drinking that's one thing, but don't get in a car with someone who's been drinking themselves.

George can't lend him one cocksucking shirt so he doesn't have to deal with that? They been friends how long? Jesus. Just ever since The Fight, that's all.

It happened a couple days after Paul and his family moved into the neighborhood. George was the local hero, eight years old, wearing jeans and boots and a pearl button shirt like his dad. What a fag he looked like. And coming on all cowboy tough, giving Paul shit about the hippie stuff his mom found for him at the Salvation Army store.

They fought for so long the kids watching started to cry. They were so scared one of them was gonna kill the other one. They beat the living shit out of each other. Went on for hours. Seemed that way. Anyway, didn't stop till Mr. Whelan drove home and saw them punching each other on the Phelps' front lawn. Pulled to the curb and came over and got a handful of their hair in each hand and yanked them apart.

That was a great fucking fight, man.

Next day they ran into each other on the sidewalk and talked about it and showed each other their bruises and scrapes and scabby knuckles.

He crams the shirt back in the drawer. Fuck this, man. Got cash on hand. Go down to Galaxy Records and buy a brand new shirt. Get that black Ozzy T with the red jersey sleeves. Yeah, man, cut the sleeves off, that'll look cool as hell.

He climbs into his shredded jeans and the dirty T and pulls on Jeff's Harley cap.

—George!

He heads down the stairs to the kitchen.

—George, let's cruise over to Galaxy, check out some tunes, there's a shirt I like on the wall over there.

———

Andy walks around the empty house.

It's after twelve. The thermometer on the back porch is hitting ninety. Mom and dad left for work first thing. Who knows when George and Paul and Hector took off.

He goes to the bathroom and brushes his teeth and fills a plastic cup with water from the tap and drinks it standing at the sink. He looks at himself in the mirror. Skin and bones and greasy, tangled hair. Mostly bones and hair. No wonder no girls like him.

Paul says he'd do better if he was bigger. *Chicks dig muscles,* he says, and flexes. Chicks like Paul OK, dig his muscles, until they get to know him. Then they get scared of his temper.

Hector says Andy needs to be himself. Chicks don't dig him when he's being himself, then fuck them anyway, he says. Chicks used to be into Hector, until he went punk and started wearing the mohawk last year. There are a couple that are still into him, funky ones with tons of black eye shadow and black nail polish and shit.

George says he just needs to be cool, not dig the chicks too much. Just do your own thing and they'll come around. And it works for him. Like most things work for George. He's the one chicks come around to talk to, trailing a couple friends. Paul and Hector get the friends. Andy gets told to go home.

That's what it's like being the little brother.

He's made out twice in his life so far. Both times with girls that were older than him. Both times at parties where everyone was drunk and stoned. Both times they found out he was at least a year younger and ignored him after and told their friends it didn't happen.

He picks up a brush and tries to run it through his hair, but it snags and pulls at his scalp. He gives up and leaves it in a tangle.

In the kitchen he finds some of last night's fruit salad and sits at the table in his underwear. He studies the bowl and estimates how much more fruit is in it than was in his bowl last night. He remembers the total numbers of each type of fruit he had in his bowl because he counted them all and he multiplies that number based on his estimate and calculates the odds of selecting any particular type of fruit if he were to do it blindfolded.

He remembers catching his dad watching him pick through the fruit. Remembers the look on his dad's face. He gets that look a lot, the *where did this weird kid come from* look.

It's not like he's trying to be different, like he wants to be weird. He just is. Not like it's easy being this way. He'd rather be like George. He'd rather be like his dad. He'd rather be like anyone else. But he's not. Because no one else is like him. No one else is this weird. And that's just the weird stuff people know about. They don't know about the stuff inside his head.

Dreams where soldiers attack their house and he sneaks around with a toy gun that shoots real bullets and he kills them all. Moments in the middle of the day where he's by himself doing homework and suddenly sees himself with a knife, walking up behind some jock who picked on him in school and sticking it in his eye while he's talking to his jock friends and then just going crazy and cutting them all up. Things inside his head that he doesn't know where they come from and he can't tell anyone because they scare him so much.

He looks into the bowl. Apples are the most likely. He closes his eyes and reaches into the bowl. Apple. He drops it back in the bowl and fishes out a strawberry.

He wishes George and Paul and Hector hadn't taken off without him. Being alone sucks.

He finishes the fruit salad, washes the bowl, and rinses his hands and wipes them on a paper towel and uses it to blow his nose.

Making sure one more time that the guys aren't lurking somewhere in the house waiting to ambush him and scare him shitless, he goes to the stereo and puts on *Madman Across the Water,* one of his mom's favorites. He turns the volume up and goes to his room and takes out a fresh piece of graph paper.

He starts to draw a new map, ignoring the grid of lines this time, drawing jagged twisting lines, caves and tunnels and dead ends. A labyrinth with more monsters in it for the guys.

After a couple minutes he stops drawing and goes back in the drawer and finds the picture of Alexandra that was in Timo's things. He looks at it, covering *Te quiero, Timo* with his thumb.

"Tiny Dancer" plays in the livingroom.

He pictures hitting Timo with a battle ax.

ImsuchadildoImsuchadildoImsuchadildo.

———

—Chester. Muchacho, it's Geezer. Got a minute? Not bad, no complaints. Well, that's a fucking lie, course I got complaints. Man ain't got complaints ain't alive. Man that can't open his mouth to bitch is . . . the word? The word when someone's out of it, asleep, knocked out, but forever? No, like that, but the other one. Someone gets hit by a hammer they go in a coma, but if the hammer hits you then you're what? *Comatose.* That's it. Man ain't got something to bitch about, he must be comatose. Yeah, yeah, then he'd really have something to bitch about, just couldn't, yeah. Hey, Chester, can we pass the fucking time later, I got something. A bond? Why the fuck else do I call you? Yes, a bond. A big fucking bond. Two big fucking bonds. Yeah, them. No, two. The little one is a minor, they released him to his parents. Too bad for him, what I hear he'd be better off staying in a cell. His old man's gonna beat the shit out of him. That's sure as hell what I'd do I was his dad. So his older brothers. Yeah, it's a load. No. No. Tell you what, no, you just put it up. Fuck do I care that's not the way you do business? That's not my problem. You, no, you put up the bond. They're not going anywhere. Only place they're going is to do some work for me. They take off, we can talk. Till then, just bond their ass out of jail. Fuck do I care how you make money? I care about you bond the fucking Arroyos and tell them to get their asses over to my place. You worry about making money off some useless cocksucker out there who isn't gonna have someone come in your office one night and hit you with a fucking hammer until you're fucking comatose.

Geezer hangs up the phone.

Fucking people. What are they thinking some times? Guy asking him, *How am I gonna make money if I don't get my ten percent?* If there was ever someone else's problem, that's it. Go around expecting other people to take care of your business for you, you get what you deserve.

He should know. Look at this shit with the Arroyos. What he gets for trusting a litter of spic puppies to take care of shit in a responsible manner.

Now it's all about doing a job yourself if you want it done right.

Gotta get the spics out on bond. Gotta get them over here and tell them some bullshit story about how it's all gonna be OK. How he's gonna set them up with a real deal lawyer who's gonna get them off. Yeah, right. Get a bunch of spic thugs off manufacturing and possession with intent to distribute and all that other shit. Fuckers are lucky the judge set any kind of bail. So, gotta tell them that fairy tale. Then gotta have them deal with these punk kids and get the rest of the stash back and . . . fuck. You ever get a break? And after the kids, gotta deal with that bitch Amy Whelan sticking her tits in his area of commerce. His markets. Knew she was gonna be trouble when she started in with the pills. Thought she got the message about not expanding her product line, turns out she's just plain stupid. Runs in that family. Seeing the experience he's had with Whelans, should have taken that stupidity into consideration with her in the first place. Well, that shit's gonna get sorted out with everything else. Gonna make a clean sweep of everything.

Including the spics.

Gonna have to take care of that before they get it through their thick spic skulls that they're fucked for life.

And do it all without pissing up Oakland's tree any more than it's been pissed up already. Fuckers don't care to hear about legal troubles or what shit your employees drop you in, just want to see the envelopes with the dollars inside. Fuck they care a lab gets busted? Rent on the town is due, pay up. The half key the brothers say was missing from their fridge will cover it. Give some space to think, get the new lab going.

Running your own business, is there anything worse?

He leans as far forward as his gut will allow, puts one hand on the coffee table and the other on the edge of the couch and pushes himself to his feet, taking the grabber with him because he won't be able to bend for it once he's standing.

Making a short mental list, a list that starts with gun and ends with garbage bags.

———

Hector comes back to the Whelans' with his mohawk reestablished. He hears Elton John playing but doesn't say anything, just turns it off, tunes the radio to KSAN, and "Baby's on Fire" comes on. He goes into Andy's room, watches him drawing one of his dungeons, and sits on the floor and looks through a pile of old comic books until he finds one with the Guardians of the Galaxy in it.

Andy barely notices him, rolling dice, sketching twisting lines, exploring probabilities, deep inside a world of small things.

George and Paul get back from the record store.

George turns off KSAN and puts the copy of British Steel he bought at the record store on the turntable. He drops the needle on "Breaking the Law" and turns it up.

Paul goes in the kitchen and finds a pair of scissors and sits at the table and cuts the sleeves from his new shirt so his arms will show when he's wearing it. He tosses the dismembered sleeves in the garbage and puts on the shirt and goes into the bathroom and looks in the mirror. It looks badass, the *Diary of a Madman* cover on the front and the picture of Ozzy lifting Randy Rhodes in the air on the back.

He remembers how he locked himself in his room when he heard the news that Randy had died. The best guitar player to come around since Jimi, dead at twenty-five. Just wanting to sit in his room and listen to *Blizzard* and *Madman* all day long, but his dad kept knocking on the door and asking if he was OK, ruining everything. Again.

It feels suddenly hotter in the bathroom. The spike digs between his eyes and knocks the air out of his lungs. He chokes and bends over the sink and presses his forehead against the cool countertop. The spike goes a little deeper. He fumbles with the cold water tap and sticks his head under the faucet and tries to breathe slowly as water runs over the back of his scalp and his neck. The spike pulls out, slowly.

He stays bent at the sink for a few minutes, turns off the water, and looks at himself in the mirror, pale, red eyed, hair dripping.

He makes sure the door is locked and drops to the floor and does a quick set of pushups and looks at himself in the mirror again with his chest and arms pumped.

Badass.

———

They hang around the house until it's too hot to stand it and then they ride to the bowling alley and blow a joint out back and go inside and eat lunch at the counter and play some video games. Andy mostly watching because he's so bad at the games it just makes him feel like he's throwing his quarters away.

Suchadildo.

They're late getting back to the Whelans' for dinner because George hits a new level on Missile Command and goes for the high score and gets it.

Mr. Whelan gives them a ration of shit and tells Paul and Hector that the kitchen isn't a restaurant where you eat whenever you want to and if they want their dining privileges to continue they can damn well be there when the family sits down. George and Andy he just gives a look and asks them if this is going to happen again any time soon and they tell him no. He tells them to empty the ashes from the Weber and get some coals going and scrape the grill, and goes inside to make the burger patties while his wife cuts tomatoes and chops iceberg lettuce and peels slices of American cheese from a yellow stack.

They eat in the backyard, sitting around an old picnic table Mr. Whelan salvaged from a building site. Right after the meal he's walking around the yard with his fourth beer in his hand, kicking stones from the ground he's going to rototill the following day, giving his sons and their friends a bad time, asking them if they have their back braces ready for the Sunday rock haul. Telling them to start drinking water now, gonna be hotter than hell. Warning that he'll be getting them up at the crack of dawn on Sunday to try and beat the heat. Laughing at the looks on their faces as they think about how much it's going to suck.

Paul helps Mrs. Whelan clear the plates. Something he always does.

—I thought Sunday was the Lord's day, sir.

Bob Whelan yanks one of the weeds he let grow over the last couple weeks.

—Young Mr. Cheney, if Jesus can get up on Easter Sunday to move a rock, you can do it *this* Sunday.

They have popsicles for dessert and the boys say they're going back to the bowling alley and they get their bikes and take off.

Bob Whelan comes up behind his wife at the kitchen sink and reaches around her and puts his hands on her tits.

—Looking good, baby.

—Stop it.

—Mmm, feeling good, too.

—You're drunk.

—Drunk? On five, six beers? Baby, the day I can't knock over a sixer and keep my wits is the day I give up beer.

—Uh huh.

—It's Friday.

—I know what day it is.

—Date night.

—I know what it is.

—Empty house.

—Not for long.

—That's my point.

—Let me wash these dishes.

—Let me help.

He presses against her back, slides a hand, cold from his beer can, down the front of her cutoffs.

—Stop it. Bob! Stop it, your hand's cold. Stop it!

He doesn't stop. And they go to the bedroom.

Part Two

The House They Came to Rob

—Cops impounded my car, vato.

—Fuck do I care about your fucking car. Ain't your fucking vato, neither.

Fernando raises his hands above his head.

—Hey, no shit you ain't my vato. Don't worry about not being my vato. Worry about the cops having my car. Worry about when I finally get it back and it still has that hole you put in the window.

—Send me a bill.

—A bill. Ese, I give a shit about the bill. I care about you broke my rear windshield.

He pulls Hector's chain out of his pocket.

—A fucking chain you threw at my car. My car. Fuck you and the bill, you broke my glass.

He lashes Hector's face with the chain.

Hector folds in half, hands over his face, face between his knees, eyes squeezed shut, mouth closed tight around the shriek that comes up his throat. He opens his eyes and watches the blood that runs out of his face and between his fingers and trickles down to pool on the warped hardwood floor between his feet while Fernando whips his shoulders with the chain, the Levi's jacket on his back the only thing that keeps his skin from being ribboned.

—Save a little for me, big brother.

Fernando stops beating Hector and looks at Ramon coming in the front door.

—What's up?

Ramon knocks the door closed with his crutch.

—Cheney got away.

—Got away? Get Timo and go find him. What if he calls the cops?

—Kid's got a half kilo of meth. Ain't calling the cops.

Fernando drops the chain on the floor.

—Hope he don't, little bro, fucking hope he don't.

Ramon leans against the wall.

—*You* hope he don't, man, *I* been in prison. Shit don't touch me. I can do that shit I have to. Worry 'bout how you handle a little real time. Where's Timo?

—Yo, ese.

Timo comes down the hall, joint between his lips, trailing smoke.

Ramon lays out his palm and they trade skin, Timo slipping him the joint.

He takes a toke.

—Thanks, bro. What's up?

—Whelan and his kid bro are out cold.

—Want to wake those bitches?

—Let's do it.

Fernando holds up a hand.

—Don't wake shit. I say to wake shit?

Ramon holds out the joint.

—Bro, take a hit, chill out. Ain't nothing. Just gonna wake them up. Ask some questions. Find out where the shit is.

—Nobody asking questions. Nobody asking questions till the man gets here.

Ramon and Timo bug their eyes at each other.

Timo smiles big at his big brother.

—Get all jefe on us, ese? What's with that? This your thing all a sudden? We all not in the same shit? We all not takin' the same bust?

Fernando takes two steps and pops Timo in the nose he broke two days ago in their last fight.

Timo screams and goes down.

Ramon cocks his fist, but Fernando has him by the neck. Ramon unclenches his fist.

Fernando nods.

—That's right, bro, relax that shit.

Ramon points at Timo.

—What the fuck?

Fernando lets him go.

—Little shit talking about we all got the same bust. He's a fucking minor. No priors. Nothing. Bust means shit to him. He's talking jail-house tough shit he gets from you. And you? Acting like it's a fucking joke? Joint don't mean nothing to you, bro? That your story now? What I remember when I went up there to visit, I remember I seen what you look like comin' down that hall, sittin' on the other side of that window. I remember you so lonely you were crying. Remember what I said that day?

Ramon touches the bandage around his thigh where the cops put a bullet in him.

—Yeah.

—Say it.

—Said. Said it was no good me being inside. Being away from my brothers. Said not to forget how it felt, not being with blood. Said outside we had each other. Inside we got nobody.

—That's right. Inside we're alone. And we're not going inside. Not you, not any of us. You want to go against those charges with a public defender? Some whitey from the county gonna get you off that shit? *The man* is gonna get us off that shit. We do his thing, he's gonna get us a real lawyer. That's what I want. Till we got that settled, you're right, I am the jefe. We all work together, but I am the boss and you gotta listen to me. Gotta follow what I say. Do that, stay together, stay on the outside. Stay family. Blood?

Ramon puts out his hand.

—Blood.

Fernando takes his brother's hand.

—Blood.

Timo sits up, fingering his nose.

—Thit's brothen again, futhcker.

Fernando helps him to his feet.

—Come on, blood, let's clean that shit up.

He takes his brother back down the hall to the bathroom.

Ramon watches their backs.

—Jefe.

He smiles, takes a few steps and, leaning on his crutch, bends and picks up the snake of bloody chain. He looks at Hector, still folded and holding his face.

—Check you out, ese, you're all fucked up. How's shit like that happen, holmes? How'd you get into this shit?

He takes a seat on the couch, leaning forward to take the hacksaw from his belt and tuck it next to the armrest. He stretches his wounded leg.

—I don't want to fuck with you while you're down, but you gotta be told, you ain't got it so bad.

He taps his thigh.

—This shit, taking a .38 in the leg? That hurts. No lie. Know what the bullet did? Skipped off the bone. Check that out. Doc said it could just as easily shattered the motherfucker. 'Stead, it skipped off the bone and went right out my leg. Told him I wanted to keep that bullet, good luck charm there ever was one. Said they can't give it to me. Said it's evidence. Evidence in the resisting arrest part of the case. Cops got a case against us, it's so big it's got fucking *parts*. Makes my head hurt as bad as my leg. Take it from me, little man, you ain't got it so bad.

He leans back.

—Still, this shit is all fucked up. This brown on brown thing? Know what I'm talking about, holmes? Yeah you do. This ain't right. Mean, here you are, three white dudes and one Chicano. And, whoa, stop the presses, who's in here getting fucked up? Two white dudes in the back room sleeping it off, other white dude ditched this shit. Cue up the same sorryass story.

He wiggles the chain.

—And us, here we are, three brothers, hermanos, the real deal lowrider vatos. Who we waiting on? That's right. White dude. In the meantime, how we spending our siesta? Beating on a fellow Chicano. That seem right? There something wrong with this picture? Know there is. Blanco Nortinos steal all of California from us, right? That's how this shit started, that's how far back. Still there's places like this, towns where we got the numbers. Still we can't seem to do shit any different than before. Ain't right, ese. All us Chicos here and hardly any Mr.

Browns in sight, and we're still fucking each other up instead of taking it to them.

He levers himself up with the crutch.

—That's some prison education for you. Lessons direct from the school of hard knocks. Santa Rita social studies.

He looks at Hector, still bent over, bleeding face still in his hands.

He looks at the chain, watches a drop of Hector's blood slowly creep from link to link.

—Anyway, whatever. Let's see how this shit works.

And he puts the chain to use.

————

—Andy. Andy.

—Leave me alone.

—Andy.

—I hurt. Leave me alone.

—Let me see your face.

—I donwanna.

—C'mon, man, just let me take a look.

—No. No.

—Andy, stop being a fag and let me see your face.

—Fuck you. Fuck you.

But he turns his head, letting his brother see his face.

—Shit, oh shit, little brother, oh shit.

Andy looks down.

—Your legs are bleeding.

—It's OK, it's just scrapes. How's the inside of your mouth, did you bite your tongue?

Andy sticks his tongue out.

—I thon thing tho.

—It looks OK.

—Thor hed ith bleeing.

—Put your tongue back in your mouth.

Andy puts his tongue back in his mouth.

—Your head is bleeding.

—They hit me with something.

—Who did?

—I don't know. I don't remember too good. Fernando or Ramon, I think.

—You tore my favorite shirt.

—That was Paul, OK? It was Paul. I told him to stop and he just. Fuck! Andy, your eye?

—What?

—Can you see out of it?

Andy blinks.

—Which one?

—The left one, your left eye. It's like, it looks like it's full of blood, like there's blood inside of it.

—Oh.

He closes his right eye.

—Yeah, I can see out of it.

—Good. OK.

—George?

—Yeah, bro?

—My stomach feels funny.

He tilts, eyes open, until he's lying on his side, shivering, and then still.

———

Paul stops running.

He looks around to see where he is. Somewhere on Locust. Turning, he can see the swimming pools at May Nissen Park a few blocks away. He's covered in sweat. Even with the sun down it's still like eighty. He gets out a Marlboro and lights it. He starts to walk, heading toward the pools.

Too bad they close at dark. Be nice to jump in the water and cool off. If they didn't have those security lights he could just hop the fence. Could do it anyway. Get over the fence and do a couple quick laps and get out. Still be plenty of time to meet up with the guys. They were lagging so hard, didn't see any of them behind him when he took off. Fucking laggers. Gonna give them all kinds of shit when they catch up. Trouble starts, you gotta jet right away.

He crosses Rincon and walks up to the fence and stands there looking at the pools on the other side.

Lameass Andy fucking up inside the house. Getting George in there with him. Well, George'll get them both out. Hector must have split around the other side of the house. Probably got his bike. Man, getting *his* bike back is gonna be a bitch. Maybe go back there right now and take a grab at it. No, that's lame. Guys'll be catching up soon. Gonna have to deal with those bikes together.

He hooks his fingers in the chainlink, closes his eyes.

And sees again his best friend's legs, cut and bleeding, being pulled through the window. And hears the screams.

He opens his eyes.

—Fuck me.

———

—Where are they?

—There's one right there, man.

—Yeah, I see him. What's wrong with him?

—He's the puta bitch that fucked up my car.

—OK. So what's wrong with him?

—I hit him a couple times.

Geezer tilts his head to get a better look at Hector's face.

—Kid's got, what, cuts on his face? What're those?

—Cuts.

—From what?

—Piece of chain.

Geezer looks where Fernando is pointing. Uses the grabber to pick up the bloody chain from the floor.

—You hit him a couple times with this?

—Once, just once.

—Kid's been hit a lot of a fuck more than once. Kid's missing teeth. He's been . . . word? When you get attacked by a wild animal, a bear, what it does to you?

—Como?

—What's the word for that?

—I don't fucking know, man.

Ramon shifts on his crutch.

—Maul. You get mauled by a bear.

Geezer drops the chain.

—That's it, kid's been *mauled.*

He looks at Fernando.

—You hit him once and mauled him like this? Remind me never to let you hit me.

Ramon pokes Hector with the rubber tip of his crutch.

—I mauled him.

Geezer pulls at the brim of his black and yellow Caterpillar hat.

—What'd he do?

—Screamed a little. Cried a lot.

—No, what'd he do that you mauled him?

Ramon pivots on his crutch and hobbles to the couch.

—Nothing. Just wanted to see what that chain'd do to his face.

Geezer watches him lower himself to the couch and stretch out his gun shot leg.

He points at Hector.

—Well, guess we know now what happens you whip some kid's face with a piece of chain. He gets all fucked up. Might want to call a medical journal or some shit, make a report, get yourself nominated for the fucking Pulitzer.

Ramon smiles.

—Nobel.

—What?

—Nobel Prize. Pulitzer, they only give that for writing stuff.

—Well, when they start giving a Nobel Prize for fucking kids up with chains you'll be a pioneer in the field, won't you?

Ramon stares.

Geezer pushes up the brim of his hat, looks at Fernando.

—'Nando, your little brother vying for top psycho in the room honors? He trying to freak me out, put me off my game?

Fernando puts a hand on his brother's shoulder.

—He's cool, Geezer. Just likes to show off a little.

—Got some macho in him, eh?

—Sure, like all of us, right?

Geezer smiles.

—Never met a Mexican worth a damn who didn't have some macho
to him.

—Sure, that's just how we are.

He looks at Ramon.

—Right, little brother?

Ramon leans back.

—Sure, ese, just me and my macho showing off.

Geezer nods at Fernando, chins waggling.

—Good enough. Where's the other ones?

Fernando points at the hallway.

—Bathroom.

—El baño, eh?

—Right. The bathroom.

—Show me.

Fernando walks around Geezer and down the hall, ignoring the slit-
eyed wink Ramon throws him from the couch.

Geezer follows him into the master bedroom, waving the grabber at
Timo on the floor.

—Jesus, everybody in this place take a beating?

Timo stays on his back, pinching his nostrils gently, trying to stop the
blood that keeps dripping from his swollen nose.

—I dinn't tate no beadin' froh nodbody.

Fernando puts his hand on the bathroom doorknob.

—He fell down.

Geezer laughs.

—Fell down on a pile of fists it looks like.

Timo looks away.

—I fell ond duh grounb libe ebberbody dubs.

—Sure, sure thing, amigo. Whatever you say.

He faces the door.

—Alright, 'Nando, open up.

Fernando opens the bathroom door.

George looks up at them, his little brother's head in his lap.

—My brother. My brother. He's hurt. I think he's hurt real bad. Help my brother. Please help my brother.

Geezer fills the doorway and peers down at Andy's bruised face and turned up eyes.

—Damn, now that's comatose if I ever saw it.

————

—Whas the matter? Whas that?

—Nothing.

—Whas that thm?

—Yeah.

—Whut time's't?

—It's late. Go back to sleep.

—Where?

—I'm gonna go give them a little talk.

—Done be too hrd. Th'r hum. L'thm go t'bed.

—Don't worry.

—Talk in the muhrn'n 'bou't.

—Don't worry. Go back to sleep.

—Hokay.

Bob Whelan watches his wife tuck her face back into her pillow and close her eyes and drop back to sleep. Still naked, he grabs his jeans from the foot of the bed. He uses the toilet in the hall instead of the one in their room, not wanting to wake her again.

She's tired. Up first thing in the morning, on her feet all day behind that cash register at the Safeway, back here to straighten up the house and get things ready for dinner.

She tried to stay up when they finished screwing around and realized the boys hadn't come home, made it till a little after midnight, but couldn't hang in there. Even after she conked out she was restless as hell. Well, she'll sleep OK now.

He flushes and puts on his jeans and goes to the front door and out onto the porch. Whatever the sound was, it wasn't the boys. But he knew that already. He knows exactly what they sound like sneaking in and out of the house. He walks to the foot of the driveway and stands there and looks up and down the street.

Goddamn kids.

Got no problem with them running around and getting in a little trouble. Learn more about life that way than by sitting around inside watching TV like so many other kids. Get in a few fights, that's how you learn to stick up for yourself. Get the crap beat out of you, that's how you learn what sticking up for yourself can cost you. Do a little drinking and smoking, that's how you learn how much you can handle. Take a ride in the back of a police car, that's how you learn the consequences of trying to get away with too much.

And that's probably how they'll be coming home. If he's lucky the cops will drive them right up to the door. If he's not lucky he'll be getting a call from the jail on North L telling him to come get his boys that got picked up at some house party where the parents are out of town and their kids got their hands on a keg and a few bottles of Cuervo or something.

The more things change.

If it was just him, he'd wait for the call and let them stay the whole night in jail, pick them up tomorrow afternoon after the yard is rototilled, bring them home and put them to work on the rock pile right away. That's how his pop would have handled it. Hell, that's how he *did* handle it.

He scratches his stomach, his index finger running along the ridge of scar at the bottom of his rib cage. Truth be told, his pop handled it a hell of a lot harder.

Paul, he knows about that kind of thing. Seen those cigarette burns on his stomach. Only one place you get marks like those.

He takes a few steps into the street, looks down the block at the dark front of the Cheney house. Man, sometimes, see that little prick out there watering his lawn, like to stroll over and give him a good one. See how he likes it. Don't even say anything, just walk up to him and put him on his ass.

A kid gets knocked around a little by his dad? Well, shit like that happens, nobody ever said life was fair. But cigarette burns? No way to explain that. Just that Kyle Cheney is a little prick. Probably ran his wife off by being a little prick. Now he probably blames his kid for her smashing up her car and dying, takes it out on him.

Prick.

Just one good punch right on the button. Might straighten him out.

No. Can't do that kind of thing. That pecker brings assault charges, a whole can of worms gets reopened. Rules broken, rules he made for himself. Promises he made his wife. That's not the way to handle it. That's not the way he handles things. Not anymore. Not for a long time.

Ain't none of his business, anyway. How a man raises his kids, that's just nobody else's business. And Paul's gonna come out of it OK. Tough little fucker. They're gonna love him in the Army. And he spends half his time down here anyway. No need to make a big scene out of helping the kid, just give him a place to go every now and then, that's help enough.

He walks over to the 4×4 and boosts himself up on the fender. He leans forward and a roll of his stomach pushes over the waist of his jeans. He looks at it. Still don't know where the hell that came from. Woke up one morning and there it was. Crap. Nobody stays young. But crap.

He freezes.

That the phone ringing inside? Nope.

If it was just him, he'd be asleep right now. But Cindy would worry. Got to put on a show for her. Make her think they're home safe and sound. Damn them. Worrying their mother, messing with his wife's sleep. And then she'll be bitchy in the morning and he'll be grouchy and they'll end up bickering tomorrow. Damn them. George should be old enough by now to get himself out of trouble. And Andy is smart enough he shouldn't be in it in the first place. Or he *should* be smart enough. Some days the kid seems like he's not so much smart as he's just from Mars. At least he hasn't gotten as weird as Hector. Yet.

He slides off the fender and walks back up to the porch.

Not doing any good standing here. Go back inside. If Cindy wakes up tell her the boys are in bed. Doesn't do anyone any good standing here getting worked up and worn out. The boys are fine. Probably in the police station right now. Getting the shit scared out of them. Do all four of them a load of good.

He sits on the edge of the porch.

Anyway, it's warm and it's quiet. Might as well wait a little longer.

————

—Where's the other one?

—Other one?

—There's four of them, right?

—Yeah.

—So, you got the Nobel Prize winning science project in the living-room, you got that one comatose, and you got his brother here. Unless Ramon learned a different way of counting in the joint, that's three.

Fernando pulls the front of his hairnet, shifts it slightly lower on his forehead.

—He ran away, man.

—He got out of the house?

—No, man, he was never in it.

Geezer takes off his hat, runs his hand over his head, and wipes the sweat on his thigh.

—And how, why was the kid outside when he ran? How did he know you were in here?

—He saw us.

—How? No. The point. This was a trap, right? I set up a trap. I saw some jewelry that should be in your possession and I did some pretty fucking clever reasoning and plotting. Impressed the fuck out of myself, to be honest. The point of it being to let them all get in the house be-fore you did anything. Grab their asses in the house. It's quiet, there's no witnesses, it's easy.

—Yeah, man, but they couldn't break in.

—What do you?

—They were taking forever to break in. We.

—Why would they?

—They don't know how to pick a lock or anything.

—What the? Why was it locked? We wanted them in the house. Why the fuck would you lock the doors?

—I thought you wanted. Well, you know, man, to make it, real. So they wouldn't know it was a trap.

Geezer slaps his hat on the side of the bed.

—They're kids, 'Nando, how the fuck would they? OK. Just. Never mind.

He puts on his hat and holds out his hand, slick with sweat from the top of his head. Fernando takes it and hauls him to his feet.

Geezer makes for the livingroom.

—Just bring the one that's awake.

Fernando goes to the bathroom.

—Get up.

George looks at him.

—Hey. Hey, man. Fernando.

—Get the fuck up.

George puts his hands under Andy's head and lowers it to the floor and stands up.

—Hey, whatever, whatever we fucked up, my brother is really hurt. No more fucking around here, man. This is no joke. We got to call, we got to get him some help.

—Get out here.

—Seriously, man. This shit between us, we can't mess around, you know, whatever, take it out on me, but Andy's. Look at him, man.

Fernando reaches out and swats the side of his head.

—Whelan, fuck you. Fuck Hector. Fuck fucking Cheney. And fuck your fucking brother. Get in the fucking livingroom and shut the fuck up.

George holds the side of his head, covering the bloody lump where Fernando hit him with the minibat while he was stuck in the window screaming. He looks down at his brother.

—I'll be back, Andy.

But Andy doesn't say anything and George steps out of the bathroom, following Fernando.

Still on the floor, Timo flips him off.

—Dode fudking loob ad me, bidch. Youd gob fudking enoudgh trubdle.

—You're a shucking cockshucker, Ramon.

—Me? No, man, never. Had mine sucked a few times in the joint. Know what, Hector? Man's mouth feels just like a woman's. Yours, with those teeth knocked out, it might feel pretty good.

—Shuck you and you mosher and you grandmosher, puta Shucking cockshucker.

—That's a long to do list you're making for yourself, joven.

—Shee ish I'm a lishle boy when I shuv that chain down your shucking shroash.

Ramon leans forward on the couch and prods Hector with the end of his crutch.

—Hey, hey, what do you think this would feel like in your ass?

Geezer comes in and points at the floor next to Hector.

—Put him over there.

Fernando shoves George and George joins his friend, his back against the wall.

—Fuck, Hector, your face is all fucked up.

—Doesh ish look punk?

—It looks fucked up.

Geezer stands in front of Ramon.

—Want to scoot over and make some room?

Ramon scoots, shifting his hacksaw.

Geezer works his way down on the couch, the thin and threadbare cushions flattening beneath him. He swipes the back of his hand under his chins.

—Why's this place got no AC?

Ramon picks at the edge of the bandage on his thigh.

—You know us wetbacks, jefe, we like it hot.

Geezer looks at the tiny spot of red that's oozed through the bandage.

—Uh huh. How's the leg feeling?

—Hurts when it's cold.

—Uh huh.

Geezer looks at him, looks away.

—You, you kids, faces front over here.

Hector and George look at him.

He shrugs.

—This is pretty messed up, huh?

Nothing.

—I said, *this is pretty messed up, huh?*

George nods.

—Yeah, yeah, it's messed up. Hey, look, man, we, you know, we, whatever we fucked up, you know, that was, it was wrong, but, I told Fernando, you know, my little brother, he's, man, he, you saw him.

—He's *comatose* is what he is, kid.

—He needs a doctor, man, sir. Just, whatever we can, like, whatever, I'll do it, but he's really hurt.

—Uh huh, uh huh. OK, good, you . . . What's your name?

—George.

—George. You got a good head on your shoulders over there. You're getting the situation exactly. Your brother is really hurt bad. He needs a doctor. And you guys, you need to do *whatever* you need to do to help him. That's a great . . . the word? For when there's a lot to say and someone puts it all together in one piece. Wraps it up?

Fernando looks at his feet.

—We get it.

—You get it, but what's the word? The word, the exact word is what *I* want to get. I give a fuck if *you* get it.

Ramon raises his hand.

—Call on me, call on me.

Geezer wipes more sweat from the back of his neck, looks at him.

—You got something to say, Ramon, say it.

—Just trying to keep my place, jefe.

—The word?

—*Summation.*

Geezer waves his hat at Fernando.

—You got a pen or a pencil, something to write with? Some paper?

Fernando goes into the kitchen.

Geezer faces the boys again.

—*Summation*. That was a great summation of your situation, George.

George looks at Hector, looks back at the fat man.

—Cool, cool. Thanks. So, you're gonna call 911?

Fernando comes back in with a yellow pencil and an old envelope.

—Here you go, Geezer.

Geezer takes them with the grabber and puts them on the arm of the couch.

—Your brother opens up his vocabulary again, I want to be able to write shit down so I don't forget it. OK. OK. George. I'm gonna do whatever I can for your little brother. I'm gonna get him whatever help we can get for him.

—Cool. OK. OK.

—I'm gonna do that just as soon as you tell me where my meth is.

—Sure. I. Your? What? I don't?

—George.

—I don't.

—George, cool it for a second. Before you say another thing, shut up and tell me the first word you just said.

—Word?

—What was the first word, when I asked you where my meth is, my half kilo of crystal methamphetamine, what was the first word out of your mouth?

—I. Fuck, man, sir, I have no.

—*Sure*. You said, *sure*. Like telling me where it is would be no problem at all. So don't go back on that, that was the way to handle this, that was the way to get some help for your brother. Tell me, just tell me where my meth is.

George looks at a mass of dusty cobwebs clogging one of the high corners of the room.

—Mister, I have, really, man, sir, I have no idea. I. *Sure* just came out of my mouth.

He looks the fat man in the eye, looks back at the spiderwebs.

—I don't know. I just want to help my brother, I just want to get out of here and help my brother and go home and.

He stops talking and starts crying, burying his face in his arms.

Geezer looks at Hector.

—What about you, muchacho, gonna tell me where my meth is?

Hector pokes his shattered front teeth with his tongue, stops staring at Ramon and flicks his eyes at Geezer.

—I don'sh know.

—Uh huh. OK. Think you can maintain for a few more questions, or you a crybaby like your friend?

Hector shakes his head. It hurts.

—I ain'sh no crybaby.

Ramon laughs.

—Shuck yoush, Ramosh. Gonna shucking kill yoush.

Ramon laughs harder.

Geezer looks at him.

—What?

—Hey, nothing, jefe, just you should have heard him before. He cried plenty before. Lost his . . . the word? Lost his *composure*. Know that one, jefe?

Geezer wheezes out a laugh and picks up the pencil.

—OK, you got me, that was funny. *Composure*. Gonna put that one down.

He licks the tip of the pencil and grips it like a dagger and slams the sharp lead down on the spot of blood that shows through the bandage on Ramon's thigh, ripping through the gauze and the stitches below.

—How about *trauma*, shitheelfuckface!?! Know that word!?! Know that word, you fuckingspicfucker!?!

Ramon grabs Geezer's hand, trying to peel his fat fingers off the pencil, unable to get a grip on the greasy, sweaty skin.

—Stop moving, spic, fucking be still and take it.

Fernando is coming across the room.

Geezer takes his chrome .32 derringer out of the pocket of his sweat suit and presses it against Ramon's nose.

—Fernando, get back over there. Fucking brother asked for it, he's getting it now. You gonna take his medicine for him? Yes? No?

Fernando shakes his head.

—Good. Get back over there.

He cocks the derringer.

—Ramon, you stop whining and wiggling right now or I'm gonna shoot your nose off. No shit, jailbird. Go back in the joint with no nose, know what's gonna happen? Someone's gonna fuck you in your nose hole and cum in your lungs.

Ramon stops moving.

Geezer keeps the derringer where it is.

—OK. Got everybody's attention? You boys. George, you there?

—Yes, sir.

—Little amigo?

—Yeah.

—Good, I want your attention here because this is . . . fuck . . . the word? When something is important to someone, when it applies to their situation? Ramon? You gonna help me out here?

Ramon stares at the pencil in his leg, licks his lips.

—Relevant?

—*Relevant!* Got it again. Damn, did you swallow a dictionary in there? OK, boys, got that? This is *relevant* to your situation.

Geezer's eyes circle the room, going from face to face, making sure they're paying attention. And once he's certain, he flattens his empty hand and slaps it down on the pencil, driving it into the bullet hole in Ramon's leg until just the pink eraser is visible, quickly turning red.

Ramon shakes, opens his mouth and sticks out his tongue, shakes, and passes out.

Fernando turns his face away, closes his eyes.

George takes Hector's hand.

Geezer wipes his hand on Ramon's plaid shirt.

—So, now that we're all clear, now that the situation has a *summation* and we know what is *relevant* here, we can all take half a second to regain our *composure*. And now you can tell me where the one fucking bag of meth the cops did not get is. Is it at your home?

George shakes his head.

—No, sir.

—Did you sell it already?

—No, sir.

—Did you give it to cunt Amy Whelan to sell for you? Cuz that's what I'm thinking. That is the, here's another one for you, the *essence*, of why I'm here. Because I have a feeling that cunt has you shits fucking around in my business.

—No, sir. No, sir, that's not true.

Geezer points the derringer at the nub of bloody pencil.

—You see this?

—Yes, sir.

—What is up with Amy and where's my meth?

The doorbell rings.

Geezer points his tiny gun at the door.

—The fuck? Who the fuck is that?

Fernando opens his eyes. Looks at Ramon, sees his chest rising and falling, looks at Geezer.

—I don't know.

—Well go check.

Fernando goes to the door, peels back the corner of the filthy curtain that covers the window, drops it, and opens the door and stands back to let Paul in.

—I got your meth, dick.

———————

—Bob? What're you?

He pulls on his other sneaker.

—Just putting my shoes on, babe.

Cindy rubs her eyes and sits up.

—What? Where are you? What's the?

—The boys aren't back yet.

—Not. What time?

She picks up the clock from the nightstand.

—It's after four. Bob, it's after four. How long?

—It's cool. They're fine. I'm just gonna take a little drive around.

Her fingers whiten around the clock.

—But. What about? You said you heard them come in.

He gets an old sleeveless sweatshirt from the laundry basket on the floor.

—I was wrong.

She pulls the covers off.

—That was hours ago. Where are?

He walks into the bathroom and turns on the faucet.

—They weren't home, Cin. OK? I got up in the middle of the Goddamn night and they weren't home, OK?

—Did you call anyone? Did you call the?

—Hey, can I? You want me to tell you what happened or what?

She walks to the open door of the bathroom and stands looking at him.

He splashes some water on his face, turns the faucet off and lets the water drip off his chin.

—OK. I got up, they weren't home. I knew they weren't home, but there's no use both of us being up worrying.

—Did you call Paul's or Hector's parents?

He takes a hand towel from the bar on the back of the door and wipes his face.

—What for? So they can worry? The boys aren't gonna sneak out of here just to sneak into Paul or Hector's house.

She grabs the hem of her T, Bob's old Texaco shirt from when he worked at the gas station. She balls the fabric and twists it.

—And the police?

He throws the towel on the floor.

—No, I haven't called the cops. If they're there, they're there.

—Bob.

—It's not that big a deal you know. Whatever kind of trouble they got themselves into, I'm not my dad. Not like I'm gonna do anything if they got picked up or had a few beers.

—Bob.

—What? What? What am I doing now? What am I doing wrong now?

She brings up her little hands, slaps his chest.

—I don't care if they're in fucking jail, you asshole! What if they're not, Bob? What if they're not? I want to know where my sons are! Right now! I want to know where my sons are, you son of a bitch. Where are my sons?

He has to take her by the wrists to keep her from slapping his face. By the time she stops he has her wrapped up tight, pressed to his chest, rocking her back and forth.

—It's OK, babe. They're OK. They probably just got picked up. Got picked up after curfew and they don't want to give the cops their name because they don't want to get in trouble or something. If they're not, listen, if they're not at the police station when I call, I'm gonna go out and get them. I'm gonna go find them. It's cool. Shhh. You're gonna stay here, OK? Stay here. I'm gonna run around like a chicken with my head cut off and make an ass of myself showing up at all the places they hang at and you're gonna stay here and be here when they come home with their tails between their legs. OK? They're just at someone's house. Some kid threw a house party last night and they all got loaded and passed out on the floor. They're gonna wake up sick as dogs and when they come home you're gonna get to nurse them and take care of them and I promise I won't give them any shit till they're feeling better. OK? OK, babe?

She pulls herself away from him.

—I'll call the cops.

He puts a hand on her shoulder.

—I'll call them, babe.

She slips under his hand.

—No, I'll call them. You should have called them when you got up, Bob. I'll call them.

He stays in the bathroom, and is standing with his toothbrush in one hand and a tube of toothpaste in the other when she makes the call and the police tell her they don't have her sons in custody.

———

Geezer's place is still dark. Just the porch light on, illuminating the spread of patio furniture and the scattered kiddy stuff.

Jeff stands in the middle of the gravel drive, staring at the Big Wheel and Hippity Hop and the big rainbow swirled rubber ball and the miniature croquet set with plastic mallets. His pupils are huge, gathering the bright colors bouncing off the toys.

Damn, those whites are intense. Not your run of the mill speed. This shit is, woof, is gonna make for an all night thing. Bad call taking it for a test run. Got the morning shift tomorrow. Today. In a few hours.

Fuck.

Where's Geezer?

Need to talk to him. Have a quick word about Amy and that crank thing.

That was a choke. Double choke. Bringing it up with Geezer was a choke. Bringing it up with Amy was a double. She chilled eventually, but it took some talking. I mean, of course he didn't go over there looking to set her up. Just that Geezer put the idea in his head that she might be moving some crank and a little of that sounded good. Should have kept his mouth shut. First Geezer's all freaked about Amy, and now Amy's all freaked about Geezer. And here he is in the middle.

Well.

It'll be cool. Just need to have a word with Geezer and put it straight. And it won't hurt to do a solid for Amy. Sure he kind of fucked up a little, but if he can put it right she's gonna be feeling pretty warm toward him. Felt good just stroking her back when she started crying. Woman has kept herself in damn good shape.

Yeah, it'll all be cool with Amy.

And the kids.

It'll be cool with them, too. Just as soon as they get their asses back here it'll be cool. Should have been here by now, drop off whatever they grabbed from the house so he can take it to Geezer. But they're not.

Smartasses are somewhere fucking around.

Probably better that the fat man's not home. If he was home, if he was waiting for the guys to show up with the score from that house, he'd be ready to blow, man. Ready to teach those smartasses a lesson.

Not that he'd really hurt them. Geezer's a tough nut, but he's got limits. He'd never go heavy on some kids. Just scare them straight like the kids in that program in the prisons. He wouldn't fuck them up. Shit, he likes kids. Keeps all these toys and shit around for the little kids in the trailer park to mess with. Parents come over here to score some meth or whatever, they can leave their kids out front to play. Don't have to take them inside where they'll see all that shit. That's good looking out for the kids on Geezer's part. Yeah, it'll be fine.

He grinds his teeth.

Just, where are those smartasses?

Getting Bob's kids mixed up in Geezer's shit. What was that? Was that the lamest move in history, or what? What was he thinking? That hard up for a couple bucks? That big a loser?

Damn it to fuck.

He kicks the Hippity Hop again, sending it up onto Geezer's porch, ricocheting off the door.

Loser.

He turns and heads back to his own trailer, where the lights burn bright and "Taking Care of Business" comes out the front door. He takes his seat on the milk crate and gets back to work on the almost completed carburetor rebuild.

Get it done and take a little ride to make sure the bike's running smooth. Cruise around, check out some of the smartasses' hangouts. Get this shit sorted out before it gets complicated.

Maybe roll past that house.

———

—So where is it?

—Let me and my friends go and I'll bring it here.

—No.

—Yes.

—No.

—Yes.

—No.

—Yes.

Geezer runs his index finger over the derringer in his pocket, tracing the swirls engraved on the stubby barrel.

—What's your name?

Paul flips him off.

—None of your fucking business.

Geezer closes his eyes, snaps the grabber open and closed a couple times, and opens his eyes.

—Kid, let me tell you, under normal circumstances, I wouldn't be going through all this just to get my hands on one measly half kilo of meth. Under normal circumstances, someone steals from me, I'd just have them knocked unconscious and dragged out by the quarry and their legs or an arm laid across the train tracks and to hell with the half kilo.

He sighs.

—But these are not normal circumstances. In these circumstances, you shits got my lab busted. In these circumstances, the new lab these muchachos were supposed to have up and running here is not up and running. In these circumstances, I now have a serious fucking problem as far as what kind of cash I have on hand to pay people over in Oakland who want to be paid when they want to be paid and don't give fuck all what my circumstances are.

He takes out the derringer.

—All of which is a long way of saying *if you want to keep your arms and legs attached to your body you better tell me where my meth is.*

Paul puts a hand under his shirt, touches the cigarette burns, thinks about why he puts those burns there, remembers what every single one stands for.

And finds that he isn't afraid at all.

He points at the derringer.

—That your dick in your hands there, fatass?

George slaps Paul's calf with the back of his hand.

—Cool it, man.

—You cool it, man, I got this.

—No you don't, no you don't, just tell him.

—I'm not telling him shit.

He points at George's head, points at Hector.

—He fucked you guys up, I'm not telling him shit.

George stands.

—Yeah we're fucked up, so stop being a dick and tell him where it is!

Paul sticks his face in George's.

—I'm not being a dick. These guys are the dicks!

—You're being a dick!

—Fuck you!

—Fuck you, dick.

—Paul! Paul!

Paul looks at Hector.

—What?

—George itsh righsh, you're being a dick.

—No, I'm fucking not!

George shoves him.

—Andy's fucked up! My brother is all fucked up and he needs help and he, he, and you fucked up! I told you to leave that shit alone! Now stop being a dick! Give them the meth! Tell them where it is! Tell them, you dick! Tell them!

Something jumps in Paul's face. Something under the skin.

He looks at the fat guy.

—You hurt Andy?

Geezer looks at Fernando.

—Andy?

—The little kid.

Geezer looks at Paul.

—Yeah, we hurt him.

—You.

Paul looks at the floor. The thing under his skin jumps a couple times, stops. The pressure builds behind his eyes. He holds it in, waits for the spike, but it doesn't come.

He looks up.

—Man, I am so pissed at you.

Geezer nods.

—Then I guess we can start talking now.

————

Her connection in the pharmacy leaves the door unlocked when he takes his break, and Amy goes in like she belongs there. She walks among the shelves with a clipboard, fills a doctor's order for erythromycin, then heads out of the antibiotics and around the steel shelves to the opiates.

She takes the huge family size bulk shopping bottle of Vicodin from the shelf, shakes ten into her palm, and replaces the bottle. She drops the pills into a Ziploc bag she pulls from her bra. Seals the bag, lifts her skirt and tucks it inside her panties. She does the same with the codeine, taking twenty instead of just ten. She looks at the Percocet and Percodan.

Percs are getting way popular. Used to be all Valium and Quaaludes and Dexedrine. Nobody wanted anything else because nobody knew about anything else. Now pretty much anyone who's had their wisdom teeth out or gone on a diet or had a few stitches just whines and the doctor writes them a script for some new pharm. It's all good for business, but damn it's a pain keeping everything in stock.

She gets down the bottle of Percocet and shakes thirty into her last baggie. The pills nest in the crotch of the big white granny undies, and she walks straight out of the pharmacy and into the nearest ladies' room. In a stall, she fiddles with a seat cover dispenser, tugging down the tops of the tissue doughnuts. Then she pulls the baggies one by one from her underwear and shoves them behind the covers and smoothes them back into place. The top one is all wrinkled and bunched. She pulls it out along with three or four more and flushes them away. Now the dispenser looks perfect. The pills will be safe until she comes back for them at the end of her shift. Fuck of a lot better than walking around with panties full of contraband. And with all the times the lockers in the nurses' changing room get broken into, there's no way she's leaving them in there. Ladies' can is the best place by far.

She washes her hands and exits.

She drops the erythromycin at the nurses' station on her floor, tells them she's taking her break, and rides the elevator to the basement cafeteria. She gets a cup of coffee, looks at a doughnut, remembers having to cover her tummy in front of Jeff and grabs a banana instead.

The cafeteria's almost empty. Just a few graveyarders like her, and a handful of family members doing all night death watches on their loved ones.

Whole hospital is depressing as hell.

At least she got out of pediatrics.

Seemed like a good idea. Thought being around the kids would make the day go quicker. Doesn't have any of her own, but she really digs kids. And they *are* fun to be around when it's just a checkup or something.

But kids that are sick? Really sick?

That's the worst.

Some mommy getting word that little Brianna has advanced stage lymphoma and is gonna die in about two months *if* they start chemo right away? Watching a scene like that, having some doctor expect her to pick up the pieces after he's dropped the news and gone on to his next patient? That is not life affirming at all. That is not what she had in mind.

Head trauma is a walk in the park after that.

In head trauma you see what's coming from a mile away. Pediatrics was like getting a fresh lesson in the fuckedupness of God on an hourly basis.

The fuckedupness of God. Defined in her own life as Geezer thinking she's dealing crank. She puts her elbows on the table and her head in her hands.

Jeff may or may not be able to convince Geezer she's cool. If he can't, he'll be worthless. Nice guy, cute, but not tough. Not tough enough for Geezer. Couple of her old men would be up for it. But calling any of them means opening the door to all kinds of shit. Call one of those guys to take care of something like this and they're gonna be expecting a lot back. End up playing house with one of those Neanderthals, riding bitch on the back of his hog, handing over the cash from her business. No fucking way.

Should get a gun.

A gun. Shit.

If only. If only Bob wasn't such a dick. She could call him. He'd take care of it. One way or another, he'd make sure she was safe.

Or maybe not. There was a time he'd have dealt with it in no uncertain terms at all. But that was a while back. And even if he hadn't put all that away, he still might not help her. Not after the crap with George.

When he found out George was hanging around her place all the time, he flipped. *I know what's going on here, Amy. I know what your business is. Can't go into the Rodeo for a beer without someone asking me to get them hooked up with you. I know you're dealing. I don't know what it is, I don't care what it is. But I can't believe, I cannot believe that you'd let children, your nephews, be around that crap. They're kids, they don't know any better unless they're told. I tell them, I tell them to stay away, that's just gonna make them come around more. So you tell them. Tell them they are not welcome. Do it. You don't do it, I hear they're coming around, and I will drop a dime on you, Amy. Sister or not, my kids are more important to me than you are. Make them go away. Do it tomorrow.*

Nothing to do at that point but run George off. Start a fight with the kid and piss him off.

Jesus, if Bob had known the kid was running her shit around for her.

Would have disowned her for sure. Christ, would have pulled one of their dad's moves and beaten the crap out of her.

—Amy.

She looks up.

—Hey, Bob.

———————

The car's still not there.

Paul tries to remember the last time he saw it.

This morning? No, it's almost morning now. Not *this* morning, yesterday morning, when they went down to Galaxy? Was it there? No. Shit. OK, think. Was it there when they snuck out of George's bedroom window and got the bikes and rode over to the house?

He thinks about the house.

Hector and George all beat to hell. That fat bastard sitting on the couch, too fat to even get up, just sitting there sweating. Fernando staying on the other side of the room, not speaking unless spoken to. Ramon. Fucking badass Ramon. Out cold. All that blood.

Andy.

Wouldn't let him see Andy. George is scared bad. Fuck kind of shape is Andy in if he's so worried about him? Hurting Andy? Who? What the fuck? What do you get out of hurting a little kid?

What do you get out of touching a kid?

—Comb on, Cheney. Whud duh fug?

He shrugs Timo's hand off his shoulder.

—Don't touch me.

—I'lb touge youd id I wad.

Paul looks at Timo's swollen nose, the bloody clogs of toilet paper sticking out of his nostrils. Don't even have to hit the thing, just slap it and he'll go down on his knees.

He turns back to his house, the mystery of the missing car.

—Just keep your hands to yourself.

Timo stuffs one of the TP plugs deeper into his nose.

—Jud ged uz in duh house.

—Shut up and I'll get us in.

—Id'z righd dere, led'z juz wog in.

—I'm trying to figure out where my dad is, OK?

—Your dab? Fug hib. Led'z go.

Paul closes his eyes, tries not to think about hurting Timo. When did he see the car?

This is Saturday morning. No car. Last night when they snuck out? No car. Yesterday afternoon when they went to Galaxy, came back, went to the bowling alley, back for dinner? No. No. No. No. Thursday night when they snuck out to case the sketchy house? No. When they snuck back in? No. That afternoon, after they went to Jeff's with the jewelry? No. Before they went to Jeff's? Before?

Yes.

He looked down the street when they came out of Marinovic's house. The car was there.

So where's the car now? Where's his dad?

—Enub uv dis shid, led'z go.

Paul thinks about the car in a ditch, his dad's chest crushed by the steering column. The car flipping down the middle of an empty highway, his dad being tossed around the interior.

Like mom. Mom. Just like mom.

Leaving him alone. To live however he wants.

No.

The world doesn't work like that. You don't get the things you most want. The car's in a garage with a dead battery his dad's too lame to replace by himself. His dad's in the house asleep.

Life just like it's always been.

—Cub on, adshole.

Cuz that's what life is like. Life's not ever gonna suck any less than it does. Shit like this never stops happening.

—OK, come on, but keep your fucking mouth shut so we don't wake him up.

—He wades ub dads hids problub.

———

He rides the elevator with her, back up to the trauma ward.

She leans into the corner farthest from him, her arms crossed.

—How long? Since when?

—They took off after dinner. Haven't come home. Cindy's worried. Told her I'd look around. Probably nothing.

—The cops?

—No. She called, but no.

—What about?

—Amy, look, I know I told you I'd. I know I told you what I'd do if I found out they were at your place. But. If that's it. Cindy's really worried. So. Look, if they're at your place, I'm not gonna do anything. I just need to know. For my wife.

The elevator stops, the doors slide open and Amy walks out, shaking her head.

—Bob. Jesus.

She goes past the nurses' station, holding up five fingers when Trudy stands and starts to collect her things. Trudy rolls her eyes, but sits back down.

Amy stops at the end of the hall and looks out the window down at the cars in the lot. Bob's reflection appears in the glass. She doesn't bother turning to face him.

—You are. Man. Bob, you are a piece, man, a real piece of work.

—Are they at your place or not?

She turns.

—No, Bob, they are not at my place. I told you I'd keep them away. And I have. Christ, man. And even if I hadn't, even if they were there right now shooting smack and fucking hookers, you think, you really think you could have said two words about them missing and I wouldn't have told you where they were? You think I would do that, put you through that? You are a piece of work.

—OK.

—And, OK, fuck you, but Cindy? You think I'd let Cindy worry like that? I like Cindy. We were friends. If you weren't such a tightass we'd still be friends.

—OK, Amy.

—You think I'd scare the mother of my nephews like that?

—Cool it, Amy. OK? I got it. They're not at your place. Sorry I asked.

She bites her lip, kicks the toe of her white shoe against the wall a couple times.

—It's cool. Sorry I lost it. I'm uptight about some other shit.

—No problem.

He looks out the window. At four stories the hospital is the tallest building in town. To the north, streetlights show him the sprawl of housing tracts and apartment complexes broken by undeveloped lots peppered with For Sale signs. Headlights on the freeway in the distance. False dawn on the horizon.

She taps the glass with a nail.

—You know they're just at someone's house. Some party.

—I know.

—Right now they're getting their stories straight.

—Sure.

—Gonna come home and say just enough of the truth so it sounds good. You remember.

—Yep. I do.

—George will do the talking. Just like you used to.

—Uh huh.

—He's gonna tell you just enough. *Sorry, Dad, we had some drinks. I know that's not cool. Andy got sick and couldn't ride his bike and me and the guys didn't want to leave him there and everyone else was too drunk to drive us home.* Right?

—Yeah, that'll be it.

—*We should have called. Andy was sick and told me not to call because he was scared of how mad you'd be. And we just ended up, you know, passing out. Sorry, Dad.* Just like me and you, right? Except we got the belt.

—That was the price of a good time.

—If you say so, Bob. I just think it was fucked up.

He crosses his arms.

—Can't change it now.

She pokes some loose hair behind her ear.

—No, can't change anything now.

—Nope. Sorry to bother you at work.

—It's cool.

They head back to the elevator. She pushes the button for him and puts her hands in her pockets and takes them out and looks at him.

—So. Look. So you know they hang out at Jeff's place, right?

He blinks.

—Loller's?

—Uh huh. Used to anyway. I think Paul's over there a lot. Maybe Hector. George and Andy were going around to see Paul there. Mess with Jeff's old wrecks. That kind of thing.

—Since when?

—I don't know. Just heard George talk about it a couple times.

—Christ.

—But, you know, he's cool. He's just . . . Jeff. Just the same as he always was.

—*Same as he always was.* Great.

She puts a hand on his shoulder, touching her brother for the first time in a year

—Bob, it's Jeff. He wouldn't let them get into any kind of trouble. He knows better. He knows better.

The elevator opens; a tired woman inside, large white teddy bear under one arm, looking at the floor.

Bob shakes his head.

—OK. OK. I'll go to see him.

—He might know where the party was last night.

—Yeah. I'll go.

—Look, Bob. I.

He puts his hand between the closing doors and they bounce open.

—Yeah?

—I. Just I got this thing going on. And.

—What?

—Nothing.

He glances at the woman, she doesn't look up.

—Something you need help with?

—Just my own problems. You got enough right now.

The doors try to close again and he blocks them.

—Ames. You need help, you call me.

—Yeah?

—Yeah. Just, just right now I got to deal with the boys. But you call tomorrow.

—OK, yeah, maybe I will. OK.

He pulls his arm back.

—Yeah, call. Whatever you need, we'll figure it out.

The doors close.

Amy walks back to the station, waves at Trudy.

—Sorry. Take an hour. I'll be fine.

Trudy scoops up her purse.

—That your old man?

—Brother.

—No kidding? Married?

—Yeah.

—Too bad. I love that hardcase cowboy thing.

Amy drops into her chair.

—Help yourself. I've had enough to last a lifetime.

———

Jeff rolls the Harley to the QuickStop lot. The teenage son of the owner is out front. He nods at Jeff then goes back to wiping down the gas pumps with a soapy rag.

Jeff straddles the bike, pulls in the clutch, twists the throttle a couple times, then jumps off the seat and brings his weight down on the kickstart. The bike pops once.

The kid looks up from the pumps and watches as Jeff adjusts a screw on the side of the carburetor, brings the clutch in again, and comes back down on the kick. He has to hammer the bitch about a half dozen times before it catches. The kid gives him a double thumbs up as Jeff twists the throttle and the Sportster roars.

He brings it back down to an idle, leans the bike on its kickstand, and walks inside the store with the kid following him. He waits at the counter while the kid circles around and grabs a pack of Camels from the rack and hands it to him. Jeff passes him a couple bucks, peels off the cellophane, lights a smoke and walks out. The kid dumps the change in the loan a cent.

Outside, Jeff swings his leg over the seat and tucks his ponytail down the back of his T. He left his goggles in the trailer, but there's a pair of geeky safety glasses in the little tool kit on the bike. He slips them on. Finds the packet of whites in his pocket and crunches one between his teeth.

He guns the throttle out of the lot, taking the Harley around the long curve of the entrance ramp that dumps him on the 580 West. The bike runs smooth and he opens it up, the cherry getting blown off the cigarette between his lips. Within a quarter mile the sweat that's been caking him all day and all night is drying. The early morning air is almost cool.

Take it up the road and back a couple times. Let the bitch clear her throat. Then hit the street and find the damn kids.

See what the fucking problem is.

————

Geezer is playing with the pencil, drawing it out of Ramon's thigh and wiggling it back in, stirring it around, watching the kids across the room try to keep from looking, try to keep from puking.

—You need to leave my brother alone, Geezer.

—What?

Fernando holds up a finger.

—He gets out of line, talks a lot of shit like he learned in the joint, I get it. Pendejo motherfucker drives me crazy. But you got to stop now with that shit.

Geezer leaves the tip of his index finger on the end of the pencil.

—You were gonna take care of it, 'Nando? Your brother was mouthing off to me, getting all macho in front of a room of people I'm trying to make an impression on, were you gonna shut him up for me?

Fernando's eyes are on his brother's face; the waxy, sweaty skin, the lids that flutter open from time to time, revealing glassy eyes.

—Sure, sure, man, some things you have to take care of, OK. But you gotta stop with the, with that thing you're doing with the pencil. You can't do that kind of shit in front of me and expect me. Family, you know? There's things, a way things have to be taken care of. Something like that, you can't do that and expect me to. I have responsibilities. So, please, I'm asking you. Please stop that.

Geezer shifts on the couch, moving his arms to pull the material of his sweat soaked sweat suit from his skin.

—That was, that must have been hard. To ask me that. Say please to me. Humble yourself like that. I know that flies right in the face of the way you people are raised. Want you to know I appreciate that. So.

He pulls the bloody pencil out of Ramon's leg and drops it on the man's lap.

—There you go.

He pats Ramon's shoulder.

—That make you happy?

Fernando's looking at the pencil covered in his brother's blood.

—Sure, Geezer, sure.

—Got something to say?

—No, I'm done.

—No, I mean something you ought to say? A little gracias maybe?

Fernando looks from the pencil to Geezer's sweaty face.

—Si, Geez. Gracias, man. Muchas gracias, man.

We have to talk.

That's what the note says. *We have to talk.* Like something from an After School Special or some public service Just Say No commercial. Found a pound of crystal meth in the toilet and he leaves a fucking note. Some dad. Some man.

Paul puts the lid back on top of the tank.

—Whud wuz dat?

—A note,

—Frub hoob?

—My dad.

—So wherdz da meth?

—My dad did something with it.

—Whud? Lide da cobz? He tabe id do da fugging cobz?

—Mellow out, man. Be quiet.

—Whyd da fug shud I bellow oud man? Da methz nod hered!

—Because my dad's passed out on the livingroom floor.

Timo points at the bathroom window they shimmied through to get into the house.

—Howd da fug do youd dow whered hed idz?

—Cuz the bathroom smells like brandy and puke.

He bangs his fist against his forehead. What the fuck! Leaving the drugs in the toilet. Know dad's a weakass, can't flush a toilet right. Know he's always poking around in there.

Retard! Goddamn retard! Leaving it in there!

Timo grabs the doorknob.

—Ledz wagge hib ub.

Paul pushes the door closed.

—No way, man. You stay in here, stay in here. I'll wake him up. He wants. He wants to talk to me. He.

—Whad da fug, Cheney, youd fugging crying?

—Fuck you.

—Fug me? Fug youd, youd crying fugging poozzy!

He puts his hand in Paul's chest, shoving him against the door.

—Fugging poozy. Alld youd guyz itz fugging poozzies!

Paul thinks about how Hector holds his fire until the last possible second, how he wears that blank peon look hicks expect from a Chicano, then unloads on their skulls. He thinks about George's mellow, how deep it is, how the only thing that can make George lose his cool is someone telling him what to do. He thinks about Andy, that faraway place he goes to inside, the way his eyes just blank out and you can't get a rise out of him no matter how much you fuck with him. He thinks about how they're depending on him, leaning on him not to fuck up, to just come over here and get the meth and get back as fast as he can. How they need him to keep his shit together.

Timo shoves him.

—Ged da fug oud ov da way, poozzy!

He pushes Timo back into the wall, the towel bar snapping in two as they slam into it.

—Isaiddon'ttouchmeyoufaggotspicmotherfuckersonofabitchfuckingshitfucker!

Timo bounces off the wall, grunts, blows one of the TP wads from his nose and forces Paul back into the hollow core door.

—Fugging poozie! Fugging pendejo, mudderfugger!

The latch pops and the jamb is peeled from the frame and the door splinters open as Timo slams Paul into it again and they both fall into the hallway.

Paul hits the floor hard, Timo landing on top of him. The wind is smashed from his lungs and he gasps.

Timo is crawling on top of him, trying to pin his arms to the floor with his knees.

—Poozies, fugging up ourd shid! Fugged up all ourd shid!

Paul brings his arms up and crosses them over his face. Timo grabs his wrists and twists and brings them to the floor and gets his knees planted on his elbows and pops a fist into Paul's neck.

—Fug you ub, fugger!

Paul twists, tries to squirm loose, tries to open his lungs, but Timo is planted on his chest, unmoving.

Timo cocks his fist.

—See howd you lide a broden nodez, poozy!

The empty half gallon brandy bottle smashes against the back of Timo's head and he goes limp, flopping forward, blood dripping from his open nostril onto Paul's shirt.

—Leave my son alone!

His dad still has a grip on the bottle's handle, a jagged rim of glass attached to it.

—Get off my son!

Shrieking, kicking Timo.

Paul pulls himself from under Timo's weight, crawling down the hall, back toward the livingroom, toward the front door.

Behind him, his dad throws the handle at Timo and kicks his inert body.

—He's my son! You can't have him! He's my son! He's mine!

Paul stops, mouth stretched, trying to find some air.

—Paul? Paul? Are you OK, son? Did he hurt you?

He tries to stand up. Can't. Crawls again.

His dad is coming down the hall.

—It's OK now, Paul, you don't have to run, I'm here, it's OK. You're safe.

His lungs start to work again, he breathes, puts his hand on the wall, starts to get his feet under him.

—Don't get up, son. It's OK, I've got you.

He's almost up. Get up and get out, that's all he has to do.

He dad puts his hand on his back.

The spike drives up from under his lip. Up, scraping the roots of his teeth, through his nose and his sinuses, splits the space between his eyes, buries itself in his brain.

—I'm here now.

Paul throws up. Falls back to his knees. Makes a noise that hurts the inside of his head. Pants. Curls up in a ball.

—I got you, son. I got you.

His dad sits on the floor, strokes his back.

—Just us here, no one to hurt you. Just you and me, son.

He lifts Paul's head and scoots so it rests on his lap.

—There you are, there you are. Look at you. Look at you. Who could hurt you like that? Who would do that? Look at you. You're just a little boy. Who could hurt you like that?

He wipes at the tears on his son's face.

—Here we are. Just like we used to be, huh? Here we are. Close again, close again.

He rubs his son's chest.

—Here we are.

Paul makes a sound, knowing it will hurt.

—No, Daddy.

What the hell is Geezer's car doing here?

Jeff takes the Harley past the house, easy on the throttle so he doesn't rattle any windows.

Looks just like it did last night. Streetlamp's still dark from that pellet George put through it. Dart's still in the driveway. Only real difference is a big one. Geezer's car at the damn curb.

He turns the corner and cruises around the block.

Thinking.

Paul wanting to talk to him on the side about some kind of drug deal. Geezer getting uptight when he saw the jewelry the guys had. Getting even more uptight when Jeff mentioned there might be a side deal to be done. Geezer getting pissed about Amy, thinking she's stepped into his crank market. Setting up a soft gig for the guys. A cherry house waiting to be hit. Waiting to be hit because his go to gang of house breakers, the Arroyos, just took a heavy bust. Paper said it was a drug bust.

Crank lab.

—Awww shiiiiiiiiit, maaaaaan!

Jeff's not home.

Bob kicks through the weeds at the back of the trailer, squeezing past the rusted fenders, old tires, and cases of empty beer bottles Jeff's yet to redeem. He stands on a rain warped industrial cable spool and looks through the window into the livingroom. Nothing but mess. He hops down and goes back to the front and bangs on the door again. Still no answer.

Almost five in the AM and Jeff Loller not at home. Doesn't mean anything. Could be with a chick somewhere. Could be finishing up a graveyard shift at whatever crap job he's holding down these days.

He looks at the cars in front of the porch.

Man's still got the same taste in cars. Cheap.

He looks around the trailer park, doesn't see any early rising retirees peeking from their kitchen windows. He jiggles the door, feels the give it has within the frame. Slam his shoulder into it and the lock will pop right open.

Breaking and entering.

That alone could be enough to bring him a world of shit.

He turns and walks off the porch and gets in his truck.

Too early for the Rodeo to be open, but someone should be there mopping up. Wouldn't be the first time Jeff slept on the pool table.

He drives out of the park, heading downtown.

———

—Where you think your friend is?

—I don't know.

—I know that. I know that, sitting there on the floor, you don't *know* where he is. I'm asking where you *think* he is. Because I don't expect you to be psychic, a mind reader, right?

George keeps his eyes on the carpet, locked on the spot between his feet.

—I don't know. Getting your stuff.

—Better be.

—Can I see my brother?

—No.

George looks up. No one's moving much.

Geezer just sits on the couch sweating and wiping and drinking glasses of water and bitching about how hot the house is.

Fernando watches his unconscious brother and fetches the water for Geezer, going back and forth from the kitchen.

Hector's sitting there. Just sitting and staring at Ramon and wincing when he swallows his own blood.

Ramon breathes and that's about it.

On TV, when they say someone's in shock, they usually sit there with their eyes open and mumble shit about how they can't believe what happened or how it wasn't their fault or some shit. But this is probably what it's really like. Just sitting there all pale and bleeding and sweating and shivering.

Kinda like how Andy looked. But that was hours ago.

—What are you staring at?

George realizes he's staring at Geezer. He looks back at the carpet.

—Nothing.

—Uh huh.

They sit there.

—Hey. George.

—Yeah?

—Amy ever tell you about the time I went over there?

—Huh?

—The cunt who caused all this trouble, she ever tell you what I told her? When she was fucking up your life by getting you to steal my meth, she ever tell you what you were getting into?

George looks up again.

—Amy?

—Kid's a genius. Yeah, her. She ever?

—She? Tell us what?

—I take it back, kid's a retard.

—She didn't. I haven't. I don't even talk to my aunt anymore.

Geezer looks at his watch.

He looks back at the kid.

—What?

—I don't talk to my aunt.

—What?

—We had a fight. I don't talk to her.

Geezer shifts so he can scratch his butt.

—What was that, kid? George? What was that?

—Said I don't talk to my aunt. We had a fight.

Geezer leans forward, sweat rolling all over him.

—'Nando, help me up.

Fernando comes over and Geezer grabs his hand and pulls himself off the couch.

—Don't talk to your *aunt*?

—No. I. She got mad at me.

—Amy Whelan is your *aunt*?

—What?

He steps closer, huge and sweaty, his face red in a way that a face shouldn't be.

—Are you telling me that cunt is your aunt?

—She.

—Your name, what's your goddamn name?

—George.

Geezer lurches at George, squeezing the grabber's handle, the claw snapping open and closed in front of his eyes.

—Your last fucking name! Your dad's fucking name!

George flinches from the grasping plastic finger in his face.

—Whelan. Like my aunt. Whelan. My dad's name is Bob Whelan.

The grabber goes limp in Geezer's hand.

—Fuck me. Jesus, fuck me hard.

————

Bob Whelan pushes through the swinging doors of the Rodeo Club and looks at the empty pool table.

Someone stands up from behind the bar, a case of Hamms in his hands.

—Closed. Closed till eight AM.

—Don't need a drink.

—Pisser's for customers. Come back in a couple hours.

Bob walks toward the bar.

—Don't need the pisser, Crawford.

The bartender squints.

—Bob?

—Hey.

Crawford puts the case of beer on the bar, wipes his hands on his shirtfront.

—Since when you a morning drinker?

Bob leans against the bar.

—Since about never.

Crawford takes a Tiparillo from a box on the register and clamps the white stem between his teeth.

—Good thing. Lose the license if I served ya at this hour.

—Like I said, not a problem.

Crawford lights the thin cigar and blows smoke.

—How you been?

—Can't complain.

—Nobody'd listen if you did.

Bob fingers a mark on the bar, initials carved deep in the wood: PWW.

—No reason they should.

Crawford points at the initials.

—Your old man, right?

—Yeah.

—Yours are around here someplace, yeah?

Bob points down the bar.

—Over there.

Crawford smokes.

—Know what, I think I could use a little hair of the dog. Care to join me? As my guest?

Bob looks over his shoulder at the near darkness beyond the windows. He thinks about the last time he had a drink at this hour.

—I'd drink a beer.

Crawford pulls two cans of Hamm's from the case, cracks them open and sets one in front of Bob.

—Mud in your eye.

They drink.

—So, Bob Whelan, what's on your mind?

—Jeff Loller still come by?

—Hell yeah.

—Last night? This morning maybe?

Crawford adjusts the class ring on his left hand. The year on the ring the same as on the one Whelan is wearing.

—Bob, when's the last time I saw you in here?

—While back.

—Jeff's here about every night.

—OK.

—All I'm saying, man, whatever your business is these days, it's not mine. And I don't want it to be. Times have changed and I don't mess in nobody else's business ever.

—Not asking you to, just asking if you've seen him last night or this morning.

—And I'm giving you your answer.

Bob nods.

—OK.

Crawford tilts his can of beer to his lips and drains it.

—Anything else?

Bob is drifting down the bar, he stops and looks at some more recent marks in the rail.

—Say, you remember that time?

Crawford crushes his can and frowns.

Bob knocks on the bar with his class ring.

—You remember. That guy who tried to take your head off with the pool cue? The one who'd played guard for Amador High. He was trying to set up shop in here, wanted to peddle his stuff out of your john. You didn't want him around. Always felt bad about coming at him from behind. Seemed the only thing to do. Way everyone was sitting around watching him beat on you. But you ended up coming out of it OK. After I took care of him. Remember that?

Crawford wipes a spot on the bar that doesn't need to be wiped.

—Jeff ain't been in.

Bob sets his mostly full can on the bar.

—Thanks. Tell him I'm looking if he stops by.

Crawford talks to his back as he heads for the door.

—That wasn't right of you, Bob, bringing up ancient history. I paid my dues already.

—Yeah. I know.

He goes out into the morning and leans against the side of his truck and tries to spit the taste of warm beer out of his mouth.

Inside, Crawford picks up Bob's abandoned beer and finishes it, looking at the triple initials carved in the oak: BW/JL/G.

He thinks about calling Geezer to tell him that Bob Whelan's poking around for Jeff Loller, but decides he's better off minding his own fucking business than getting messed up with those three madmen again.

————

Geezer looks at Fernando.

—Bob Whelan's kids? You got your shit, you got *my* shit mixed up with Bob Whelan's kids?

Fernando shrugs.

—Their dad's a construction worker or something, so what?

Geezer spits.

—You fucking retard. You retarded spic.

He looks at George.

—Spic thinks your dad is a construction worker.

George wipes his nose.

—He is.

Geezer points at him with the grabber.

—Yeah, that's right, loser Goddamn construction worker. Could have been a winner. Could have, Jesus, gives me . . . word? When your heart beats too fast? *Palpitations.* Gives me palpitations thinking about it, what we could have had.

A thick throbbing vein splits his forehead in two.

—Could have had it all. 'Stead I got spic retards doing business for me and most of the money flying away over the hill into Oakland.

He jabs the grabber in George's direction.

—Your dad had kept his shit together, we could have had the whole fucking town.

—Geezer!

Geezer stops. Looks at Fernando. Points at Jeff, standing by the open front door.

—Thought you said the door was locked.

Jeff takes a step into the room, leaving the door open.

—What the hell are you doing, man?

—The hell are *you* doing, Jeff?

—I was cruising past. I saw your car.

Geezer lowers the grabber.

—And you just ask yourself in?

Jeff points at George and Hector.

—Jesus, Geezer.

—Close the door. Lock the door.

Jeff shakes his head.

—No. I. No way, man.

Geezer squints.

—What?

—No way, man. I'm.

He points.

—Those are kids, man. Kids. I mean, to hell with them being Bob's kids. They're kids period. You can't.

Geezer nods.

—Jeff, close the door, man. Yeah, they're kids. You think I did this shit to them? You've seen my place. Who loves kids? Who loves kids? *I* love kids. This shit? Who else is in the room, Jeff?

He points at Fernando.

—You see who else is in the room and, seeing *him* in here, you assume, you make the assumption that *I* would do this?

—Man, don't.

—Wait. You wait. I've been accused, of hurting kids I've been accused. What other . . . the word? Shit. The word when you have no other choice, it's the only path you have?

—Recourse?

Geezer scratches his calf with the grabber.

—That's it. *Recourse.* Being accused, I have no recourse but to defend myself. Fernando, close the door, will you.

Fernando takes a step toward the door, toward Jeff.

Jeff shows him the ten inch crescent wrench he took from the Harley's tool kit.

—Stay over there, Fernando.

Fernando stays put.

—Don't want to be waving a wrench at me, Loller, not unless you got a gun in your other hand.

—I ain't a kid, man. I was skinning knuckles on motherfuckers' teeth when you were flunking kindergarten.

—Hey, makes two of us.

—Just stay over there.

—Whatever you say, pendejo.

—Yeah, fuck your mother.

Geezer grunts.

—Jeff.

—Don't talk, Geezer. Seriously, man. I mean, all the respect in the world, but just, you know, shut up.

—Jeff.

—No, I mean it. Telling these kids 'bout that shit. Beating on kids. That's fucked up. So just can it. I don't want to hear.

—Kids! Kids! Kids! We were barely older than they are. Being a kid matters what kind of shit you get up to? And these kids are just the tip of the iceberg.

—They're thieves, Geezer! They're punkass thieves. They. You know, I'm not a, whatever, a scientist or something, but I figured out what you're thinking. And there's no one moving in on you, you paranoid son of a bitch. Man, Amy Whelan isn't running some game on you. She's not into your business. She's doesn't want anything to do with Oakland. So, look. I'm taking the kids out of here. I got to. I'm like a friend of the family, sort of. I've. That kid, that's Bob's oldest, man, I remember when that kid was a baby, man.

—Jeff, my man, you think you know what you're talking about, but you don't. Alright, you don't know shit about the deal, I believe that, you've never had a clue. But you expect me to think it's coincidence? My lab gets busted? Just as I'm trying to set up a new lab, increase the profitability of the venture here, have a little something on the side that Oakland doesn't know about, just as I'm doing that, some kids stumble in and screw things up? Oh, and hey, the kids just happen to be Amy Whelan's nephews? Just happen to be Bob Whelan's kids? I'm gonna believe that shit? Let me tell you, I never, I never believed for a second he was out of it for good. I always knew he'd come back around. Pounding nails when he could be pounding skulls? Bob Whelan? That was never gonna last. Scratching out whatever he makes when he could have the fat of the land? No, uh uh, I am an obese, foul mouthed and racist motherfucker, I am white trash to my Tony Lamas, but I am not that stupid. You, look, close the door and let me explain a few things to you about profit and loss and the kind of money we're talking about. The kind of money we're talking about, kids don't just stumble in and screw things up. It's common sense. It's counter . . . the word?

Jeff hefts the wrench.

—I don't know the word, man. Just shut the fuck up before I forget myself and put this through your fat face.

Geezer shrugs and draws an invisible zipper closed across his lips.

Jeff sees Ramon.

—Fucking A.

He looks at Fernando.

—Your brother looks like hell, man.

—No shit.

—Yeah. Well. Go lay down on the floor on your face or I'll bust your teeth out.

Fernando lies down on his face.

Jeff crosses to the boys.

—I am sorry about this, Geezer. Seriously, I will make it up to you. But you know, after you cool off, I think you're gonna thank me. You were getting away from yourself here. Once you get a chance to sit back and think about it, you'll know this is the way to handle this. These kids, they're punks, smartasses, but they're not like a part of a conspiracy kind of thing. They fucked up. They fucked up and they learned their lesson. Thing we got to do now, we got to get them home and safe and put this behind us. Make up some story 'bout how they got in a fight or something. Keep Bob out of this. That's what we got to do now.

He squats in front of George and Hector.

—Hey, George. You OK, man? Hector, you look like, man, you look like the Hunchback, man. No, no, I didn't mean that, you're OK. Gonna. Jesus.

He looks over his shoulder.

—Fuck, Geezer. Kids.

Geezer keeps his lips zipped.

—Jeff.

He looks at George.

—What's up, man, ready to split? Where's your bro? Where's Paul?

Let's get you guys out of here. Know who's gonna patch you up? Your aunt. How good is that, having a nurse for your aunt when shit like this comes down? C'mon, guys, take a hand, let's get up.

—Jeff.

—I ever tell you, me and your dad, I ever tell you the time we went toe to toe with those Angels? The real deal. Angels from the Oakland chapter, out here making trouble. Me and your pop, we came out of it looking a hell of a lot worse than you do. Those Angels though, when we were done with them, they made us look pretty.

Geezer unzips it.

—Right, tell them another one. Like you had anything to do with what those Angels looked like when that went down. Kids, listen to me, this guy, he threw a couple punches, got knocked down and stayed down.

—Fuck you, Geez.

—You, George, your old man, he wrecked those cocksuckers. Had this baseball bat he used to carry with him, the handle sawed off, wrapped in tape, had nails driven through the head of it, galvanized. Know why he used galvanized nails?

Jeff stuffs the wrench in his boot top and takes each boy by the hand.

—Shut it, Geezer.

Geezer laughs.

—Said he used galvanized nails so the blood wouldn't rust them.

He coughs, chokes, laughs again.

—No shit, kids, that night, he laid the law down on those Angels. Ever see a guy try to talk when he's got nail holes in his cheek? Blood just sprays all over. Funny as hell.

Jeff squeezes George's arm.

—Don't listen to him, he's full of shit.

—Hey, hey, I'm just finishing the story you started. If you'd been up to finishing it, I'd have kept my mouth shut. Like Bob, if he'd been up to finishing what he started that day, none of us would be here, yeah? These spics wouldn't be anywhere near this business if Bob had taken the bull by the horns. His kids never would have crossed paths with the Arroyos, right? And me and you, shit, we'd be working together. Working with Bob. Kids, your dad had done the right thing and stood behind the message he sent that night, if he'd gone over the hill to Oakland and finished the job on their ground, you wouldn't need to be ripping off my crank, you'd have it running hot and cold from your taps. But he had better things to do. And don't come on all noble about *kids*, Loller, you were pissed about it just as much as I was.

Jeff lets go of the boys' arms, takes hold of the wrench again and rises.

—Shut up! It's past! It's over! No one else thinks about it anymore but you.

—You don't think about it, Jeff? You telling me you don't think about it every time you put on that Security Eye uniform?

Jeff bites his lip.

—The way it is is the way it is and.

—*The way it is is the way it is.* You lameass hippie loser.

—Fucking shut up, man.

—Jeff!

He looks down at George.

—What, George, what?

—He's got a gun.

Jeff is turning his head when Geezer shoots. The bullet takes him in the jaw and blows the bottom of his face onto the wall and he falls on top of George and Hector.

Hector throws up, the vomit burning the torn flesh inside his mouth.

George blinks, trying to clear his eyes of Jeff's blood.

Fernando gets up on his hands and knees.

—Shit, Geez.

—Shut up. Get the other one. Get the comatose kid in here. We're gonna get to the bottom of this shit right now.

Fernando heads for the master bedroom, staring at Jeff's ripped face, bumping into a wall on the way.

Geezer waits till he's gone before breaking the barrel of the derringer and popping out the spent shell casing.

—You kids, you don't know it, but you just saw a hell of a shot.

He digs an extra round from his pocket and drops it in the empty chamber and snaps the little two shot gun closed.

—Hitting someone in the head from across the room with a gun like this? That's some shooting. That's marksmanship.

George is pulling up the tail of his ruined concert T, wiping his face.

Hector is using his feet to push Jeff's body away from them.

Geezer places the gun on his massive thigh and takes off his hat and wipes his head.

—Ever see a dead body before? Like that, messy and fresh? No, course you haven't. George. I'm talking to you. You listening?

—I?

George gives his face a final wipe. Opens his eyes, the lids sticking together slightly.

—I'm listening.

—Good, get attentive. 'Cause this body, if I don't get answers to my questions, it's going to be the first of many. You're going to see a life-time's worth of corpses in no time. 'Nando! Get the fuck back in here with the kid's brother.

George starts to get up.

—Hey, leave Andy.

—You wanted to see your brother, kid, you're gonna see him. 'Nando!

—We don't. It was just his bike, man. Sir, it was. They stole his bike.

—Save it. And sit the fuck down. 'Nando! There you are, what the fuck?

—He ain't there.

Geezer picks up his gun.

—What?

—Kid's gone.

———

Bob takes the long way home, covering streets he missed before. Coming around the back way, he sees Kyle Cheney's car parked two blocks from where it should be. Man's car maybe broke down on his way to work. After five now, could be he's up. For that matter, could be Paul's home. Could be Andy and George are the only ones missing

He passes his own house and parks in front of Cheney's.

There's no answer when he knocks.

He walks down a couple houses to Hector's. Mrs. Sanchez will be up for sure. Getting breakfast together. Just ask her if the boys have been around. And watch her get as panicked as Cindy. No, not yet, there's no need for that yet.

He turns and walks to his truck, stands with his hand on the door, looks down the street to his own home.

Go down there and tell Cindy.

Can't find them. Don't know where they are. I don't know where our sons are.

He lets go of the door and squats, dips his head between his shoulders. God. Don't know where the boys are. Don't know where they are. Don't know if they're safe.

A nightmare of fathers.

Man's first job, keep his family safe. No reason to be if you can't do that.

A car turns the corner and he stands, rising quickly so he won't be seen like this. The car goes past, a stranger at the wheel.

He wishes he'd had a real drink at the Rodeo instead of a beer.

He opens the door and climbs inside the truck and starts the motor and puts it in gear so he can drive down the block and tell his wife.

Across the street, something gleams behind a bush.

He gets out of the truck and walks over there and finds two bikes stashed behind one of the huge pampas grass bushes the new couple put in when they bought the corner house.

One bike is Paul Cheney's Redline.

The other is George's Mongoose.

He turns and stares at Kyle Cheney's house.

———

It's exactly like being invisible.

Being in a room of people, almost in plain sight, and none of them seeing you, that's exactly like being invisible.

Andy clenches his teeth.

No, that's not right, it's not *exactly* like being invisible. Well, it could be, but he's in no position to say. Never having actually been invisible. It's more precise and accurate to say that it's exactly as he imagines being invisible would be.

There, no one could fault him for that usage.

The fat guy stops yelling at Fernando.

Something's happening.

He wants to look up, lift his face from where it's tucked against his chest and take a look at the room. But he knows the movement will expose him. The trick to it, to folding up here on the floor just at the end of the couch, the trick is to be still. That's why he hides his face, even the movement of his eyes would draw attention.

It took forever to get here.

Getting from the bathroom to the kitchen hadn't been that hard. Using all the stuff going on in the livingroom, moving down the hall and across the edge of the room while the fat guy was arguing with Fernando, that had been pretty easy. But getting out of the kitchen and in here had been really hard.

Once Jeff showed up it happened fast. Everyone focused on Jeff. It was like a magic trick. Legerdemain. Everyone is watching one thing, while what's important is happening somewhere else.

And once Jeff and the fat guy started talking, it was so easy to stay perfectly still, not to move at all. Just to listen to the story of their father.

When the fat guy said the thing about his dad hitting people with a baseball bat with galvanized nails in it, he knew right away why the nails were galvanized. It's exactly the way he would do it, too. He thinks about making a bat like that. You'd also want to make sure the wood was well sealed so the blood didn't seep in and make it swell. If that happened, it would eventually crack. That's probably the way their dad did it, he's good at making things.

He pictures hitting someone in the head with something like that. You'd have to be pretty strong, it'd be heavy, and the nails would get stuck in the bone and it would be hard to pull free. And, yeah, the fat guy is right, blood would spray out of those holes in your cheek if you tried to talk, the air pressure inside your mouth would make that happen.

It sure sounds like a real story, like something that really happened. And if it did, that might mean he's not as weird as he thinks he is. Well, still plenty weird, but maybe not so scary weird. Because he's thought about doing stuff like that, but it sounds like his dad really has done stuff like that. So maybe it's not so bad to have those things in your head. Or, at least, maybe there's a reason for them getting in there.

When the gun goes off he only moves a tiny bit. Just enough to look and see what's happened to Jeff. Then he closes his eyes again. Because it's not his brother or Hector, and he can deal with that. Plus, having his eyes closed keeps the room from spinning. Sure his head still hurts and his left eye still feels loose in its socket, but as long as the room doesn't spin around like he's been drinking Thunderbird all day long he can deal with it.

Now the fat guy is talking again.

—Get that loser out of here.

He opens his eyes and the room stays still. Fernando is right in front of him, pointing at Jeff's dead body.

—I'm gonna get stuff all over me.

—There's garbage sacks in the bag I brought. Wrap him and put him in the garage. And when you're done, you're going and finding Timo and the big kid and drag their asses back here.

—Geezer, maybe it's time.

—'Nando, I just told you what time it is. I put a bullet in that loser's face. That told everybody what time it is. It's time to start taking me very fucking seriously and giving my words a little . . . shit . . . a little . . . shit! Word? For what holds us to the ground. Totally basic word. Someone say it before I go crazy.

George whispers.

—It's gravity.

—Yes! Give my words some *gravity*. Jesus. Is that so hard? What else do I have to do?

They all watch Fernando wrap Jeff in the bags.

He should move now. Too long in one place and he'll become visible again.

So he leans slowly to the side, unfolding into the space between the back of the couch and the wall, the space he didn't hide in because he knew they'd look there, and he worms to the other side, careful not to rub the bulge in the back of the couch that is made by the fat guy, and they're all still watching Fernando, and he gets on all fours and crawls quickly into the front hall that spins around him and he squeezes between a big dead plant in a big pot and a couple stacked cardboard boxes and when Fernando drags the bagged body into the garage and leaves the door open he follows him and settles next to a rusted out old bathtub with claw feet and stays there until Fernando goes back in the house and closes the door and leaves him alone with all the chemicals and stuff that are just like the ones Fernando and his brothers had back in their garage and everything spins and he goes asleep again.

———

—Bob Whelan. Bob Goddamn Whelan.

Geezer scoots his ass around on the couch, trying to ease the rash on his sweaty buttocks. He watches Fernando tromp around the house and out to the back yard, looking for the comatose kid. He looks at the two huddled against the wall.

—If I'd been smart, smarter, I would of told the Oakland crew not to listen to him. He decided to get out of the trade, decided he didn't want to take it any further than running the grass and acid and all that hippie shit, told the Angels the town was theirs he just wanted out; when that little negotiation took place, I should have told them not to listen, told them a head case like Bob Whelan will never leave the life, never get tired of kicking the shit out of people, should have told them to do everyone a favor and put him out on the train tracks. Now look what I got. Got his kids on my hands. His kids.

He makes the grabber into a fist and bangs it on the floor.

—Kids! Fucker. He made, you know, he made a speech? Went over the hill, made me and Jeff go with him so it'd be like an official peace conference the way those bikers like it. Made us go with him even though we didn't want to give up the town to those fuckers, even though he knew they might just say fuck the cease fire and start breaking bottles on our heads the second we walked into their clubhouse.

He takes the grabber by its aluminum shaft, raises one butt cheek and scratches it with the claw.

—Goddamn rash. Goddamn house. Goddamn no AC. My place, I got a swamp cooler. Ever been in a trailer with a swamp cooler? You haven't. Like a fucking ice box. I love it. Turn the thing off for maybe two months in the whole year. Meter man comes around from PG&E, his eyes spin around in his head. Tells me there's an *energy shortage,* I should *conserve.* I tell him, *I pay the damn bill, how I use the energy I pay for is my fucking business.* Got that swamp cooler, what else I got, I got a 32 inch color Zenith with HBO and Showtime. You know anyone else got both HBO and Showtime? No. Got the Spice channel, too. All the Playboy specials and the Emmanuel movies. Got the fridge full of cold cuts and sourdough rolls and sliced Swiss cheese. Got a freezer full of frozen sausage pizzas and Häagen-Dazs. The cupboard full of pork rinds and Funions and Ding Dongs.

He raises the other cheek and scratches.

—Love my trailer. Never get a heat rash in that thing. Never break a sweat. My whole life in this town I've been sweating and itching till I got that trailer and that swamp cooler. And now, now it is at risk, my castle is at risk because fifteen fucking years ago I was stupid and didn't tell the Angels not to listen to your dad's fucking speech about how he was done forever with the business. Kids! All his crap about his three year old he doesn't want around this shit, his *new baby boy in the hospital* he wants to be with. Bullshit! And here, what do we have here? Here we are finding out how much his kids mean to him. They mean he got to raise his private little gang to send to fuck me up and bust my lab and put me in the shit with Oakland! Fucker! Should have killed him myself!

He throws the grabber on the floor.

—Fuck.

He waves his hand at the boys.

—George.

—Yeah.

—Come here and pick that up for me.

George gets up, stumbles, takes a couple steps and picks up the grabber and holds it out to Geezer.

—Our dad didn't tell us to do anything. He wouldn't do anything like that.

Geezer takes the grabber.

—Kid, you got no clue what your old man would do for money, a piece of pussy, or just to fuck someone up because he thinks it'd be fun.

He holds out his hand.

—Help me up. Maybe get some air on my ass, stop this itching.

George takes Geezer's hand and pulls him to his feet, lets go and wipes his palms on his jeans.

Geezer plucks the seat of his sweat pants away from his ass.

—So, your friend, he gonna come back with my half key so I can salvage something here? Say he got away from Timo, he the kind gonna call the cops, knowing it'll mean you guys are gonna be dead? He gonna call your dad?

George shakes his head.

—He won't call my dad.

—Cops?

—No.

—Good. Now go sit down and keep your mouth shut because when I hear you I think about you and I get pissed and I can barely keep from shooting you.

George goes and sits down next to Hector and takes his hand. Hector doesn't move, his eyes are open, looking at Ramon again, but he doesn't move at all.

Fernando comes in from the back yard.

—He's not out there.

—You sure?

—I went all around the house, looked under all the bushes. Timo and Cheney took a couple bikes. The other two are out there.

—Where is he then?

—I say he's in the house.

He kicks a pile of carpet remnants.

—He's somewhere in all this shit. We put the bathroom window back together after they got in. It's still together. The other windows are all locked. He didn't come through here, walk out the front door.

Geezer holds out his arms.

—OK, so?

—He's a scrawny brat, he's hiding under something. Behind something.

They both shut up. They look at the couch.

Geezer cocks the derringer, waves Fernando toward the couch.

Fernando looks at the floor, picks up Jeff's wrench, runs across the room, jumps on the couch and throws the wrench into the space behind it.

—Fuck.

Geezer comes over.

—Get him?

Fernando reaches behind the couch and comes up with the wrench.

—He ain't back there.

—Hey, hermano.

He drops the wrench, looks at Ramon.

—Ese.

Ramon sticks out his tongue.

—Got some water?

—Hang on.

He heads for the kitchen.

Ramon pokes his leg, watches blood leak out of the hole. He picks up the blood crusted pencil from his lap and looks at Geezer.

—Yo, boss, want your pencil back?

————

Paul looks better.

Without those torn up jeans and that bat eater's heavy metal T shirt, he looks much better. He looks almost like a boy again. Like he did when he'd run around in his shorts all the time. Always barefoot. Never wanting to put on a shirt. Used to be so much trouble getting him properly dressed for dinner someplace out.

Kyle Cheney sits on the floor, leans his back against the front of the couch, and puts his son's head back in his lap.

Paul coughs and gags, but he doesn't throw up again.

Kyle pats his cheek.

—See, it's getting better, isn't it? I can tell. I can always tell when your migraines are getting better because you stop throwing up. Soon, you're going to be thirsty and then hungry. That's how it's always been. Now we know, know we can get through it, know it will pass. But when they first started, I was so scared. And in fairness to your mother, she was scared, too. You know it's hard for me to talk about her at all, let alone to say something nice, but it is true. She was scared. You crawled under your bed and wouldn't come out, and when I touched you, you screamed. And then when you started throwing up, we didn't know what to do. When we moved your bed so we could get to you, I thought you would try and run away. Your mother wrapped you in a blanket and I drove to the hospital. It took forever to get a doctor. And months before they could say what was wrong. I thought the worst, of course. That's your father for you, thinking the worst. I thought a brain tumor. I thought I was going to lose my son forever. Migraines were a relief. And I know that's not what you want to hear, but considering what I thought it was, migraines were a relief. Coming out of nowhere like that, never a sign until you were almost eight. And every one was a major event at first. Getting you into your bed, drawing the curtains, getting a towel and a bowl of ice water. Keeping the house as quiet as possible. Your mother, well, fair is fair and this is the truth too, she couldn't keep at it for long. Help to get you into bed and then go somewhere else when she got tired of helping. Not that I minded. It was nice to have time alone. Have you all to myself.

He checks the cords around his son's wrists and ankles, making sure they're snug.

—Those still OK? Sorry. I know it's not what you want to hear, but you would have hurt yourself, running around while having a migraine. You would have run into a wall or into the street and gotten hurt. You're safe this way. I'll keep you safe as long as I can. I know, I know I can't forever, but now, now that we're together, now that I have you to myself again, I'll keep you safe as long as I can. Because, Paul, this is not what you want to hear, but, Paul, people wouldn't understand. These drugs, these drugs you hid, people wouldn't understand that boys can get confused. If they don't have guidance, they can get confused. And I can't, well, if this is the kind of thing you get into when I'm not around to keep an eye on you, well, then, we'll have to handle things differently from now on. And, you are not going to like this, I know, but if a little less freedom is what it takes to keep you safe, then so be it.

Mr. Cheney reaches inside his open bathrobe and scratches his stomach and looks at his son's sweaty face.

—You know what you need? A haircut. A real haircut. Not a trim. A good old fashioned haircut like you used to have.

He finds the scissors he used to cut the cord.

—A good old fashioned haircut like the ones you had when you were a little boy.

At first he thinks it's an earthquake.

When he's grabbed by his hair and the fabric of his robe and pulled from under his son and thrown across the room, he thinks it must be an earthquake. The biggest he's ever been in, much bigger than the 7.0 that hit a few years back. Maybe it's the Big One, finally come to tear California in half.

It's only after Bob Whelan has crossed the room and picked him up and thrown him again that he realizes how much worse it is.

Whelan lifts him by his armpits, shaking him.

—Where are my boys? Goddamn you, you sick sonofabitch! You're not doing this! You don't do this! No one does this!

Slamming him against the wall with every word.

—Where! Are! My! Boys!

———

Forcing the back door of the house, all he could think was what a B&E bust would mean for him. For his family. It's been years since his last bust, years since clearing probation, but the stories would come back, stuff George and Andy would be bound to hear about. The stories he's kept them from hearing, about what kind of man he is. They'd never listen to him again. His crap about responsibility and hard work, they'd never listen again.

Then he stepped into the house and closed the door behind him and started for the livingroom where he could hear the sound of *The Price Is Right* on the TV.

Seeing the body face down in blood, seeing the bloody shards of glass, he'd almost screamed. In the darkness it could have been anyone. But it's not George or Andy. It's a Mexican guy. One of those Arroyo boys. Knocked out and bleeding.

And then a voice from the livingroom, too soft, almost lost in sound of the TV.

And he remembers watching *Helter Skelter* a few weeks ago with George and Andy. They showed it in two parts on KTVU because it was so long. He and George liked it. Andy had nightmares.

He remembers that Charles Manson is in prison in Vacaville, just a few hours away. They say he's always trying to escape. He sees in his head words written in his sons' blood scrawled across the livingroom walls. Crazed junkie murderers in an orgy in the livingroom. Those hippie friends Paul's mom had around all the time.

And he has to shake his head to get the craziness out.

And coming out of the hallway, and walking past the dining room table covered in the uncorrected papers of Kyle Cheney's students, and standing behind the couch and looking down at his neighbor cradling his bound and naked teenage son, he realizes there are things nearly as bad.

———

—What's that you got, boss?

—Keep your seat, Ramon.

—Keep my seat? Boss, you tell me how to do anything else I'll do it. *Keep my seat.* You hear that, ese, telling me to keep my seat? Know what it feels like, my leg?

—Just stay on the couch.

—My leg feels like nothing. No lie, ese, like nothing. Felt like all kinds of something when boss put the pencil in it. Feels like nothing now. What you think that mean, ese?

Fernando gives him the water glass.

—I don't know, bro.

—Can't be good, is what I think.

Geezer waves the derringer again.

—Fernando, just stay over there.

—Givin' him some water.

—He has it, you go over there.

—Want me to look for the kid?

—Just sit over there.

Fernando goes and sits on an upended orange crate with several broken slats. The old dry wood creaks.

Ramon empties the glass in one long swallow.

—Otro vez, bartender.

Fernando starts to rise.

Geezer shakes his head.

—No. No more water.

Ramon tilts back his head, opens his mouth wide and shakes a last few drops from the glass onto his tongue.

—Ahhhhh. No problem, boss, that took care of it.

He rubs the glass against his forehead.

—It hot in here?

Geezer scratches his ass.

—Yeah, it's hot in here. Didn't think a beaner noticed the heat.

Ramon smiles.

—Sure, sure we do. We feel the heat. Know what you do about the heat? Got to dress light. All that sweat on you. That's cuz you're wearing a sweat suit. Sweat suit means sweat, boss.

—Fuck you. I'm wearing a sweat suit because I have some proper AC in my place. In my place a man could freeze without a sweat suit. I didn't bother changing into my tropical suit because I thought this place would be further along. I thought it'd be cool at least.

Fernando shrugs.

—Hey, man, you said get another lab set up. You didn't say it had to be climate controlled or some shit.

—Fuck sake, 'Nando, I say keep it like a swamp? Come over here, I didn't figure I should be wearing my . . . word? The hats, but not called a hat, the ones explorers wear in movies. Like Livingstone? No, wait, I got it! *Pith helmet.* Didn't think I needed a pith helmet to come over here.

Ramon taps the pencil against the side of the glass.

—Boss?

—What?

—Never answered my question.

—What?

—What you got there?

—It's a gun.

—Yeah, no shit?

—No shit.

—Why you waving it all around at us? We're your people. Employees. Got us out on bond. Things gone sour while I was asleep?

Fernando points at the blood and bone on the wall.

—He killed Loller.

—The biker security guard guy?

—Yeah.

—Maaaan, that's too bad. He was alright.

He looks at Geezer.

—Why you do something like that, boss?

Geezer taps the grabber against his leg.

—Because he fucked with my shit.

Ramon nods.

—Yeah, man, I see that. But, hey, bro?

—Yeah?

—You saw him shoot the guy?

—Yeah.

—Whelan and Hector saw?

—Yeah.

Ramon holds out his arms.

—Shit, ese, you all are like witnesses to murder one. Know what they say in the joint about when you kill someone?

—No.

—Say, *no witnesses, ever.*

He raises an eyebrow at Geezer.

—That why you got that gun in your hand, boss? Thinking you got some witnesses to deal with? Once everything is sorted out here with the meth and shit, you got some other shit to sort now?

Fernando stands up.

Geezer points the grabber at him.

—Sit back down, 'Nando.

Fernando is staring at his brother.

—You know, ese, that's some of the smartest shit I ever heard come from you.

Geezer lowers the grabber and points the gun.

—Sit down, 'Nando.

Fernando sits.

Ramon holds up the pencil.

—How about that, boss?

He taps the pencil against his chest.

—First, I got *your* point.

He waves the pencil at the guys and his brother.

—Now, I'm making a point of *my own*.

—You're an asshole, Ramon. A jailbird asshole and you don't know what you're talking about.

Ramon looks at the pencil.

—Check it out, it's a Number 2.

He taps the tip against his thigh.

—Think you filled in the bubble completely?

—A fucking beaner spic wetback asshole.

—Ooooooh, that's a lot of racial stuff. That's a lot of, get this one, racial *epithets*.

—You fuck your mother.

—Man, you ever seen my mother? You ever saw her, you wouldn't talk like that. My mother is one mean ugly bitch.

Fernando snaps his fingers.

—Don't talk like that, ese.

—You know what I can't figure out, bro?

Fernando shakes his head.

—What?

Ramon holds up a hand, four fingers in the air.

—Me and you and Hector and Whelan over there, all four of us sitting and being scared of boss here, and him holding that gun that only shoots two bullets.

Geezer licks his lips, gestures with the grabber, pointing it in the air.

—OK, OK, you got a point about the witnesses thing, Ramon. And I'll admit, all things being the same, I'd be trying to figure out how to deal with that issue. But we're kind of beyond that now. We're at a point of shit being so fucked up that we can just forget about what happens with the cops. Right now, getting that half kilo so we can hand it to Oakland and keep them happy is a more pressing problem. Most of all, before we worry about the cops, we got to worry about them.

He points the grabber at George and Hector.

—And what we're gonna do when psycho Bob Whelan shows up looking for them.

Ramon shakes the pencil from side to side.

—Oakland. Whelan's dad. These things, they sound like *your* problems. Bro and me, we got to worry 'bout how you're not mentioning lawyers anymore. We got to worry 'bout getting out of town, it looks like. These kids, looks like they got to worry 'bout getting from this house alive.

He taps the pencil against his forehead.

—All of us, we got conflicting *agendas,* ese. 'Cept one thing. The four of us, we all got one thing in common.

He leans back and crosses his arms.

—None of us like you.

—You are so fucking dead, Ramon.

—See what I mean, guys. Ese, vato Hector, Whelan, let's rush him, eh? Tell you what, if it means this fat pendejo cocksucker dies, I'll go first, I'll take one of those bullets.

The crate shatters under Fernando's ass and Geezer jumps and the gun goes off.

George and Hector, still holding hands, squeeze, and their knuckles go white.

Fernando scrambles up, a big splinter jutting from his right buttock.

Ramon looks at the bullet hole in the plaster two feet from his head.

—I know your vocabulary sucks, boss, how's your math?

———

It's no real surprise that his dad can't tie a knot worth shit.

Once he starts twisting his wrists back and forth, once his dad isn't touching him and the pain stops and he can move, pulling his hands and feet free is pretty easy.

Mr. Whelan has his dad shoved into a corner, holding him by the throat.

—Youyouyouyouyoufucker! My kids! Where?

Paul gets up and goes to the dining room table and picks up one of the big hardbound computer textbooks and comes back and hits Mr. Whelan in the back of the head with it and Mr. Whelan hunches over and Paul hits him again and he falls on the floor and his dad slides to his knees coughing.

Paul drops the book.

—Sorry, Mr. Whelan. You can't hurt my dad like that.

Mr. Whelan doesn't move.

Paul finds his clothes in the garbage bag under the kitchen sink and puts them on, but his boots aren't in there and he has to go back to the livingroom to find them.

—Paul.

—Yhuh huh.

—Thank you.

—Hunh uh.

He puts on his socks and his boots.

—We're going to have to, I know this isn't what you want to hear, son, but we're going to have to leave town. I know that's going to be hard for you. You have friends here, a school. But it will be hard for me, too. And sometimes a change is good for everybody.

Paul gets up and adjusts his shirt and brushes back his hair.

—Hunh uh.

Mr. Cheney pushes himself up the wall, pulling his robe closed.

—So let's not put it off. Let's dive in. You go start packing a bag and I'll get some things together that we need. And, it won't be all bad, we'll be on the road for a bit. I can teach you to drive.

Paul looks around and sees what he wants and picks up the bag of crank.

—I know how to drive, Dad.

His father comes toward him.

—Well, I guess that doesn't really come as a surprise. But you can always use practice. And I'd like to see your traffic safety skills before I feel comfortable about you driving on your own. Why don't we, let's get some things together, and we can get started. I'll drive the first leg and then you can take over and we'll see how you do. How's that sound?

Paul looks at his father.

—I got to go somewhere.

Mr. Cheney reaches for him.

—No, Paul, I'm going to have to put my foot down here. I'm not letting you get in any more trouble. It is time for you to listen to your father and do what he tells you.

Paul steps away from the outstretched hand.

—I got to go, Dad, my friends are in trouble. I got to help them.

He starts for the door.

Mr. Cheney rushes around him and blocks the hall.

—No, Paul. No. I appreciate you wanting to help your friends, but this is not the time.

—Get out of my way, Dad.

—Don't speak to me in that tone.

—Get out of the way.

—Paul.

Paul shoves his father out of the way and walks past him.

—Leave me alone.

Mr. Cheney comes after him, grabbing at the back of his shirt.

—Paul, Paul, you have to listen to me, son. There's things. You don't really understand things. Me. I'm your father and you don't even understand me.

Paul turns, knocking the hands away.

—Don't touch me. I don't want you to touch me. I want you to leave me alone. Just leave me alone.

—I. I. Leave you. I. Paul. I. Leave you? Paul, I. I, don't. You, can't you try, try to understand? I. I love you. I've always loved you. You. You are what I. I just love you so much and I don't understand why, why you can't see that. Why you won't see that? Paul, listen, I, I can make you happy, I can make you so happy. I can make you, you can love me, you can. You do. I know you do. I can feel it. I can. You just don't know how much you love me. And I love you so much.

Paul slaps his father.

—Be quiet, Dad.

—I love you.

He slaps him again.

—Just be quiet.

—I do, I do, I love you.

—Dad, listen to me.

His dad listens, a hand on his burning cheek.

—Yes, son?

Paul spits in his face.

—I don't love you, Dad. I never loved you. Ever.

He turns and pulls the door open.

—Go away, Dad. Run away. You're in a lot of trouble, so run away. If you don't, I'm gonna kill you or something when I come home.

He goes out and closes the door behind him.

Kyle Cheney grabs the doorknob, twists it, starts to pull the door open, and closes it before he can see the street outside.

He walks back to the livingroom and looks at the mess. The boy unconscious in the hall. His neighbor on the floor. He sits at the dining table and picks up an uncorrected test and a red felt tip pen and makes a few marks on the paper. Some of his son's spit rolls down his chin and onto the table.

He gets up and goes to the bedroom and dresses in brown corduroys and a blue and pink madras shirt and blue socks and a pair of brown moccasins. From the nightstand he takes a photo of himself holding his five year old son; crouched behind him, arms around his middle, Paul squirming. He takes the picture from its frame, folds it in half and slides it in his breast pocket and gets his keys and checkbook and ID and walks past the wounded bodies and out of the house.

The sun is cracking the sky above the Altamont.

He walks around the block and finds his car and gets in and starts it and drives to the QuickStop. He doesn't have any cash, but the man lets him write a check because he recognizes him and because he has ID. He takes his bottle and gets in his car and takes a long drink and sits and thinks for a minute.

If he closes his eyes, he can remember exactly where it was his wife's car slipped the embankment. He can picture what the car looked like when he got the call and drove until he saw the flashing lights of the police cars and ambulance and fire truck. He can remember the elation.

He starts his car and pulls it onto the freeway and drives fast.

———

—Seriously, boss, why the hell you bring a gun with only two bullets?

—I got more.

Ramon laughs.

—I'm not lying, guys. I don't think I can walk much, but I bet I can hop on one leg. After he shoots me, the rest of you got no problem.

—Shut the fuck up.

—Fernando, you promise me, you guys, too. Whelan, Hector, you all promise me you'll kill this fatass, and I'll get up and hop right at him and make him shoot that last bullet at me.

Ramon looks at the bullet hole in the wall again.

—Hell, I could get lucky, he might miss.

Geezer puts his back in a corner of the room, Fernando and Ramon to his right, the kids to his left.

—Gun can be reloaded, asshole.

—Yeah, how fast? Whelan, Hector, you guys in? Want to play some chicken with fatass?

George is shaking.

Hector pulls his hand free of George. He picks up the length of chain crusted with his own dry blood and stands up.

Ramon claps.

—That's it, vato, that's what I was talking about before, homies sticking together.

Hector stares at him, swallows more blood.

George grabs at Hector's hand.

—Sit down, man. Sit down.

—No.

George watches the barrel of the derringer swing in his direction.

Geezer thumbs the hammer back.

—George, I promise you, these spics try to rush me, you're gonna be the one taking the bullet.

Ramon sits up.

—Hey, I like that even better. You mean, I come at you, me and my brother and Hector come at you, you're gonna blast Whelan? Ese, hear that?

Fernando yanks the splinter out of his butt.

—Yeah, I heard it, bro.

George is pulling on Hector's hand.

—Sit down, man, I don't want to get shot, sit down.

Hector edges down the wall, out of his reach, watching Ramon.

Ramon's hand dips between the couch cushions and returns, holding the hacksaw.

—Yo, boss, look what I left lying around.

Glass shatters as Paul throws the bag of meth through the sliding door, making the hole Hector punched in it big enough to climb through.

—I got your shit, fatass, let my friends go.

———

Bob stands slowly, the lump on the back of his head throbbing. He goes to the phone and picks it up. He dials 9, but sees something he'd forgotten and doesn't finish. He hangs the phone up and goes to the end of the hall and walks over the broken door, his foot punching a hole in it, and finds a glass and fills it with water and goes back to the boy on the floor in the hall and pours the water in his face and throws the glass over his shoulder and bends and takes the boy by his hair and slaps him.

—You, fuckhead, wake the fuck up, you little piece of shit, wake the fuck up. Where are my sons? What the fuck is going on and where the fuck are my boys?

———

The garage pitches and rolls and Andy thinks he's going to go back to sleep, but he doesn't.

He folds the plastic back around the parts of Jeff's head that are still there. It's weird, how it looks almost exactly the way it looks when he imagines shooting someone in the face.

He gags. But his stomach has been empty for awhile now and nothing comes out, but it makes his eye and his head hurt.

He stands up and pokes around in the chemicals and glassware and trash and piles of broken furniture and crap and finds a bent piece of rusted rebar with a clot of broken cement jutting from its end.

He swings it back and forth a couple times.

He sees himself standing behind the door when someone comes out to the garage as he brings the rebar down on their head and it gets lodged in there and they fall down and pull the rebar from his hand and it cuts his palm as it jerks free and he has to wiggle it back and forth to pull it loose from the hole in the skull of the dead body on the floor.

He swings it a couple more times, raising it above his head and letting gravity pull it down in an arc. He guesses at its weight and thinks about the density of bone and resiliency of flesh and figures that swinging it like that you wouldn't have to add much force to it at all to create enough momentum to shatter bone and cause sufficient trauma to a person's brain so that they wouldn't get back up. Swinging it from the side like a bat will take more force. He tries it. The bar wants to slip from his hands, but it doesn't.

He wonders how long it will be before someone realizes that he must be in the garage because they've eliminated everywhere in the house and then they come out to look for him.

Then he hears a gunshot.

And then breaking glass.

And then the screaming starts.

————

George watches as the bag of crank hits the floor and pulls Geezer's eyes from him, the aim of the derringer drifting away, and he jumps at the fat man who is reaching for the drugs with the snapping claw of the grabber.

The bag is about the same size as a football.

Fernando sees George making a move and dives and rolls and cuts George's feet from underneath him and tries to cover the bag with his body, but it's snagged on the end of Geezer's fucking grabber and is pulled away from him.

Ramon gets his crutch planted in his armpit and shoves himself forward, a stream of blood pulsing from his leg, pivoting on the rubber tip of the crutch to face Paul as he comes through the hole in the glass door, and being totally blindsided when Hector whips the chain across the side of his head, ripping his ear open.

George flies, his legs suddenly out from under his body, and plows head-first into Geezer's gut and Geezer grunts and jerks the grabber and the claw rips the plastic bag and it falls and he lets go of the derringer as he tries to grab the meth, but both drop to the floor, the bag spilling dirty yellow crystals.

Ramon swings the hacksaw backhand, the blade tearing through Hector's black jeans and into the meat at the back of his knee. Hector's leg folds and he goes down, swinging the chain, watching it wrap around Ramon's crutch, and yanking as he hits the floor, bringing the jailbird down on top of him.

On the floor, Fernando lunges and wraps his fist around the shaft of the grabber as Geezer moves to snatch up the fallen derringer. He wrenches it free of the fat man's sweaty hand and throws it across the room and curses all the saints as George flops on top of the gun.

Geezer looks at the floor, at the bag spilling his meth, at his favorite gun disappearing under Bob Whelan's son, and at his grabber across the room. He doesn't even try to bend and pick anything up. Knowing he'll never be able to rise without help, he heads for the door.

. . .

Paul sees Geezer running. He wants to hurt him. Hurt him so bad for sending him to get the meth, for sending him home. He runs past Hector and George, struggling on the floor; going after the fat guy, crying.

George covers the derringer as Fernando comes down on him, driving his elbow into the back of his neck. George's face goes into the floor and he feels Fernando's hands digging under his chest, going for the gun, grabbing his thumb.

Fernando wrenches, and George's thumb breaks.

Geezer's hand slips off the doorknob. He screams and wipes the sweat off on his chest and twists the knob as the big kid comes charging after him. He swings his arm and catches Paul in the balls with his huge fist and the boy folds and falls and Geezer is out the door.

He chugs to his Seville, gets in, fumbles the key into the ignition and the AC comes to life with the engine. He hits the gas and the engine roars, and he almost plows head on into a 4×4 rounding the corner. He cuts down the street, thinking about money and where to get some.

Hector has one end of the chain in each hand, stretching it across Ramon's neck as Ramon sprawls on top of him, one forearm shoved under Hector's chin as his other hand feels for his dropped hacksaw.

George goes blind from the pain of his thumb breaking, he can feel it as Fernando grabs his other thumb, but this time he just pulls George's hand to the side and worms his fingers around the derringer.

Curled around the pain between his legs, Paul watches as Andy comes through the door from the garage, something dangling from his hand.

.   .   .   .

Ramon has the saw. He twists his head, trying to keep Hector's chain from biting through his throat and plants the blade on the back of Hector's wrist. But he never draws it across the skin to shred the tendons. Instead he goes limp as something impossibly heavy hits the back of his head, and his body falls away from him.

Fernando pulls the gun from George's hands and rolls off and flips over just in time to see the little Whelan kid put his foot in the middle of Ramon's back and twist an iron bar and pull it from the hole in the back of his brother's head, something heavy and red dragging at the end of it.

Andy stumbles backward as the rebar jerks free from Ramon's skull. Everything is working pretty much the way he thought it would. He turns, but Fernando isn't on top of his brother anymore. So that was a miscalculation. One of the risks of entering a situation that is inherently chaotic. He watches Fernando point the derringer at him. He looks at the two barrels, and watches the hammer snap down. And nothing happens. And he knows this is not random chance, remembering the sound of the gunshot he heard, he knows this is a product of order, of things working as they should. And he moves to maintain this order.

The kid is coming at him. He's running, hefting the iron bar, raising it above his head. Fernando pulls the trigger again. But the hammer isn't back and the gun doesn't go off again. He pulls the hammer back as the kid gets closer and pulls the trigger and the gun still doesn't go off. And he realizes that you must have to pull it back further to fire the second barrel. And then the kid is in front of him and the iron bar hits his hand and shatters the bones and the gun is gone and the kid is raising his bloody weapon over his head.

.   .   .

It looks different, which is obvious, but it also feels different, which is less obvious. When the chunk of concrete at the end of the bar crushes Fernando's face, it both looks and *feels* different from when it crushed the back of Ramon's head. Less resistance. More blood.

Coming onto the porch, dragging Timo Arroyo behind him, Bob stares through the open front door and watches as his young son brings the bar down. His strange and incomprehensible boy. The boy he changed everything for, the boy he has nothing in common with, nothing to share with, killing a man twice his size.

He watches the teenager next to him watch his brother murdered.

He takes him by the throat and squeezes, and slams him into the side of the house.

—Keep your fucking mouth shut.

He releases him.

—Run.

Timo doesn't move.

Bob slaps him.

—Run.

Timo runs.

And Bob Whelan walks into the house and he gets the boys on their feet and makes them help Andy out to the 4×4 and he finds the Coleman fuel in the garage and he spills it over the blood and the bodies and he sets it all on fire, burning the house the boys came to rob.

Part Three

A Normal Life

The phone rings.
   —Hello. Yes? Hello.
   —Cindy.
—Yes. Yes, what is it, what?
—Cin, it's Amy.
—Amy. What? Amy, Bob's.
She remembers what Amy's job is.
—Amy, why are you calling?
—It's OK, honey, it's OK. They're here at the hospital, but they're OK.
—Oh, oh.
—Sweety, listen to me, don't jump in a car. Wait for.
—Are they, what's wrong with?
—Honey, listen, don't drive yourself. You have no idea how many parents kill themselves rushing to the hospital. Get a neighbor to. Cin? Are you there? Cindy?
The phone dangles from its cord. Cindy Whelan is already outside getting into her car.

———

Bob knows the cop.
The cop that comes to the emergency room to file a report when he shows up with four beaten boys, Bob's ridden in the back of his car. Old timer. One of the ones who knew him when.
—What's the word, Bob?

—Same shit, different generation.

—What'd they get into?

—My oldest, George, tells me they scored some acid from some guys that were hanging around the bowling alley.

—Acid dealers are over at the Doughnut Wheel.

—Older guys, from over the hill, they all had Raiders gear.

—Black guys.

—Yeah.

—Probably from Alameda.

—Don't know.

—So?

Bob takes a sip from his coffee cup and looks down the hall to see if his sister is coming back with any news. Hector's mom and little sister are still sitting across the room, heads bowed, rosary beads passing through their fingers. No sign of the kid's dad or brothers.

—George said it was just plain blotter paper, no acid on it. They got pissed. Rode around looking for the guys' car and found them getting drunk in May Nissen Park. Started talking shit and saying they wanted their money back.

—The Cheney kid, right? Fucker's got a mouth on him.

—I don't know.

—Yeah, I've had him in the car. He likes to mouth off.

—Well, whatever it was, these dealers beat the hell out of them.

—And you?

—George called from a pay phone and I went and got them and brought them here.

—They didn't call us.

—In a fight with some guys that ripped them off on a drug deal, they didn't call the cops.

—Uh huh. OK.

Bob looks at him.

—So you gonna go find the guys or what?

The cop underlines something on his notepad.

Bob remembers how the fucker put a hand on the back of his neck and slammed his head against the door as he put him in the back of the car the last time he was ever cuffed. How he laughed about it.

—Tell you, Bob, I'll head over to the park, take a look around, try to get over there before it gets too crowded, but what the fuck do you expect me to find? Think some coons from Alameda are gonna hang around after they did something like that to some white kids and one of our Mexicans?

Bob stands up.

—That's bullshit, man. Did you see my kids?

—Easy, Bob.

—They. George's hand is all fucked up. Andy.

He looks in his coffee cup.

—He's a mess. He. Fucking do something.

The cop closes his notebook.

—Bob, I appreciate your kids getting hurt. I can only imagine. But, honestly, you should not be acting all outraged citizen with me.

—What the hell is that?

—Just saying, if you had boys that weren't out scoring acid in parking lots at two in the morning you wouldn't have a problem like this.

—Don't fucking.

—Can it, Bob. You use that kind of language again, I don't care what's up with your family, I'm gonna remind you what it's like to get booked.

He taps his index finger on Bob's chest.

—Want to take a ride? Try on some bracelets again? One of those orange jumpsuits? It's the weekend. Take you in now, no one gonna see you till Monday. Don't got no friends at the station anymore, Bob. Those days are over. Your money's no good over there now.

He shakes his head.

—Reformed punk or not, you're still a punk. You got punk kids that hang out with punk friends and what they got was in the cards for a long time. So you just calm down and take a seat so you can be sure to be here if they need you. Yeah?

Bob looks down, takes a seat.

—Sure. Sorry.

—Yeah.

He tugs at his belt, shifts his holster.

—It's a busy morning. There's stuff going on. Got half the force and emergency services at that fire over by Junction. Another fucking crank lab. Town this size, we got two crank labs going at the same time. Damn drug war here. Me, I say we got guys like you to thank for that. So, when I get the chance, I'll take a look at May Nissen. When the kids are feeling a little better, someone'll get descriptions of the black guys and their car. And then we'll decide if we're gonna do anything about your kids being out after curfew looking to score. OK?

—Sure.

—Best to the family, Bob. They're in my prayers.

Bob watches him leave, remembering the times they shook hands, the folded bills passing between their palms, and then goes to find George to tell him again what to say.

That night, in the ICU, he has to stop walking when he comes in and sees Andy, his head and face buried in bandages, his mom sitting next to him. He has to stop and remind himself where he is. When it is.

———

He remembers the way it was before. The bags of Colombian Gold shoved inside plaster lawn gnomes and jockeys and Christs, coming across the border at Tijuana, driving nonstop back up here, swapping shifts at the wheel with Jeff, chewing whites and drinking warm beer and shots of mescal the whole way. Dumping the shit at Geezer's, the fat boy weighing and bagging and pinching off shit on the side that they never even fucked with him about because there was so much goddamn money.

The parties.

People cramming the house, spilling into the yard and the street, the cops closing their fists around the hundreds he slipped them and closing off the block with sawhorses. Football games at midnight in the middle of the street, high as hell. Cindy on the lawn, dropping the strap of her halter to nurse George while she tried to help Amy deal with her latest loser boyfriend. Cindy, just the best looking lady on the scene, baby or no baby. The best woman in town, and his pick of any others he wanted.

Always action at the house.

People coming by, scoring dime bags and quarters, shooting the shit as they rolled up a joint to smoke before they hit the road. Cash piling up. Until you spent it. Just blowing it like the fucking wind.

And the fights.

Guys saying they got shorted, getting in your face, learning the lesson that you don't talk to Bob Whelan that way. Not in his house. Not nowhere. Dealers from the central valley trying to bring their Mexican Brown in from Tracy. Busting in the front door of their pad and running riot, swinging the bat, busting the place to shit, setting it all on fire and watching them run.

The changes.

Geezer showing them numbers and talking about smack and coke and speed. Talking about profit margins. Like it was supposed to be a business. Like it was supposed to be something where you punch a clock. Like he loved it for more than the fun and the freedom and the fights. Like he loved anything more than getting fucked up and fucking and blood on his knuckles.

And then the Angels.

Seeing them down at the Rodeo Club. Dealing their shit in the lot. Eyeballing him and Jeff and Geez. The Angels letting them know they *knew* whose town it was, and they didn't give a fuck. Sending a message about changing times.

And then showing the Angels they were wrong. Giving that parking lot a coat of red paint.

And Andy.

Walking into that hospital room the same night, seeing that thing they took out of his wife. And realizing he did love something more than all that other shit.

Fucking family man.

Who could have seen that coming?

The ride out to Oakland with Jeff and Geezer.

Carrying the bloody colors he'd stripped from the Angels after he beat them down. After Jeff dragged him off and kept him from killing them all. Walking into their clubhouse and laying the colors at the feet of their president. Telling them he was done. The town was theirs.

Telling them they'd never hear his name again. Taking the beating their warlord put on him in retribution. What it took from him, what it took to keep from rising up each time he was knocked down, what it took to keep from doing what came so natural. What it took to kill that thing inside.

And how killing it hasn't protected anyone.

———

He stands in the doorway now and she turns and looks at him.

He remembers his wife by the side of the incubator. How she turned and looked at him then. What she told him he needed to do to keep her. How he turned and walked out of the room and did it.

She doesn't tell him what he has to do this time. He's already on his way.

To Dress and to Butcher

The double is almost a triple by the time Amy heads for home.
She stops at the AM/PM on the corner of Rincon and Sunset and grabs a couple packs of cigarettes, a two liter of Diet Pepsi, and four Cocktail in a Can 7&7s. Except they call them 77's on the can because of lawsuits and shit.

Some asshole has blocked half her driveway with his Seville and she has to drive over the corner of the lawn to park her car. Saturday night and there's no curb space on the whole block because somebody's having a lawn party a few houses down. She leans against the fender of her Mustang and listens to "Total Eclipse of the Heart" coming from the stereo they've got set up on the porch over there. She thinks about joining the party. Couple of her customers live down there. She can see a few Harleys at the curb. But then she gets another whiff of herself.

Shower.

Nothing before a shower. And once she has a shower she won't be going anywhere but her chair and she won't be doing anything but drinking a couple 77's and dropping a lude and crashing.

She takes another look at the Seville, almost rakes her key across the door to teach the asshole a lesson, but doesn't have the energy to get that angry.

She's been angry all day. Angry and scared.

Poor Andy.

He had the look. When they called her down to Emergency and she saw him on the gurney, thought that was it. But that was just the start. Bob grabbing her and telling her to keep an eye on George and Hector and Paul, not to let them talk to anyone. Bob, up to something, sure as shit. And that can't be anything but bad news.

Having to sit with Cindy while he dealt with the cop. The doctor explaining to her what a burr hole is and how they were going to have to drill a few in Andy's skull if they were going to have any chance of taking the pressure off his brain. Got to give it to the girl, she took it. Signed the form just like that and cried her tears and went to see how they were doing with George's stitches and his thumb.

She unlocks the front door, blocking it with her foot so the cat can't get out, dumps her purse and the AM/PM bag on the couch and goes down the hall dropping her clothes and the baggies of pills on the floor behind her. In the shower, she finds some dry specks of blood on her forearm and scrubs them away. She toys with the loofah but doesn't have the energy to use it. Shampooing takes it all out of her.

Out of the shower, she grabs an ankle length red cotton nightgown from the back of the door and drops it over her body and folds her hair inside a towel turban. She looks at the AC, but the heat is finally breaking so she leaves it off and goes around opening windows and the sliding glass door, pulling the screen door closed so the cat stays in. A couple oscillating fans get the air moving around.

She passes through the kitchen long enough to open a can of cat food and fill a glass with ice. The cat runs in and starts eating. She scratches it behind the ears with her bare toes, then goes and grabs her grocery bag off the floor, hits the play button on her turntable, and settles into the basket chair.

She closes her eyes and listens to the music.

Joni Mitchell always works. Hardly ever take *Blue* off the turntable unless there's company.

Her eyes still closed, she reaches inside the bag and takes out one of the 77's, opens it and pours it in the cold glass. She takes a sip. The cat lands in her lap and nuzzles till it finds its spot. She keeps her eyes closed, too tired to lift her lids.

Those kids.

What the hell did those kids get into? What kind of shit did they fall into for Bob to be lying to a cop? Jesus, he gets caught in a lie to a cop, he'll never get right again.

Those kids.

Doctors won't know what the deal with Andy is for at least a couple days. If the sweetheart makes it he may never be a super genius again. George should be OK, but he was as freaked as she's ever seen anyone, until they stuck a needle in his arm and settled him down. ER doctors took one look at Hector's face and started calling around to USF and Stanford, looking for a plastic surgeon who could do the stitching without turning him into a freak. And Paul. Just sitting there, staring at the wall, not talking to anyone except when they asked him where his dad was and he said he didn't want to see his dad. No problem there, the man still hadn't showed up by the time she left.

Whole town coming apart at the seams today. Boys beat, mutilated. Bob up to some shit. Fire on the edge of town, some drug thing gone wrong. Reporters from the *Tribune* and the *Times* and even the Oakland papers coming around when the bodies came in. Asking questions about the local dealers. Shit. It's like signs and portents. Everything telling her it's time to cut her losses and get the hell out of the game. Sell off the shit she brought out tonight and just wash her hands. No reason she can't make do on her salary. The Mustang is paid for. The time share she can unload.

The cat jumps down from her lap.

She realizes she can't feel the breeze from the fans. She opens her eyes.

Geezer points the kitchen knife at her.

—Fans all you got, you got no AC?

Her drink spills in her lap.

—I'm not dealing crank, Geezer. I told Jeff. I don't know who you've been talking with.

Geezer laughs.

—Jeff. Yeah, Jeff. Forgot about him. Funny.

—I told him.

—Amy, you remember when I came over? Made the special trip over here to talk to you. Remember?

She doesn't say anything.

—That guy you had hanging around, your boyfriend or whatever, the one with the lip on him, had so much to say. What was his name?

Amy wonders if her cat ran away when Geezer came in through the screen door.

—Eddie.

Geezer shifts the knife in his hand.

—Yeah, Eddie. His nipples ever grow back?

—I. I never sold any meth. Ever. I do my thing.

—What's that look like when it heals, a man with no nipples? Hey, could you have sewed them back on if I hadn't dropped 'em down the garbage disposal?

—Never, Geezer. Not a single gram. I swear. I don't even do the stuff myself. I don't even like selling my pills to your customers.

—Where's your money, bitch?

—I don't.

He takes a step closer.

—This the same knife I used on him? This the same . . . word? God-damn it! A thing. A tool. The word for a tool.

—I.

—Don't fuck with me. The fucking word?

—Cleaver?

—No, not a specific fucking tool. The word for tool, a thing you can use, a fancier way of saying it.

—I.

He stomps, walks in a circle, face reddening.

—Goddamn spics! Goddamn kids! Goddamn word!

—Kids.

He stops.

—Got it! *Implement.* Is this the same *implement* I used to cut that guy's nipples off with?

—Kids?

He comes closer, waving the knife.

—No! Don't pull that shit. That fucking, *kids, what kids?* crap. Fucker, that fucker your nephew tried that shit. I know, I know. I don't need to be told, I know. You, you shit where I eat, that's what you did. You and your fucking brother. I'm all fucked up, and if I'm all fucked up, everybody's fucked up. Money. Money now. Money now and I won't cut off as much. And where's the AC? Is everybody in this town a . . . word? Damn! Damn.

Lizards and snakes? Fucking things that are cold blooded and like the heat? What are they!? What the fuck are they!?

—*Reptiles*, Geezer.

Geezer licks his lips and turns his head and looks at Bob.

—I keep getting snuck up on today.

Bob nods.

—I know how you feel.

Geezer sees what Bob's holding, he drops the knife.

—You know what makes me laugh the most, Bob?

—What's that?

—They kept telling me, Loller and your kids, they kept saying you had nothing to do with it. Loller telling me I'm paranoid. *There's no conspiracy, Geezer. They're just fucking kids*. Like I'm an idiot. But, and I'll give it to you, Bob, I never saw it coming. I mean, when it was in front of my face, I got it. But I never saw it coming.

—That right?

—Never. But now, now, I see everything, and what I'm thinking is, you're gonna need help. Dealing with Oakland. Making it right. And I know how to deal with those guys. And you'll need an extra hand, with Loller not around. 'Cause it's a mess right now, but I see where you were going with it, what you were aiming for, and I can help you to put it together so it can still work.

—Geezer.

—Bob.

—You got no clue what you're talking about.

Geezer wipes some sweat from his upper lip.

—Oh.

—My boy, my oldest, the one that isn't in a coma right now, when he mentioned a stupid fat sonofabitch, I didn't bother to ask for a name. Know why?

—Not really.

—Because you're so stupid and greedy and predictable and low. If I'd thought about it for half a second, I'd even have figured you for coming over here. As it is, I just feel lucky I needed to talk to my sister. You cool, Ames?

—Uh huh.

Geezer blinks as some sweat rolls into the corner of his eye.

—You know, Bob, things may not be what you think they are. You know your son there was running for your sister here? You know that?

Bob shakes his head.

—I did not know that.

—All I'm saying is, so *you're* not looking to get back in the business, no second thoughts, but *this one* here? She's got something cooking. And your kids, and I don't mean to say anything bad about them, but maybe you don't know everything they got going on for themselves.

Bob hefts the sawed off bat with the galvanized nails pounded through its head.

—Remember?

—Uh huh.

—I keep it in the toolbox on the truck. Sometimes a job site gets robbed, copper piping and PVC and whatever, the contractor might ask a couple of the guys to sleep over at the site and keep an eye on things. So I got this in the toolbox. Not that I've ever done more than show it to a couple kids tried to jack some insulation.

He tosses the bat lightly, spinning the handle.

—All that stuff, my sister and my kids, I don't care right now. All I care about, the only thing on my mind, is if you've talked to anyone. Does Oakland have any idea my kids were mixed up in this shit? My sister? Have they heard my name, Geezer?

Geezer raises both his hands.

—Bob, they have not. I am deep in shit, last thing I wanted to do was bring up your name. See them go on a rampage. I didn't tell them anything except I was taking care of the problem.

Bob looks at the bat, lowers it, looks at the fat man, the man who was a friend.

—What a Goddamn mess, Geez. My kids are in a mess. And I don't want any more. I want my kids safe. That's all I ever wanted. I never lied about that. I just wanted my kids safe and a normal life.

—Sure, Bob. I mean.

—Shut up.

—OK.

—So I want this to end. Now. But if I kill you here in my sister's house, it's gonna cause more problems and, Jesus, I have no idea how the hell we'd move your body, you fat son of a bitch.

—Yeah, that's true.

—So get out.

Bob moves to the side, clearing the way to the door.

—Go on, Geez, get out, leave town, go away, and never, never say my name to anyone. Go on.

Geezer nods, claps his hands twice and nods his head again and makes for the door and as soon as he's taken a single step past him Bob raises the bat and swings it and embeds the nails in the back of his neck and hits him over and over while his little sister curls in her chair and hides her face.

When he's done he goes out to the truck and gets some tools. Grateful for the things his father taught him how to do on the ranch. Like how to dress and butcher a steer, when the occasion rises.

Blisters

They tell George he can go home on Sunday.

He tells his mom he'll stay and keep her company with Andy, but she says that as soon as his dad gets back she wants him to go home and get some rest.

And the truth is, sitting in the ICU with Andy is fucked up. Not just because they don't know if he's ever gonna wake up or what he might be like if he does, but because looking at him makes him think about the house and what happened inside. And thinking about his little brother doing those things makes him have to get up and go to the drinking fountain again and sip some water.

He could go see Hector, but Hector's mostly too doped to talk because they have his face all sewn back together. Say he's gonna have scars no matter what. Say he's gonna need crutches because of the way his leg was cut. Say he may need a cane for his whole life.

Paul's gone.

Came to George's ward late last night and stuck his head inside the sheet wrapped around his bed. Said not to jerk off in there because everyone else on the ward would hear it. Told him that when Andy and Hector wake up to tell them they're fags. Said his dad is dead. They identified his body in his car in a wreck off Collier Canyon Road. Said they found some stuff, some pictures and stuff at his house and some things, and they were gonna take him somewhere to talk to the cops or something but that it's all bullshit and he'll see him later. He cried the whole time, but he talked like he wasn't crying at all. And then a chick cop stuck her head in and took him away.

So on Sunday George waits in the ICU until his dad shows up, comes in and takes his mom in his arms.

George watches as she presses her lips against his dad's lips and whispers as they kiss and pulls her face from his and takes his hands and touches some scratches on the backs of his hands and pulls them to her eyes and wipes her tears across them. Then she pulls him across the room to Andy's bedside. His dad looks at Andy and then looks at George and tilts his head at the door.

His mom grabs him on his way out and hugs him and he hugs her, his cast clunking into her back.

Outside they get in the truck.

—You want anything before we go home?

—No.

—Stop at the store and pick something up if you want.

—No.

—Cops want to talk to you some more?

—Yeah.

—When?

—Said at the station tomorrow.

—I'll take you over.

—OK.

—Know what to say?

—I know.

—Don't mouth off to them.

—I know.

—If someone saw you guys go in the house, if they bring up the house, ask you about anything but the black guys and what happened with them, don't say anything at all.

—I know.

—They mention any of that stuff.

—I know, Dad. You're not the only one ever talked to the cops before.

Bob pulls the truck over, puts it in park and looks at him.

—Something you want to say?

George looks out the windshield at the sunny day. He puts his hand in front of the AC vent and feels the cool air.

—No.

—Now's the time. You don't say it now, you never say it. After this, whatever happened in the past is in the past. After this, what happened last night is what we *say* happened.

George thinks about who Geezer *said* his dad was, and about who he *is*.

He turns and looks at him.

—Let's go home, OK?

Bob puts the truck in first.

—Home it is.

At home George goes straight upstairs to his room and takes off the stupid OP shorts and the crap "First Blood" T his mom got him from the gift shop because his clothes were trashed and she hadn't brought any for him to wear home. He gets out some cutoffs and his B.O.C. shirt and puts them on and sits on the side of the bed and looks at the floor and starts thinking about the inside of the sketchy house again and gets up and walks around the room until he hears something banging in the backyard.

He stands at the window and watches his dad.

He's already tilled the yard and tamped the dirt and rolled sheets of heavy plastic over it. Now he's going around with a mallet and a handful of stakes, pounding them through to the ground, dimpling the plastic with them so it won't peel up later.

He watches.

When the stakes are all in and he's walked over the whole yard and looked at the ground to make sure it's even and flat and nothing bulges from underneath, Bob Whelan goes to the front of the house for a shovel and the wheelbarrow that are in the garage.

He parks the barrow next to the pile of rocks and starts shoveling.

George comes out of the house and gets another shovel from the garage. He tries a couple grips until he finds one that hurts a little less and will let him work with one thumb and half his right hand in a cast.

He starts shoveling rocks.

—When'd you do the rototiller?

Bob dumps a shovel load of rocks in the wheelbarrow.

—First thing, sunrise.

—Neighbors must have loved that.

—Job needed to get done.

—What's that smell?

—Lye.

—That's like acid or something, isn't it?

—Put it down so weeds won't grow and punch holes in the plastic.

George stops, tries a different grip, goes back to shoveling.

Bob points at his hands.

—You should wear some gloves.

—Won't fit over the cast.

—On your good hand.

—I'm fine.

—Gonna get blisters.

—I'll live.

George shovels, awkward by his father's side, working hard to bury what needs to be hid, even if he doesn't know it's there.

Things to Make Them Feel Better

Paul gets there first.

He stands in front of the benches, away from the Mexican family with their twined cardboard boxes, and shoves his hands deep in his pockets, scanning the sidewalk for a butt.

—Hey.

He looks up as George and Hector cross the street.

—Got a smoke?

George pushes his bike, going slowly so Hector, walking with his cane, can keep up. He leans the bike against one of the benches, drops Hector's backpack next to Paul's duffel bag and takes a fresh pack of Marlboros from the breast pocket of his Levi's jacket.

—Here. For the ride.

Paul catches the box, slaps it into his palm a couple times and peels the cellophane.

—A going away present, you shouldn't have. Fag.

He pulls one out and offers it to Hector.

—You allowed to smoke, Quasimodo?

Hector smacks him in the shin with his cane.

—Fuck you.

Paul gestures with the cigarette.

—Seriously, aren't you supposed to avoid it? Isn't there a risk of infection with all that shit?

Hector snaps his new silver teeth.

—Shit's close enough to healed, just give me the fucking smoke.

Paul hands him the cigarette and lights a match.

—Careful you don't burn your face, might end up uglier than you are.

Hector leans close to the match and lights his cigarette, the scars on his face livid.

—Least my scars came from a fight and not from picking zits.

Paul tosses the spent match.

—My scars came from your mom's pussy hairs grinding in my face.

George picks at a loose thread sticking from the Scorpions patch on his shoulder.

—You guys are such a cute couple. You guys should skip LA and go to SF. Go to the Castro. I hear there are some cool bars in the Castro for guys like you.

Paul flips him off.

—I'll go down there and tell all your boyfriends you'll be in soon.

They smoke.

Hector looks at the family on the bench, catches the little boy staring at his face. He sticks his tongue out at the boy and the boy laughs and sticks out his tongue. His mother catches him and tugs his hair and whispers in his ear and he starts to cry.

Hector looks down the avenue.

—What time?

Paul pulls the schedule from his back pocket and runs his finger down it.

—Two thirty seven.

George kicks a rock into the street.

—Any trouble getting out of the home?

—Hells no. Fucking place. All the kids are juvies or head cases. Think the staff'd be more careful about who can go where and shit. Just raised my hand in group therapy and said I needed to piss and went and got my bag and jumped out the window.

George blows some smoke.

—Group therapy.

—Group bullshit. The counselors think they know shit. But they don't. They keep saying about how you need to talk about shit. I keep saying, *talk about what? Talk about what a dick my dad was and how happy I am he's dead?* Fuck that. They don't know shit.

—My folks still want you to stay with us.

—That's never gonna happen, dude. Counselors say for my own

good I need a controlled environment. Just means they want me to say things they want to hear that make them feel better about shit before they let me live where I want to live.

—So say it.

—Fuck no. You say it. I stay, I'll just be sitting around that place till I'm eighteen and they have to leave me alone. Why do that there? Won't change what I do in the spring. Still gonna join up on my birthday.

—Not without a diploma.

—Fuck that. Don't need to be a high school grad to enlist. Just have to pass the GED. They'll sign me and let me take the test a couple months later.

Hector shakes a finger.

—Don't forget to study.

—Who studies for the GED? I'm not a retard.

He pitches his butt into the gutter.

—'Sides, gotta look after you, cripple.

Hector sees the bus come into view several stoplights down.

—Then get my bag, bitch.

George picks up both bags and brings them to the curb and dumps them at Paul's feet.

Hector raps the tip of his cane against the pavement.

—What's up with Andy?

—Home. Doing school stuff.

—Still not going to classes?

—No. Says he can finish quicker if he does the work on his own. Little fucker's gonna be done with the whole year by January the way he's going.

Hector checks the bus's progress.

—Cool.

Paul picks up his bag and hefts it onto his shoulder.

—He know where he's gonna go?

—No. Wants to work with me and my dad once he's done. Until the fall. Then he'll go to college wherever.

—He fuck up my bike yet?

—Not yet.

—He will.

—Probably.

—You tell him we're going?

—No. I'll tell him later. He just would have wanted to come down here. Probably try and sneak into your bag.

—Yeah, my *nut* bag.

The bus pulls up and squeals and hisses and stops and the door opens.

George reaches in his pocket and pulls out some cash and holds it out.

—Here.

Paul looks at it.

—What the fuck is that?

—Some money.

—Don't want your money.

—It's cool. I'm making plenty on weekends. This is what's left from, you know, what Jeff gave us.

Paul picks up Hector's backpack.

—Don't want it.

Hector grabs the money.

—Thanks, man. Guitar money.

They move back as an old couple is helped out of the bus by the driver.

Paul watches the money go into Hector's pocket.

—He remember anything yet?

George shakes his head.

Hector touches a scar that cuts across his upper and lower lips.

Paul spits.

—Good.

The Mexican family stands by as the driver stows their boxes in the luggage bay and then they file onto the bus.

The driver looks at the three of them.

—That all your bags?

Paul nods.

—Yeah.

—Want them down here or with you?

—We'll keep 'em with us.

The driver slams the bay door closed and straightens and stretches his lower back.

—All aboard, then.

Hector puts his arms around George.

—Be cool, man. See my mom, tell her I'll write her a card. Tell her I'm just tired of being in this town. Not gonna die here. Tell her I'm cool. Same for my sister.

—Yeah. Sure.

Paul kicks Hector's cane.

—You wanna start getting on now, crip? Gonna take you like an hour.

Hector lets go of George and hooks a thumb at Paul.

—Sure you don't want to come? Just so I got company besides dickhead?

George shrugs.

—Nah. Stay here. Do my thing. Graduate and all that shit.

—Cool.

Paul holds a bag in either hand.

—Don't think I'm putting these down to hug you, fag.

George puts his hands in his pockets.

—Dude, I'm not hugging your runaway ass.

Paul grins.

—Runaway. Man. Why'd I wait?

Hector pokes him with the cane.

—Dude, let's jet.

Paul steps up onto the bus.

—Tell Andy he can keep my bike. Tell him not to fuck it up or I'll come back and kick his ass.

The door sighs closed and the bus pulls away, Paul and Hector sticking their hands out the window and flipping George off as it turns onto North L and disappears.

He rides by the school and watches as classes get out. A chick he knows bums a smoke off him and asks why he hasn't called since the party last week and he says he's been busy and tells her he'll maybe call her this weekend and he rides off.

There's no cars in the driveway at home, too early for his folks to be back from work. Paul's old bike is in the garage. He rides in circles out front and looks at Andy's bedroom window and thinks about going in and telling him about Paul and Hector. But then he'll have to hang around with him. And that's not what he wants to do right now.

Right now the sketchy house is in his head.

And he doesn't want to see his brother.

He rides back toward the school, looking for that chick.

Dead Man's Cap

Andy studies the dungeon, rolls the twenty sided one more time, looks at the number, and fills a trap with boiling acid. Then he puts it away, adding it to a pile of dungeons he's made since he got out of the hospital. None of them explored.

He looks at his textbooks, flips physics open, reads ten pages and flips it closed. Read it already. Read all of them already. Need some new ones.

Home study is OK. It's better than the alternative. Things were bad enough when he was just the freaky brain kid skipping grades. Being the freaky brain kid with the Frankenstein scars all over his head isn't an option. It's not like people really give him shit or anything. Just stare. Maybe want to ask questions about what it feels like and what it's like to get beat up like that and what a coma is like. Better to stay at home and take the state tests.

He looks out the window and watches George ride around out front before turning and pedaling away.

His head itches.

He thought it'd stop after the last of the stitches came out, but it didn't. Wherever the hair is growing back itches. The parts where no hair is growing back don't feel like anything.

Too bad George didn't come in. It sucks being alone all day. Well, being alone is OK, but not seeing his friends sucks. But that's the way it's been.

They just act kind of weird around him these days. Like they don't really know him or something. Which is stupid.

He gets up and goes out to the garage and wheels out Paul's Redline and looks at Jeff's old Harley cap hanging from the handlebars. It's the one Paul always used to wear. The one he left in George's bedroom.

He puts it on, takes it off, puts it on, thinks about Jeff. What a bummer it is that he's dead. Tries to remember the last time he saw him. Can't.

He rides.

It'd be good to see George. See anyone after being alone all day. Once their folks head off to work it's just him. One of them sometimes comes home at lunch, but not nearly as often as they did at first. They've gotten used to him being OK now. Used to the idea that he's alive and not brain damaged after all those doctors kept telling them not to hope for too much. Which is cool. They were way too all over him for the first month. But it'd be nice to see George and hang out. And George is mostly OK with that. He doesn't care what Andy looks like. Doesn't care how weird he is, doesn't think he's any different now.

At least he tries to act that way.

He rides to the firebreak and goes over the jump. His old bike was so heavy you could barely catch an inch of air. The Redline flies. No wonder Paul loves it so much.

It was weird at first, riding Paul's bike. Still, Andy wouldn't have ridden it at all if George hadn't said Paul told him it was OK.

Some other kids show up at the jump. Andy takes it one more time and heads off. They watch him ride away.

It's nice and cool. If he takes the cap off the breeze will make his scalp itch less. But he hates the scars.

—Andy!

He glides over to the curb.

—Hey, Alexandra. What's up?

—You know, school.

—How is it?

—You know, the same.

She shifts her books from her chest to her hip.

—Andy?

—Uh huh.

—Um, can I look at your head?

—Sure.

He takes off the cap.

—Can I see the top?

He lowers his head.

—Gross.

—Yeah, I know.

—Did you really die? I mean, die and then they like brought you back?

He looks at her.

—Who said that?

—Kids.

Andy looks up at the sun until he sees spots and then looks back at her.

—No. I didn't. I was in a coma. And they thought I might die. But I didn't.

—Um. Did those Crips really torture you?

Andy tries to blink the spots from his eyes.

—Who said they were Crips?

—Everyone.

—I don't think they were. I mean, my brother said they were just some black guys. I don't remember.

—You don't remember any of it?

Andy thinks about what he remembers.

—No. They hit me really hard.

—Are you going back to school ever?

—No, I don't think so. I just got caught up with everything I missed. If I work hard I can finish all the requirements for my diploma by January.

—Wow. I wish I could graduate early. I suck at math and science.

Andy bends and scratches his shin.

—I could help.

—Yeah?

—Sure. If that's cool. I could.

She holds up her books.

—Algebra?

—Yeah. Sure.

—You'd have to . . . Um. I can't go to, you know, I can't go to a boy's house.

She looks up.

—I mean, not even to study, you know. So. You'd have to come over.

—OK.

—OK.

They look at everything but each other.

She fluffs her hair.

—So, you need a number, or?

—No, I know it.

—OK.

She starts to walk away, backward, looking at him.

—Call me after dinner?

—Sure.

—Cool.

She turns and runs.

Andy pushes off from the curb, the cap in his hand so he can feel the cool air on his head.

He crosses Murrieta, takes Delaware over to the elementary school and zigzags through the little kids on the blacktop. A teacher yells something at him, but he ignores her and rides off the schoolyard onto Rincon.

Aunt Amy's car is in her driveway, but he doesn't stop to say hi. It's OK for them to go over there now. Now that their dad has made up with her and she's stopped selling pills. Not that their dad said anything about the pills to them. He probably still doesn't know what George was doing over there in the first place. But things are cool with her now. As long as their dad doesn't find out that she stopped selling the pills because she makes so much more money off the meth she's dealing.

He rides past without stopping. He'll see her this weekend when she comes over for dinner.

When he turns the corner onto North P it's like someone has thrown a rock through the surface of the day. The face of it shattering, the pieces falling to the ground, revealing another day behind it.

Weird.

Down the street, Timo is bunny hopping a bike on and off the curb.

Really weird. Like he can almost remember some things.

He looks at the sign on Fernando's old front lawn, the one telling people the house will be sold at auction by the state. Tries to remember something about that house. Or is it another house?

Then the day puts itself back together and the stuff behind it is gone.

Andy raises an arm.

—Hey, Timo.

At the sound of Andy's voice Timo flinches. At the sight of Andy he almost dumps the bike. He wrenches the handlebars to the side, rights the bike, and pedals blindly into the intersection at the next corner, almost getting creamed by a beat up '64 Ford that roars by.

Andy watches his back disappear down the street and imagines the arc Timo's body might have made if he had been traveling the necessary velocity to have intersected with the Ford, and he flinches when he sees the spray of blood that would have exploded from his head when it hit the ground.

George rides up.

—Hey.

Andy smiles.

—Hey, what's up?

—Over by the park with some chick, saw you go by.

—Cool.

George nods down the street.

—That Timo?

—Yeah.

—He fuck with you?

—No. Saw me and took off. I was gonna maybe say something about his brothers and stuff. How much that must suck.

George looks at the Arroyos' old house.

—Yeah. Don't do that. Don't talk to him. It sucks his brothers died, but he's still a dick. Stay away from over here.

—OK. I was just riding around.

—How's the bike?

—Fucking awesome.

George spits on his thumb and rubs some dry mud from the Redline's handlebars.

—Take care of it.

—I am.

George stands on his pedals and pumps a couple times and pops a wheelie and starts to ride away.

—Let's go home. It's almost dinner time.

Andy looks back at the Arroyo brothers' house.

George yells.

—Hurry up, I'll teach you some tricks after we eat.

Andy looks away from the house.

—Cool.

He pulls the dead man's cap down low over his mutilated head and follows his brother home.

Please turn the page for an exciting preview of
Charlie Huston's

The Mystic Arts of Erasing
All Signs of Death

Available from Ballantine Books

PROLOGUE

I'm not sure where one should expect to find the bereaved daughter of a wealthy Malibu suicide in need of a trauma cleaner long after midnight, but safe to say a trucker motel down the 405 industrial corridor of oil refineries and chem plants in Carson was not on my list of likely locales.

—Ouch. That looks painful.

I touched the bandage on my forehead.

—And if that's what it feels like to look at it, imagine how it feels to actually have it happen to you.

The half of her face that I could see in the chained gap between the edge of the door and the frame nodded up and down.

—Yeah, I'd imagine that sucks.

Cars whipped past on the highway across the parking lot, taking full advantage of the few hours in any given Los Angeles county twenty-four-hour period when you might get the needle on the high side of sixty. I watched a couple of them attempting to set a new land speed record.

I looked back at Soledad's face, bisected by the door.

—So?

—Uh huh?

I hefted the plastic carrier full of cleaning supplies I'd brought from the van.

—Someone called for maid service?

—Yeah. That was me.

—I know.

She fingered the slack in the door chain, set it swinging back and forth.

—I didn't really think you'd come.

—Well, I like to surprise.

She stopped playing with the chain.

—Terrible habit. Don't you know most people don't like surprises?

I looked over at the highway and watched a couple more cars.

—Can I ask a silly question?

—Sure.

I looked back at her.

—What the fuck am I doing here?

She ran a hand through her hair, let it fall back over her forehead.

—You sure you want to do this, Web?

That being the kind of question that tips most people off to a fucked up situation, I could very easily have taken it as my cue to go downstairs, get back in the van and get the hell gone. But it's not like I hadn't already been clued to things being fucked up when she called in the middle of the night and asked me to come to a motel to clean a room. And there I was anyway. So who was I fooling?

Exactly no one.

—Just let me in and show me the problem.

—Think you can fix it, do you?

I shook my head.

—No, probably not. But it's cold out here. And I came all this way.

She showed me half her smile, the other half hidden behind the door.

—And you're still clinging to some hope that a girl asking you to come clean something is some kind of booty call code, right?

I rubbed the top of my head. But I didn't say anything. Not feeling like saying *no* and lying to her so early in our relationship. There would be time for that kind of thing later. There's always time for lying.

She inhaled, let it out slow.

—OK.

The door closed. I heard the chain unhook. The door opened and I walked in, my feet crunching on something hard.

—This the asshole?

I looked at the young dude standing at the bathroom door with a meticulously crafted fauxhawk. I looked at bleached teeth and hand-crafted tan. I looked at the bloodstains on his designer-distressed jeans and his artfully faded reproduction Rolling Stones concert T from a show that took place well before he was conceived. Then I looked at much larger bloodstains on the sheets of the queen-size bed and the flecks of blood spattered on the wall. I looked at the floor to see what I'd crushed underfoot, half expecting cockroaches, and found dozens of scattered almonds instead. I listened as the door closed behind me and locked. I watched as Soledad walked toward the bathroom and the dude snagged her by the hand before she could go in.

—I asked, *Is this the asshole.*

I pointed at myself.

—Honestly, in most circumstances, in any given room on any given day, I'd say, *Yeah, I'm the asshole here.* But in this particular scenario, and I know we just met and all, but in this room here?

I pointed at him.

—I'm more than willing to give you the benefit of the doubt and say that *you're* the asshole.

He looked at Soledad.

—So, yeah, he's the asshole then?

She twisted her hand free and went into the bathroom.

—He's the guy I told you about.

She closed the door behind her.

He looked at me.

—Yeah, you're the asshole alright.

I held up a hand.

—Hey, look, if you're gonna insist, I can only accept the title. But seriously, don't sell yourself short. You got the asshole thing locked up if you want it.

He came down the room in a loose strut I imagine had been meticulously assembled from endless repeat viewings of Tom Cruise's greatest hits.

—Yeah, I can tell by the way you're talking. You're the one fucked with her today. Made jokes about her dad killing himself. You're the asshole alright.

The toilet flushed, Soledad yelled over it.

—He didn't make jokes!

The dude looked at the closed door.

—You said he made jokes.

He looked at me.

—Asshole. Fucking go in someone's home, there's been a tragedy, go in and try to make money off that. Fucking vulture. Fucking ghoul. Who does that, who comes up with that for a job? That your dream job, man? Cleaning up dead people? Other kids were hoping to grow up to be movie stars and you were having fantasies about scooping people's guts off the floor?

I shifted, crushing a few more almonds.

—Truth is, mostly I had fantasies about doing your mom.

He slipped a lozenge of perforated steel from his back pocket, flicked his wrist and thumb in an elaborate show of coordination, and displayed the open butterfly knife resting in on his palm.

—Say what, asshole?

Say nothing, actually. Except say that maybe he was right and I was the asshole in the room. Certainly being an asshole was how I came to be there in the first place.

PHOTO © VIRGINIA LOUISE SMITH

CHARLIE HUSTON is the author of the Henry Thompson trilogy, The Joe Pitt casebooks, and the *Los Angeles Times* bestseller *The Shotgun Rule*. For Marvel Comics he has written *Moon Knight*, as well as special annual issues of *The Ultimates* and *X-Force*. He lives with his family in Los Angeles. Visit him at www. pulpnoir.com.

CHECK OUT THE FIRST TWO
HENRY THOMPSON THRILLERS FROM

CHARLIE HUSTON

In Huston's brilliant and
blazingly paced debut, Henry
Thompson becomes very
important to some very
dangerous people when he comes
into possession of a
very large amount of money.

**"Huston has come up with a wrong-
man plot worthy of Hitchcock."**
—*Entertainment Weekly*

Henry is lying low, hiding
out on a Mexican beach,
until a Russian backpacker
shows up and starts asking
all the wrong questions.
One desperate move later,
Henry is back on the run.

**"Huston writes dialogue so
combustible it could fuel a
bus and characters crazy
enough to take it on the road.
Passengers, line up here."**
—*New York Times Book Review*

Ballantine Books Trade Paperbacks • www.ballantinebooks.com
Visit the author's website: www.pulpnoir.com

DON'T MISS THE THIRD
HENRY THOMPSON THRILLER FROM
CHARLIE HUSTON

Reluctant hitman Henry Thompson has fallen on hard times. His grip on life is disintegrating, his pistol hand shaking, his body pinned to his living room couch by painkillers, and his Russian boss isn't happy about it. So it is time for Henry to redeem himself in a big way.

"Among the new voices in twenty-first-century crime fiction, Charlie Huston . . . is where it's at." —*The Washington Post*

Ballantine Books Trade Paperbacks • www.ballantinebooks.com
Visit the author's website: www.pulpnoir.com